JAN - 2003

The Bishop

AND THE

Missing L Train

**Center Point
Large Print**

**This Large Print Book carries the
Seal of Approval of N.A.V.H.**

ॐ श्री गणेशाय नमः

ANDREW M. GREELEY

The Bishop
AND THE
Missing L Train

CENTER POINT PUBLISHING
THORNDIKE, MAINE • USA

BOLINDA PUBLISHING
MELBOURNE • AUSTRALIA

For Roisin, Kyle, Colum, Conor . . .

This Center Point Large Print edition is published in the year 2002 by arrangement with Thomas C. Doherty Associates, LLC.

This Bolinda Large Print edition is published in the year 2002 by arrangement with Thomas C. Doherty Associates, LLC.

The text of this Large Print edition is unabridged. In other aspects, this book may vary from the original edition. Printed in Thailand. Set in 16-point Times New Roman type by Bill Coskrey and Gary Socquet.

US ISBN 1-58547-254-9
BC ISBN 1-74030-829-8

U.S. Library of Congress Cataloging-in-Publication Data.

Greeley, Andrew M., 1928-
    The bishop and the missing L train / Andrew M. Greeley.--Center Point large print ed.
    p. cm.
    ISBN 1-58547-254-9 (lib. bdg. : alk. paper)
      1. Ryan, Blackie (Fictitious character)--Fiction. 2. Catholic Church--Fiction.
    3. Chicago (Ill.)--Fiction. 4. Bishops--Fiction. 5. Large type books. I. Title.

PS3557.R358 B49 2002
813'.54--dc21

                                                                                    2002071608

Australian Cataloguing-in-Publication.

Greeley, Andrew M. (Andrew Morgan), 1928-
The bishop and the missing L train / Andrew M. Greeley.
1740308298
1. Large type books.
2. Ryan, Blackie (Fictitious character)--Fiction.
3. Bishops--Fiction.
4. Catholic Church--Fiction.
5. Detective and mystery stories.
I. Title.
813.6

British Cataloguing-in-Publication is available from the British Library.

Several years ago, some folks in the Big Apple actually stole a subway train and hid it for a month. Things like that happen in New York City. In Chicago, for reasons I will not divulge lest it present a challenge to evildoers, one could not steal or hide an L train. Hence the mechanics of the theft of a train on the Brown Line described in this story are fantasy and not science fiction.

Since, as the inimitable Cindy Hurley observes, Rudy Giuliani is not mayor of Chicago, and neither is Ken Starr, it is most unlikely that Chicago police in the real world would behave like some of them do in this story.

Bishop Ryan has asked me to assure the readers that all the characters in the story are also fantastical.

Notre Dame's women's soccer team has had a very distinguished history. They are always very good and very exciting. However, the account of their season in this story and especially the battle royal with Stanford is fictional. Also imaginary are the parishes of Forty Holy Martyrs and St. Regis.

BLACKIE

1

"One of our L trains is missing!"

Sean Cronin, Cardinal priest of the Holy Roman Church and, by the grace of God and abused patience of the Apostolic See, Archbishop of

Chicago, swept into my study with his usual vigor. Since he was not wearing his crimson robes but a gleaming white and flawlessly ironed collarless shirt with diamond-studded cufflinks, it would not be appropriate to describe him as a crimson supersonic jet. Perhaps a new and shiny diesel locomotive.

"Tragic," I said, pretending not to look up from the Dell 300mx computer on which I was constructing the master schedule for the next month in the Cathedral parish.

"And Bishop Quill was on the L train!!"

He threw himself into a chair that I had just cleared so as to pile more computer output on it.

"Indeed!" I said, looking up with considerable interest. "With any good fortune we will find neither the L train nor Bishop Quill."

Out of respect for his status among the missing, I did not refer to our lost bishop by his time-honored nickname, imposed by his unimaginative seminary classmates—Idiot.

"You South Side Irish are innocent of charity," he replied. "You have any tea around?"

Normally he would have appeared at night in my study and commandeered a large portion of my precious Jamesons Twelve Year Special Reserve or Bushmill's Green Label before he assigned me another cleanup task. Auxiliary bishops play a role in the Catholic Church not unlike that of the admirable Harvey Keitel in *Pulp Fiction*: they sweep up messes. However, it was morning, a sunny early autumn morning to be precise. Banned from coffee by his foster sister Nora Cronin, he was reduced to pleading for tea to fill his oral needs.

Before I could wave at my ever present teapot, he spotted

it, stretched his tall, lean frame to the table on which it rested (surrounded by the galleys of my most recent book, *There Is No Millennium*), and poured himself a large mug of Irish Breakfast tea.

"Great!" he exclaimed with a sigh of pleasure. The pleasures of being a cardinal these days are, alas, few and simple.

I waited to hear the story of the disappearance of the L train and its distinguished passenger. He continued to sip his tea, a tall, handsome man just turned seventy, with carefully groomed white hair, the face of an Irish poet, the political skills of a veteran ward committeeman, and the hooded, glowing eyes of a revolutionary gunman.

"So what was Idiot doing on an L train?" I asked, realizing that I was missing one of the lines in our routinized scenario.

"Your brother auxiliary bishop," he said with radiant irony as he played with the massive ruby ring on his right hand, "was mingling with the poor on the way home from his weekly day of ministry in the barrio. Preparation doubtless for the day when he succeeds me." Milord Cronin laughed bitterly.

"He will never be able to learn Spanish that does not cause laughter among those who know the language."

"That, Blackwood, is irrelevant to the present story. . . . His limousine driver was to pick him up at the Kimball Avenue terminal of the Ravenswood Line and drive him back to his parish in Forest Hills."

"Brown Line," I said in the interest of accuracy.

"What?" he exploded, a nervous panther looking for something to spring upon.

7

"The Ravenswood Line is now known as the Brown Line."

The Ravenswood Line is the Ravenswood Line, Blackwood," he insisted with the sense of shared infallibility that only a cardinal can muster and that rarely these days.

"Arguably."

"So the train never arrived." He extended his tea mug in my direction and, docile priest that I am, I refilled it. No milk. The valiant Nora had forbidden milk as part of her virtuous campaign to keep the Cardinal alive. "And Bishop Quill never arrived either."

"Remarkable."

"The chauffeur became concerned and called the CTA, which, as one might expect, assured him that the train had arrived at Kimball and Lawrence on time—that's a Korean neighborhood now, isn't it, Blackwood?"

"An everything neighborhood—Koreans, Palestinians, Pakistanis, some Japanese, and a few recalcitrant and elderly Orthodox Jews who will not leave the vast apartment buildings they built so long ago."

"Safe?"

"Much safer than many others I could mention, some of them not distant from this very room."

"Who would want to abduct Gus Quill?"

"I could provide a list of hundreds of names, with yours and mine on the top."

"Precisely. . . . Anyway, the chauffeur then called the Chicago Police Department and apparently reached your good friend John Culhane, who called me about midnight. They have determined the L in fact never arrived at the terminal. Rather it has disappeared into thin air and, Commander Culhane assured me an hour ago, so has the Most Reverend Augustus O'Sullivan Quill."

Deo gratias, I almost said. Instead I took a firm stand for right reason and common sense.

"L trains do not disappear," I insisted. "Neither, alas, do auxiliary bishops, though sometimes they are treated as if they do not exist. . . ."

Milord Cronin waved away my self-pity.

"The CTA is searching frantically for their missing train. The police are searching frantically for the missing bishop. He was the only one on the train at the last stop. The driver has disappeared too. The media have the story already. I hear there are cameras at the terminal and up in Forest Hills—"

My phone rang. The Loyola student who monitors our lines until the Megan show up after school asked whether the Cardinal was in my room.

"Who wants to talk to him?"

"Mary Jane McGurn from Channel Six."

"I will talk to her," I said, as though it were my rectory.

"Hi, Blackie. What's happened to my good friend Idiot Quill?"

"Mary Jane," I whispered to the Cardinal, my hand over the phone.

Although Ms. McGurn was Sean Cronin's favorite media person—he having a weakness for pretty and intelligent women (what healthy male does not?)—he shook his head. "I'm not available for comment, am I?"

"You're in prayer for the repose of his soul?"

Milord winced.

"What was that question again, Mary Jane?"

"Our mutual friend, Bishop Quill, has apparently disappeared. Do you or Cardinal Sean have any comment?"

"Only for the deepest of deep background, Mary Jane: like bad pennies, auxiliary bishops always return."

Milord Cardinal favored me with a wry smile.

"Is the Cardinal available?"

"I think not."

No one in the media had much regard for Augustus O'Sullivan Quill. Mary Jane held a special grudge since the day he told her on camera that she should be home taking care of her children.

"The crews are descending on the Cathedral rectory at this moment. I'll be there in five minutes. We're going to want a statement about the disappearance of Bishop Quill."

"You may quote the Cardinal as saying that we are confident that Bishop Quill will be found soon."

Milord Cronin tilted his head slightly in approval of my statement.

"Nothing more?"

"Nothing more."

"Off the record?"

"We are praying for him."

"Yeah," she snorted, "so am I!"

I gently restored the phone to its base.

"We cannot permit this, Blackwood!"

"Indeed."

"Auxiliary bishops do not slip into the fourth dimension, not in this archdiocese."

"Patently."

"Especially they do not disappear on L trains that also disappear, right?"

"Right!"

"You yourself have said that we will be the prime suspects, have you not? Don't we have powerful reasons for wanting to get rid of him?"

"Arguably," I sighed. "However, as you well know, in the best traditions of the Sacred College we would have dispatched Idiot with poison."

Actually neither the State's Attorney nor the media would dare suggest that the two of us could easily do without our junior auxiliary.

"This is not a laughing matter, Blackwood," he said sternly.

"Indeed."

"The Nuncio and the Vatican will be all over us. They do not like to lose bishops."

"Even auxiliaries?"

"We have to find Gus before the day is over." He put his tea mug on the rug and rose from the chair.

"Ah?"

He strode to the door of my study, a man on a mission.

"That means you have to find him."

I knew that was coming.

"Indeed."

He paused at the door for the final words.

"Find Gus. Today. See to it, Blackwood."

He disappeared, not in a cloud of dust, since we do not tolerate that in the Cathedral rectory, but trailing an invisible cloud of satisfaction.

I sighed loudly, saved the file, and turned off the computer. Time for the sweeper to get to work.

TOMMY

2

I 'm a professional gambler. I earn a decent living from this behavior each morning of the week. Then I return to my apartment in the John Hancock Center, do my daily workout, swim in the pool, and eat a modest and healthy lunch. Next I turn to the second section of my day. I turn on my big-screen television and surf the sports channels in Chicago, of which there are five. On any given day one can find almost all the forms of athletic competition that human ingenuity has devised—from hurling, which is a slightly organized version of the Irish tradition of the faction fight, to grown men riding tiny cars fit only for children in mud flats. I do not care what the competition is, no real sports freak does. I choose sides as soon as I have selected the afternoon's entertainment and make imaginary bets, as we professional gamblers always do.

When the contests are over, I make myself an adequate and tasty supper and begin to read. What do I read? Anything and everything. History, biography, popular science, mystery, fantasy, literature, classics, best-sellers—whatever looks interesting. There's a Borders bookstore across the street from my apartment. Every week or two, I amble over there on an impulse-buying expedition and collect a dozen or so books. Just now I am reading *Finnegans Wake*. With a translation. I retire early because one needs to be well rested when one enters my casino in the morning. A casino otherwise known as the Eurodollar pit in the

Chicago Mercantile Exchange, the place where the word "derivative" was born. I have been very successful there, more successful than I let anyone know, so that there is no reason to want to punish my success. I don't know why I'm a good gambler in such a complex, not to say convoluted, environment. I always got A's in math in school. My mind, however shallow, is agile. I am alleged to be a good judge of people and their motives. I am not greedy. Bears win, bulls win, pigs lose. I usually follow my instincts and they're usually correct. When they begin to be consistently wrong, then I'll find something else to do. Or retire early and watch TV in the mornings too.

I avoid the bar scene on Division Street only a few blocks away from where I live. The predatory beasts who prowl there, of whatever gender, frighten and repel me. My sisters say that I am a recluse. I concede that this is partially true. I do occasionally go out socially. Thus I had dinner last week with my good friend Peter Murphy and his mountain person (as she calls herself) bride Cindasue. I am impressed with their happiness. I reflected that it would indeed be pleasant to take someone like Cindasue to bed with me every night.

My sisters and my stepmother (completely in league with them when it comes to my case) contend that I am on my way to becoming a typical Irish bachelor. Perhaps they are right. I do not reject the genetically driven obligation of our species to assume the role of spouse and parent. I realize that sometime that obligation will overcome my reluctance. I will meet someone at a wedding or at the opera or perhaps even at the Exchange who will quite overwhelm me. She will, of course, have preselected me. We will think we are in love and perhaps we will be. We will marry. What happens then will be problematic. Marriage is a far greater risk than anything we face in the Eurodollar pit.

My family says that I don't like women and I don't trust them. That is not true. I like my stepmother very much, which is almost against the rules. I also trust women—up to the point where their agenda and my agenda are incompatible. They tend to talk these days about negotiating the differences, which means that you lose. I recognize the validity of both agendas for which our species is programmed. I would in principle be ready to sacrifice most of my agenda for the pleasure of having a woman in bed with me routinely. But I digress. . . . That's not the reason why I don't trust women. There are other reasons which I do not intend to write down at this time. Maybe I read too much.

In any event, my present difficulties began one rainy autumn afternoon when after lunch I curled up with a pot of Irish Afternoon tea and began to surf the sports channels. One game promised a contest between Notre Dame and Southern California. I didn't think it could be a football game at midweek. While I had received a better education at Georgetown than I would have received in the shadow of the Golden Dome, I had no fundamental prejudices against their athletic teams (unlike Domers, who rejoice whenever we Hoyas lose).

It was a soccer match, indeed a woman's soccer match on a cold and wet field somewhere in the shadow of the Touchdown Jesus, who seemed to be the only one watching the game. Soccer is not one of my favorite sports. When they had the World Cup here a couple of years ago I did not attend a single match. (Why go to any athletic contest when you can watch it on a large-screen television in a cozy apartment with a pot of Irish Afternoon tea next to you?) Despite the worldwide enthusiasm for the sport, in my personal hierarchy it ranks only above hockey and yacht racing for being marginally better than watching grass grow.

I was about to surf elsewhere when I found myself fascinated by the intensity of the play. The woman warriors, in a cold rain and before an empty stadium, were playing with a dedication and abandon that I had rarely observed. There was none of the macho ego, the phony cool that marks so many male athletics. These young women held nothing back. They were so fiercely competitive that they would have put even Michael Jordan to shame. Young lionesses, I thought, remembering a TV program about the frolicking and hunting lionesses in the Serengeti who wrestled with one another and charged after prey while big old Simba watched with an occasional sleepy yawn.

Fascinating. Surely there was some evolutionary advantage for the species in producing mothers of this sort.

Two things were soon apparent. Notre Dame, already leading 2-0, was pounding a game USC into the mud. And the principal lioness was a young woman named Christy Logan. Wet from the rain, her blue-and-gold Irish uniform covered with mud, her blonde hair in a ponytail, this Christy Logan person, chewing gum fiercely, was nonetheless one of the most beautiful women I had ever seen.

Head lioness. Perhaps the kind that would growl even at Simba.

I realized that she was very dangerous and that the best

thing I could do was to turn to some other program. It would be most unwise to fall in love with a lioness in a TV soccer match. However, I reasoned, it was most unlikely that I would ever meet her—pardon the expression—in the flesh.

The camera focused on her often, capturing the many moods of her mobile face—anger, amusement, sympathy, determination. Especially determination. She also laughed a lot, especially at her own mistakes. It developed that Christy had been a consensus All-American during her junior year and would surely be one again this year as well as a member of the United States Olympic soccer team.

Fearsome!

The announcer said that she was from Chicago, Illinois. A warning that the odds had gone down substantially on my never meeting her in the unquestionably lovely flesh. I knew I should turn off the program and warm up my tea.

However, I must confess that I was no longer interested in the match but only in Christy Logan as she urged on her pride of lionesses, raced down the field, booted another goal by the hapless and helpless Trojan goalie, and picked up from the mud the various unfortunate Lady Trojans (as they are called by the announcer in violation of the norms of political correctness) who had fallen in combat.

The announcer, incidentally, never called the home team the Lady Irish or even worse the Lady Fighting Irish. Heaven forfend!

I admit that I engaged in the male's age-old propensity to undress mentally an attractive woman—shapely if sinewy and muddy legs, narrow, narrow waist, neatly shaped rear end, and exquisite breasts that even the soccer sweatshirt could not hide. And a sharply etched face that seemed to demand careful and respectful caresses, the kind of bones that my stepmother would say would guarantee durable beauty. Queen Maeve leading her warriors into battle.

My fantasies ran out of control. I imagined her in the shower after the match was over.

Too much, I told myself and firmly turned off the television. After I had boiled the water, and put new tea into the pot, I returned to the TV with the firm intention of cruising immediately to another channel. When the screen came up, a picture of a fiercely grinning Christy Logan filled it. Maeve had won another battle. Despite the mud on her face, she was unbearably beautiful. The match was over. The Irish had won again, on their way, the announcer said, to a possible national championship. The picture faded to a commercial. I turned sadly to a wrestling match.

She was in the shower now, I realized. Then I forbade myself to revel in that image. It would nonetheless haunt me through the rest of the day and the night and into the beginning of the session at the Exchange. Even Christy Logan could not distract me from the demands of Eurodollars, which had the advantage over Christy that they did not exist in the real world.

Given the law of six degrees of separation, I told myself as I walked home from the Exchange, it ought not to be difficult to find someone whom I knew who knew her. One of my sisters went to Notre Dame. She might know her. Or I could drive down to the Dome and sit in the rain and watch her play.

I knew I would do neither of these things. I didn't need a female lioness no matter how gorgeous.

That Sunday at the family dinner out in Oak Park, which I usually attend, the women members left me alone, more or less. They spoke rather in fury about the asshole bishop, as they put it, who had come to Chicago. We had lots of reasons for not liking him. I felt rage stirring inside me. Not typical or appropriate behavior.

"I happened to catch your soccer team on the tube the other day," I said cautiously. I instantly regretted it because I did not want to learn anything more about Christy Logan.

"Aren't they totally cool?" Amy gushed. "We're number one!"

"So the announcer said."

"Did you notice my friend Christy Logan? She's All-American!"

"Is she the little kid with black hair?"

"No way! She's like the totally gorgeous blonde that's the team captain!"

"Blonde . . . ," I said thoughtfully. Six degrees of separation had just fallen to two.

"She's Dr. Logan's daughter, isn't she?" Beth asked, trying, as Irishwomen and Irish politicians do, to locate everyone's origins and genealogy.

"She's like a great kid, really! I mean, you know, she's very smart and very funny and very, very sweet."

"A lesbian, I suppose. . . ."

Total outrage all around the table.

Even Beth, my stepmother, who often takes my side, was shocked.

"Tommy, that's a terrible thing to say. Women athletes are no more likely to be lesbian than men athletes are to be gay. And there's nothing wrong with it if they are."

"She certainly isn't a lesbian!" Amy insisted hotly.

"I think Tommy is trying to make up his mind whether he wants an introduction, Amy."

All too accurate.

"He'd want her to be a lesbian," Amy insisted. "Then she wouldn't be any threat to him."

Again all too accurate.

To change the subject somewhat, I insisted that soccer was too rough a game for women to play. I didn't believe it for a moment. The lionesses could take care of themselves. However, my claim stirred up another firestorm of controversy.

"You're not serious, Tommy. Sometimes, however, it's hard to tell when you're serious and when you're not."

How had everyone in this crowd figured me out so well?

Returning to my apartment in the evening, I marveled at how my family had re-created itself. Beth had made common cause with my three sisters in the program of taking care of Dad. It had worked very well. My father had been disastrously unlucky in his first marriage and very fortunate in his second. Luck of the draw? He really had no way of knowing either time, especially the second, since he'd been so traumatized the first time around. Much safer in the Eurodollar pit. Nor had the damn Catholic Church been any help at all. In fact, it had made matters worse. How could it believe that he and Beth were living in sin, when she had so clearly healed him and remade him and had time to love the rest of us?

If God would guarantee me a wife like Beth, I'd marry that person tomorrow. No guarantees.

My fantasies of Christy Logan in the shower returned, to

be replaced by fantasies of Beth in the shower. Are erotic images of your stepmother incestuous? I didn't think so, but they weren't a good idea. I picked up *Finnegans Wake,* with which I had been struggling all week. No twelve books this week.

Someday I would have to tell Beth what a wonderful job she had done. The sisters, as much as they loved her, probably had not thought to say thank you.

I put Jimmy Joyce aside for a moment and went to my desk. I would write one draft and send it to her personally, not post it on the family e-mail site.

Dear Beth,

Thanks again for the family dinner this afternoon and for protecting me from the schemes of Amy and Lisa and Marie. I also want to thank you for something that I suspect none of us have thanked you for yet. You have healed my father and made him a whole man again. You have healed our family and made it a family again. Moreover you have worked these miracles with grace and style. I don't know quite how you managed these wonders against all odds. But we'll be forever grateful to you. Even though we don't quite know how to say it—and I have to retreat to mail to even try to say it—we'll always love you.

Tommy

I read the letter over once. Just the right note. She would show it to Dad and the sisters and there would be hugging and crying and Beth would say, "See, didn't I tell you that Tommy was a sweetheart!"

Then I went back to Jimmy Joyce.

Having done my good deed for the year, I concluded that Christy Logan was no longer even a remote option. If she were a friend of Amy's, she would be ex officio, a coconspirator. I did not want to find myself surrounded on all sides without an escape hatch. No more fantasies and no more women's soccer on television.

Beth called me two days later and, in the midst of much weeping, thanked me and praised me as the nicest young man. My three sisters then called, independently perhaps, to say much the same thing.

"You don't miss much, son," my father said, changing the message somewhat.

"That's why I'm a successful trader."

The week was tough. No time for fantasies. I lost a lot of money on the first three days, broke even on Thursday, and won everything back and a lot more on Friday. I loved every minute of it. We professional gamblers do.

There were no women's soccer games on the sports channels. I admit I looked for them.

My priest, the one who had wrestled me back into the Church, had often argued that I was a prisoner of my illusions, which were created by my troubles with my real mother, for whose problems I had assumed too much responsibility. He had urged me to work out these illusions with a therapist. I admitted that he was probably right and that I would seek out a shrink someday to work out my anger and my fear. But not quite yet. Someday, he had warned me, God would clobber me and force me into shedding my illusions. Fair enough, I had said. I didn't believe, however, that God gave enough of a damn about me to try anything special.

This illusion was about to be proven spectacularly false.

After picking through the poor Friday afternoon fare on the sports channels, I decided I would yield to my only serious indulgence. I rode down in the elevator, walked by the Water Tower plaza, crossed the Magnificent Mile, passed Borders, and entered that den of iniquity known as the Ghirardelli chocolate store and ordered a chocolate malted milk, a sinful concoction for which they are notorious.

I put *Finnegans Wake* and the translation on a table and sat down to wait for my order number to be called. I noticed a young woman with blonde hair and a baseball cap sitting next to me. As is required, her hair was in a ponytail emerging from the back of the hat. Pretty, I thought. Then I looked again. She was wearing a blue-and-gold Notre Dame jacket with SOCCER on the back (not WOMEN'S SOCCER, be it noted). My head began to whirl. This was either a dream or an epiphany of sorts. Cautiously and without seeming to stare, I searched for the embroidered name which ought to have been on the left breast of the jacket. Her shoulder blocked my view. I waited for her to shift, or to turn a page in the book. No luck. Then a number was called. She put a bookmark in place and carefully closed her book—which was by Annie Dillard—and rose up to collect her treat, which was the same as mine.

The embroidery read *Christy, Captain.*

I closed my eyes, hoping that the world would stop spinning. It didn't. I opened my eyes, just as she returned to the table. Even in jeans, sweatshirt, and running shoes, she was an impressive apparition, bigger than I had expected, but still perfect. The spinning accelerated.

I staggered over to the phone and made a call.

"Cathedral."

"Hi, Megan, it's Tommy."

"Hi, Tommy, how's your love life!"

They all knew who I was. I'd been there often enough while I was wrestling with the Holy Roman Church.

"Disastrous, Megan, until you agree to marry me!"

"You're too young, Tommy. Want to speak to the Bishop?"

"If he's in."

"For you he's always in, Tommy."

The little witch was ten years younger than me. Maybe she was right, however; maybe compared to her I was still a juvenile.

"Father Ryan."

"Tommy, Father."

"Ah."

"Do you think God picks on some people?"

"Like yourself?"

"Yes, like me."

"I'm sure She does. One may safely assume that She doesn't like your attitude."

"Well, last week I happened to catch a Notre Dame soccer game on ESPN. Their captain is a fierce but gorgeous young woman—"

"One Christy Logan, All-American."

"That's right. Well, I'm kind of impressed by her, if you know what I mean."

"I think I can guess."

"But I feel safe because I'll never meet her, right?"

"So God has arranged it that you have met her."

"I'm at Ghirardelli's and have ordered a malted milk."

"Highly virtuous behavior."

"And she's sitting at the table next to me!"

"Remarkable!"

"She's even more impressive than on television."

"Astonishing."

"Do you think God has done this to me?"

"Beyond a shadow of a doubt."

"So I have to talk to her?"

"Certainly God leaves us free even when He pulls one of these spectacular dirty tricks and then respects our right to decline. Both God and I, however, are betting that you will indeed talk to the exceptional Christy."

"Yeah," I said. "I don't want to upset God."

"Wise young man."

I picked up my order and sat down next to "Christy, Captain" and took a deep breath. She glanced at me and then returned to her cautious consumption of the malt and serious consumption of Ms. Dillard.

I'm not exactly Leonardo DiCaprio, but my siblings insist that most young women consider me "cute." That word has so many meanings in the womanly lexicon that I don't quite know how it applies to me. Nonetheless, I was discouraged by her brisk dismissal of my presence.

"Aren't you violating your training regimen, Ms. Logan?" I said brightly.

She glared at me, a kind of twisted frown that said, How did this worm crawl into Ghirardelli's?

"That's one of the worst come-ons I've ever heard," she snarled.

"I'm not trying to pick you up, Ms. Logan," I said, smiling as best I could. "I don't pick up young lionesses."

"That's a little better." The frown slipped away, but she was still not happy with me. "Original, anyway."

"I happened to see you and your colleagues bury the so-called Lady Trojans in the mud last week—"

"You were down there?" she asked in amazement.

"No, I watched on TV."

"Then there were three of you, counting my mother and father."

"I was impressed, as anyone would be, by your team, and I noted with satisfaction that you were not the Lady Irish but simply and definitively the Irish."

She smiled. Ghirardelli's, the Water Tower, Loyola, Borders, Ralph Lauren, the new Hyatt, and everything else around evaporated.

"The problem was"—her smile turned into an impish grin—"were we the Lady Fighting Irish or the Fighting Lady Irish? So we decided that we were simply the Irish and that was that. Fighting is unnecessary."

I gulped. I was no longer an insect.

"And for the hapless Lady Trojans, useless."

She smiled again.

"We're number one and we will be at the end of the season."

"And win at the Olympics."

"Absolutely. . . . How come you're reading two books at the same time?"

"I read one with the left eye and one with the right eye."

"Silly." She grabbed both my books. One doesn't resist a curious lioness. "*Finnegans Wake*. That's a great book!

The title is a three-way pun you know. Does it mean that the Finnegans all wake up? Or does it mean that it is a wake for a man named Finnegan? Or is it a call for the Finnegan clan to wake up and go forth in battle? The lack of punctuation suggests the first, but he probably meant all three, you know?"

God had made me read that book and bring it over to Ghirardelli's, no doubt about it.

Before I could answer, she continued, "Do you know what the story means?"

"I'm trying to figure it out. . . ."

"WELL, I think it's about old age and dying. Jim and Nora are getting older. He wonders what it would have been like if they had stayed in Ireland and bought a hotel. Their physical love is ignited again and he realizes that life is stronger than death. It's really about resurrection and Easter and the river of love that never stops running."

She paused expectantly, waiting for my reaction.

Where had this young lioness come from?

"I hope you're right. If you are, it is a very beautiful book."

"Well, I've been wrong, once or twice. . . . What do you do? Are you still in school?"

"I'm a professional gambler," I said.

"Options or Merc?"

"Merc."

"You survive?"

"So far."

"Just barely?"

"A little better than that."

"You must do pretty well if you can spend time watching

Notre Dame soccer in the afternoon."

"I channel surf the sports channels when I come home from the Merc."

"Cool. . . . And in the evening?"

Objection, your honor.

"Read. I don't like the bar scene."

"Neither do I," she agreed. "You finished your malt already."

I had indeed.

"Fascinated by your lecture on *Finnegan*."

She laughed, a warm, amused, faintly self-deprecating laugh.

"I talk a lot—I'll get you another one. I need a refill too. Don't look so shocked. I'll run it off on Monday. We virgins need something sweet every once in a while."

In her absence I tried to regain my aplomb. She was quite overwhelming. Perhaps God had a sense of humor.

She returned with a malt in either hand, two nourishing breasts, I thought, and then warned myself that if I permitted myself to slip into fantasies, I would never survive the rest of our conversation.

"In fact," she said, placing our drinks on the table and sitting down, "when I hear about all the problems my friends have with sex, I think chocolate is much safer. You can always run it off."

"Right," I said.

"Now"—back to business again—"what's this about lionesses?"

I tried to line up my argument.

"I noticed how intense the players were on both teams, especially yours. Most male athletes try to be macho cool about everything. Men soccer stars seem to celebrate themselves. Running around the pitch when they score a goal. You guys were into the game completely. Everything about you was involved. You didn't care what the audience thought."

"Such as it was."

"Reminded me of M.J."

"Maybe that's also the difference between the way men and women love."

That stopped me cold.

"Anyway, what about the lionesses?"

"I thought of a TV program I had seen about—excuse the expression—lady lions. Whether they were nursing their cubs or playing with the cubs or pretending to fight with one another or chasing game, they were sleek and lovely and graceful and implacably involved. While big old Simba watches and chews bones and yawns."

She nodded. "I've been to the Serengeti."

And I've only watched it on television. "Poor metaphor, maybe."

Her quick smile again. I held on to the table.

"Nice metaphor. . . . So you think I'm like a lady lion?"

"Uh, up to a point. You're not about to club me with a massive paw."

"Don't count on it."

"I'll be careful," I said sincerely.

"Nothing in this conversation has caused you to think any differently?"

"You mean that you're not like a lioness? No."

"What's your name, anyway?"

"Tommy."

"That's very nice, Tommy. You are kind of weird but definitely nice."

"Thank you, Ms. Simba."

"Where do you live?" Still collecting the facts.

"Around the corner, in the John Hancock Center."

"Really, my parents' apartment is in Water Tower! We're neighbors!"

"You're the girl next door!"

She pondered that and grinned.

"No, you're the boy next door."

"Fair enough."

"I'm in for the weekend. Get away from the books and team and relax. . . . Are you going to invite me to dinner tomorrow night?"

This young lioness actually seemed to like me. Be careful, Tommy! She and God are in conspiracy.

"Can't," I said.

"Oh?"

"Nope, if I'd picked you up, I would have invited you to dinner, but since I didn't pick you up, I can't. If I'd known—"

She waved the phony problem away. "So I'll ask you. Tommy, can I take you to dinner tomorrow night?"

"You certainly can, Christy."

"We'll eat at my father's club in the Ritz-Carlton. Neighborhood dinner."

"Grand."

"You know where the entrance to the apartments is?"

"Sure."

"Six-thirty?"

"Fine."

We both slurped up the last drops of our second malts.

"I have to go home. My folks are having a party."

"I'll walk you home."

"That's not necessary. It's only half a block. . . . But this is a weird afternoon. So why not."

So, oblivious to the rest of the world, I escorted her to the stoplight and then held her arm as we crossed the street.

She glared at me and then smiled. I was getting used to the process: first the twisted scowl and then the radiant smile.

"You are the weirdest boy I've ever met, Tommy." She shook hands with me at the door to the lobby of the apartments, some of the most expensive floor space in Chicago. "But you are sweet. See you tomorrow night at six-thirty."

"I'll be here. . . . Does this club serve really nice food?"

"What does a man know about nice food?"

"I'm a cook."

"Far out!"

BLACKIE

3

Following Milord Cronin's injunction to see to the rediscovery of the bishop and the L train, I boarded the State Street subway at the Cathedral corner and rode down to the Loop, where, after an exhausting climb from the subway to the L, I found a Ravenswood Line train waiting for me. I did not like the story of a missing L train with a missing bishop on it. It hinted of monumental evil, something huge, twisted, and depraved. No useful purpose would be served by pondering it before I arrived at the Lawrence Avenue terminal, which would doubtless be swarming with cops, busy about much useless work. The solution did not lie at Lawrence and Kimball.

I thought of Thomas Flynn and his newfound morning star. I would have liked to be able to claim credit for the happy juxtaposition of the two of them in their moment of great grace in Ghirardelli's, a shining sacramental temple for perhaps a half hour. Alas for my ego, a higher power than I had pulled off that very slick trick, for which She was to be congratulated. Tommy was still free to hide in his dark world of angry illusions. However, unless my judgment in such matters is completely wrong (which it never is), the radiance of that aforementioned morning star would soon drive out the darkness.

I sighed to myself. Tommy Flynn did not know how lucky he was. I then turned to enjoy the remarkable ride to Lawrence and Kimball. The Ravenswood L (a.k.a. The Brown Line) goes nowhere. Nonetheless it provides a fascinating jaunt through Chicago. Lawrence and Kimball is in the heart of the city, even if it wasn't ninety years ago when the line was built. (The original charter of the "Northwestern Elevated Railway" proposed a line to run to the Cook-Lake County line.) The ride to Lawrence and Kimball, however, is not merely a journey to nowhere, it is also a journey through places where no one goes.

Having loaded passengers at the Merchandise Mart, the train turns abruptly a couple of times, as if to throw off those who might be trying to follow it, and then slides along the thin borderland that separates the Gold Coast from the slums. To the right are the pastel high-rise luxury apartments near the lake, to the left the grim red brick buildings of the Cabrini Green projects. Only the Brown Line and greensward separate the two districts, whose history is steeped in mythology and sociology. Contrary to what one might expect from Chicago School sociology, the Gold Coast is encroaching on the slum. One wonders if in the future the Brown Line might be renamed the Gold Line.

Then the train eases its way across North Avenue, by St. Michael's Church, and into what was once a German and Swedish neighborhood and is now West Lincoln Park (also called by some DePaul, after the university that abuts the L track). In this thoroughly rehabilitated old neighborhood, the L engages in some of its unique tricks. It slips through bathroom windows, sneaks down hallways, creeps out through second-floor doorways, and roars off with a furious rumble that no one seems to notice.

There are those who claim that the Ravenswood does no such thing, save perhaps late at night. However, those who know the neighborhood disagree, as do those who, new in the neighborhood, still hear the noise when the train thunders by and shakes windows and light fixtures before it slips in and then slips out again. One should be careful in leaving one's bed for the bathroom late at night because one never knows when one will encounter an L train exploding down the hallway. Or perhaps it is only a ghost train from yesteryear; there is no record of anyone ever being run over on a late-night trip to the bathroom. Moreover, no one has ever found any trace of third rails on a hallway floor the next morning. Ghost trains or not, living next to the Ravenswood is like living on a perpetually active earthquake fault.

At Fullerton, the Red Line emerges from the ground as it rushes on its long trip from Ninety-fifth Street on the south to Howard Street on the north. The Ravenswood does not particularly like such cosmopolitan company. Just north of Belmont it turns left and heads out into the land of the ethnics—leaving the Red Line (and the Purple Line, about which the less said the better since it goes to Evanston, the Prohibition Suburb) to go their appointed ways—which include Addison and the disgrace of Wrigley Field. As it jogs west and then north and then west again before its final turn north, the Ravenswood becomes absolutely unique. When the trees are in foliage, a rider who is not quite sure where he is might suspect that he has been whisked away to a strange and mysterious foreign land and is now riding on the top of a vast rain forest. The trees, many of them a hundred years old, crowd in on both sides and arch over the narrow tracks. Occasionally, the rider catches a glimpse through the thick leaves of picturesque homes below in dark shade, which seem like almost magic dwellings on a protected enchanted island.

Sometimes there are clearings and one sees wooden two-flats, usually with siding of one sort or another, sometimes two on one lot, as was the custom in Chicago until 1940. (The first house was built on the front of the lot and then moved to the back to make room for the second house.) Usually, however, the back house has been torn down and replaced by a garage that was ample for the cars of the 1930s but is rarely large enough today. Occasionally a line of yuppie town houses appears and is swallowed up again in ethnic homes. Then gradually the brick two-and three-flats appear with their Tinkertoy back porches and stairways. The lawns in the backyards are carefully trimmed and lined with neat beds of flowers. Sometimes inflatable pools replace the lawns. Patio furniture, umbrellas, and grills line the yards. Now and then the furniture is on the porches, even on the small third-floor porches. Before one has time to marvel at the back porch, backyard lifestyle that has emerged at the edge of the alley, the forest closes in again. Then suddenly one crosses the North Branch of the Chicago River, lined by thick greenery on either side and looking like a jungle stream. A single motor launch rests at a small dock beneath the tracks. Mr. Kurtz, are you there?

Finally, as if exhausted, the train sinks to ground level, sneaks down side streets and back alleys, and then, after one last turn north, slows to a halt at Kimball and Lawrence, Albany Park, once a Jewish neighborhood and now Chicago's Little Korea.

The passengers—students, office workers, some commodity traders who boarded at LaSalle and Van Buren—slip off the train, some of them saying good-bye to the friendly Hispanic American who is the train's "operator." An observer wonders if they appreciate the wondrous ride through a Chicago where nobody goes.

Despite the fortunes of transit magnates whom Theodore Dreiser made immortal, public transit in Chicago has always been a financial swamp. The federal government has spent hundreds of billions of dollars in subsidy of the automobile and thus surrounded the cities with ugly suburbs. Public transit, however, which would have held the cities together, struggles along with poor service and little money, mostly because poor and nonwhite people ride it.

The L train to nowhere should indeed have been extended to the county line. We would not then need the hopeless, concrete nightmares of expressways that have to be repaired every couple of years.

When I arrived at the Kimball terminal, scores of Chicago cops were milling around on the tracks, on the platform, and in the terminal itself, not doing much, trying unsuccessfully to stay out of each other's way, and making life difficult for harmless and ordinary riders of the Brown Line. Since I was my usual unobtrusive self, I walked through them and came upon Commander John Culhane.

"Blackie," he sighed, "I figured you'd show up."

"L trains," I said firmly, "do not disappear."

"It wasn't a train," John, a trim man with rimless glasses, salt-and-pepper hair, and intense blue eyes informed me. "Only a single car on the last run of the day."

"In Chicago, John, as you well know, an L train is an L train even if it's only a one-car train."

He grinned, and for a moment the tension lifted from his open Irish face, "That's a gotcha, Bishop! . . . Three passengers left the train at the previous stop. We've found them. They each tell us that there was only one person left in the train, a priest with purple around his Roman collar and purple socks. . . . Did he really wear purple socks?"

"I'm afraid so. Arguably purple underwear too."

"There was no one else on the train except the driver."

"Who is where?"

"Nowhere that we can find. His name is Hector Gomez, married to Maria Carmela Gomez and father of three, an utterly respectable Latino family man. He did not come home from work last night. He lives only a few blocks away, so he usually walks home after the last run. As you can imagine, Maria Carmela is frantic."

"And the L train?"

"CTA hasn't found it yet. They claim that they will before the day is over. Unlike New York, where someone hid a subway train for a month, there's only a few places to hide an L here."

"Ah?"

"A cut-up in the Skokie Swift route, an unused connection between the subway and the L on the Near South side, and a couple of other places."

"And the Bishop?"

"Last seen sleeping over his breviary at the previous stop, which is only three blocks away."

"Someone could have turned the train around and taken it elsewhere?"

"At that time of night, sure. You throw a switch and the car heads back towards the Loop or wherever anyone wants to take it."

"So someone, or more likely some group of ones, could stop the train at one of the crossing streets, seize the driver and the Bishop, change a switch somewhere in the area, and ride off in the moonlight."

"I know it's impossible, Blackie, but since it has been done, it can be done."

"*Ab esse ad posse valet illatio,* as we used to say in the mother tongue."

"Absolutely—whatever that means."

"Such an accomplishment would require considerable resources, imagination, and ingenuity," I observed.

"So we assume. Since those are a given, we must find a

36

motive. Who would want to kidnap Bishop Quill?"

"And in such a spectacular fashion?"

Again I had the feeling that we were in combat with very great evil, almost diabolic. One could presumably hire thugs—very skilled thugs who were familiar with Rapid Transit trains—to carry out the kidnapping of the train and the bishop. There was notable risk in such a daring venture, but there were more than enough men in Chicago who were willing to take such risks, if the pay was adequate. Nor would they be likely to brag about their accomplishment. However, there had to be a mastermind who had the money to pay the thugs and indeed to conceive the whole plan.

"It's possible," John suggested, "that the target was not the Bishop, but the train. Some environmentalist crackpot who doesn't like the noise of L trains at night."

"Part of the Chicago air. Those who live near the tracks do not even hear them."

"Someone new in the neighborhood?"

"And with the money and the nerve to carry out this project?" I said with a sigh. "There may be one such. If there is, surely your agents will discover him soon."

"So it looks more like the Bishop was the target, doesn't it Blackie?"

"Arguably."

"What kind of a guy was he? Did anyone have reason to dislike him?"

Although I was a bishop and I was breaking the rules, I knew I had better tell the truth from the very beginning.

"As the adolescents would say, there are tons of people who dislike him, though I cannot see that any of them have sufficient motive for this, uh, venture."

For a fraction of a second, I thought I saw a picture of the explanation. As so often happens, it vanished before I could recognize it.

"He was a cruel man?"

"Cruel and self-deceptive, a bit of a borderline personality, I fear. His cruelty was perhaps not intentional, though it seems not unlikely that he enjoyed it. He had persuaded himself, in these matters, that he was following the will of God—as discovered in church during prayer—and/or the will of the Holy Father."

"For example?"

I told him the Megan story.

"Sounds like a real creep. Sean made him put the posters back up?"

"Rather, he dispatched him to Forest Hills, where he wore out his welcome on arrival by dismissing the parish staff, terminating the sports program, and wandering through the school warning of mortal sin."

"We still have that in the Church, do we?"

"On occasion."

"So they would hate him up there?"

"Oh, yes."

"We have a lot of work to do," he said grimly. "Who else?"

"You might put Milord Cronin and his elusive éminence grise at the head of the list. He has caused us no little embarrassment."

Culhane threw back his head and laughed loudly.

"Sure, you and Sean put together this plot to stop the embarrassment and didn't realize that it would cause more embarrassment. You're clever enough to think up something like this, Blackie, but you're far too clever to try it. . . . Who else?"

"I learned that his brother Peter has been substantially embarrassed in his brokerage activities by the Bishop, whose nickname, by the way, has been, since time immemorial, Idiot."

"We'll have to talk to the brother anyway."

"Moreover he was in contact with a certain prominent religious movement for money to build his own TV station, a matter about which he has spoken openly. The good bishop always assumed that those who listened to him without making a commitment agreed with him. They found him embarrassing and will find his disappearance even more embarrassing."

"A lot of embarrassments, huh, Blackie?"

"Indeed."

"Mike find out about all of them for you?"

He was referring to my cousin Michael Patrick Vincent Casey (in our family called Mike the Cop, as if to distinguish him from another Mike in the family, though there is no other Mike). A former commissioner of police and a world-famous expert on police procedure, Mike, in his spare time (when not painting), presides over an organization with the harmless name of Reliable Security, in which many cops of all genders and races moonlight. In addition, he is a charter member of the North Wabash Avenue Irregulars, a group of folk who occasionally compensate for my limited insights and mobility.

"Who else?"

"You put him on the Bishop?"

I sighed in loud protest at the injustice of it all.

"I asked him to, ah, keep his eyes and ears open and me informed. I expected trouble from our friend Idiot but not this kind of trouble."

"Anyone else?"

"Bishop Quill was a member of the Sacred Roman Rota, the Church's appellate court, before he was transferred to Chicago, very likely to get rid of him. He made it his practice to reverse all annulment judgments that came before him, a practice not likely to endear him to the people who were involved in the cases."

"You'll have to explain that to me."

Someone shouted, "Hey, boss, we've found the driver!"

"Alive?"

"Yeah, but drugged."

"Excuse me, Blackie, I'll be back."

I opened my cell phone and punched number 5, which I remembered to be the Cardinal's private number. In fact, it was the number of my sister Eileen Ryan Kane, the federal judge. I left a message on the answering machine.

I pondered the problem, remembered that the Cardinal Archbishop of Chicago used to enjoy Illinois 1 as his license plate, and pushed 1.

"Cronin."

"Blackie."

"What's going on?"

"The train is lost, the bishop is lost, the driver who was lost is now found, alas in a drugged condition. Apparently the train was hijacked just before it came to the terminal here at Kimball and Lawrence. The Bishop and the driver—"

"Motorman, you mean."

"No, they don't have those anymore since they decided they did not need conductors. The motorman is now called the driver because he is responsible for the whole train. He looks out the window to make sure that everyone is on before he closes the doors."

"Saves money at risk to the passengers."

"The sorry truth is that rapid transit, no matter how convenient, especially for working people, has always lost money. The government subsidizes automobiles by building roads, but it refuses to subsidize rapid transit. But what do I know. . . . In any event, the Bishop and the driver were the only ones on the train. Now the driver has been found."

"Gus is dead?"

I pondered that.

"Arguably, but I think not. If you were trying to punish Gus, would you not rather keep him alive so he witness the ruination of his career?"

"I wouldn't think that way."

"Someone might, however, someone mad enough to come up with this scheme."

"We have problems, then, whether he is alive or dead?"

"Alas, it would seem so."

"Well, I hope he is alive. I don't like to see anyone dead."

A sentiment that did him credit.

"I will report back."

I strolled over to the counter at the entrance of the terminal and purchased two Hershey's Cookies 'n' Creme candy bars and one Diet Coke. The smiling young Korean American woman behind the counter told me she was a student at Northwestern Medical School and she attended Sunday Mass at the Cathedral. She alleged that she loved my stories and asked for my blessing, which I willingly gave.

A medical student who worked part-time at an L station refreshment counter. As I always said of these nonwhite immigrants who have swarmed into our city and our country, it is a shame that they lack the good, old-fashioned American work ethic.

John Culhane rejoined me.

"We've taken him over to Augustana Hospital. He's mostly unconscious. Won't be much use to us for a while. Probably won't remember anything."

"Where was he found?"

"In an alley a mile or so down the line, behind a trash can."

"So . . . if I were the CTA and if I were looking for a lost one-car L train, I would look on one of the side tracks at the Lake Street Yards out at Desplaines Avenue in River Forest, just across Harlem Avenue from Oak Park. Quiet, peaceful place. And the Brown Line goes around the Loop and fits nicely into the Green Line, as we now call the venerable Lake Street L. It would be a nice touch for the kind of mastermind with whom we're dealing."

John looked at me for a moment, his eyes narrow. Then he waved a sergeant over to us.

"Roy, have one of our guys sneak out to River Forest and see if the missing car is on one of the side tracks out there. You got the number of the car?"

"Yes, sir."

"If it is, call me and we'll tell the CTA where they can

find their car."

Then he turned back to me.

"You think the Bishop will be in the car?"

"Perhaps. I hope so. But I think it is unlikely. Our mastermind would not make things so easy for us. . . . Incidentally, John, you did me an injustice a few minutes ago when you said I was capable of elaborating a master plot. Arguably that is true. But you implied it would be a plot like this gross and rather clumsy one. I would be far more devious and subtle. I would not permit my vanity to betray me."

"Point taken," he said. "This guy will give himself away because he's so pleased with himself."

In a way that prophecy would prove to be true, but not in the sense that John had intended.

4

The Gus Quill problem had blighted the end of summer a couple of months before. The Lord Cardinal had come into my room quietly, almost timidly. He didn't even raid my liquor cabinet.

"We have a new auxiliary bishop," he said as he sank into my easy chair, which I had vacated temporarily in search of a recent report on the finances of the Cathedral parish.

"We do not need one. We already have four."

"Five," he said mildly.

"Four," I argued, counting on my fingers. "Pete, Jaime, Tony, and Steve. That's enough."

"You didn't count yourself. You never count yourself."

That was true. I take it to be exceedingly improbable that

I am a bishop.

"Who is this new sweeper?"

"Gus Quill," he whispered.

"Idiot Quill!" I shouted in dismay.

"That's a cruel nickname, Blackwood." He shook his head in disapproval.

"I didn't make it up," I said in self-defense. "He is an admirable man in many ways, hardworking, pious, sincere, kind according to his lights, which are pretty dim, and delusional."

"Delusional?"

"I went to the seminary with him, if you remember. He lives in a world of his own fantasy, favored by the mighty and the powerful."

"I suppose he even thought that he would become a judge in the Sacred Roman Rota and then come home as a bishop."

I sighed loudly. Milord Cronin had a point.

"You should not have agreed to take him," I protested.

"I told them that I didn't need him and didn't want him. They said I had to take him because no one else wanted him. I continued to say I didn't want him. They continued to say that of course I would take him."

Cardinal Sean Cronin's greatest weakness is a soft heart. In most men, that is to say, those that don't have to deal with the Vatican dicasteries, that would be an unalloyed virtue.

"Why are they so eager to get him out of Rome?"

Milord Cronin leaned back in his chair as I freed the chair in front of my computer from a stack of floppy disks.

"They wouldn't say. Or, rather, they talked as if I understood why. The Romans work that way."

"Presumably the Signatura overturned too many of his Rota decisions."

"I wouldn't be surprised. He must finally have become an embarrassment."

Most marriage annulments are granted locally, with an appeal to a review court in a nearby diocese routinely made and routinely granted. Then if one party wants to appeal to Rome the case goes to the Sacred Roman Rota. This happens rarely because normally both parties are happy to be free to marry again, though sometimes one party is furious at the Church for granting the other that freedom. Occasionally, someone appeals to Rome because they are angry both at their former spouse and at the Church. Some of the judges on the Rota love to take apart the local decision and reverse the annulment. Then the party that has had the annulment revoked can appeal yet again to the Apostolic Signatura, the Church's sort-of Supreme Court where yet another reversal is possible. Idiot Quill had an unblemished record of voting to reverse every annulment that came before him. The judges in the Signatura, no fans of the American annulment machine, had often reversed Quill's reversal. I make no case for the annulment machine, which is an attempt to deal with a pastoral problem that has turned into a juggernaut. If the Pope would permit divorced and remarried Catholics to receive the sacraments, the demand for annulments would virtually disappear. In the absence of such change, fervently pushed by German bishops, many priests simply give that permission on their own.

I sighed loudly. "So now he'll be an embarrassment to us."

"More than you can imagine. He's telling people that the Pope himself is sending him here as my successor to clean up the mess in Chicago!"

"What!" I rose from the chair in righteous anger not at all like me.

"Cool it, Blackwood," Milord Cronin said. "He's not a coadjutor with right to succession, much less an apostolic administrator. I don't doubt that some of the Vatican bureaucrats hinted at that just to get rid of him. I checked to make sure. My contacts over there thought it was hilariously funny. They assured me that Saddam Hussein had an equal chance to replace me."

I sat down, still, to my shame be it said, furious.

"What makes him think that he's destined to replace you?"

Sean Cronin, thanks to the stern injunctions of the Lady Nora, was in better health than he had been for years. Moreover, he was the picture of physical fitness and could easily pass for fifty-five instead of seventy. The odds were excellent that he would survive till his seventy-fifth birthday and then some. The Vatican doesn't send in successors that long before a change.

"The Pope ordained him a bishop and was very nice to him."

"The Pope ordained fifty bishops a couple of weeks ago and was very nice to all of them. That's the way he does it."

Sean Cronin raised a hand, "Cool it, Blackwood. You yourself said that Gus lives in a fantastical world. Somehow a lot of his delusions have come true because he believes them so fervently. This is just one more. . . . He came home a couple of days ago and told some of his friends and relatives up on the North Shore that he would be more or less in charge. His appointment will be announced tomorrow at seven. He's called a press conference at the Chancery at ten-thirty."

"Without asking you?" I rose again in fury.

"I said COOL IT! We can't let this man upset us or we'll blow it. I'll be there with all the other auxiliaries and take over the press conference. You'll take the calls from the media between now and then."

I cooled it, indeed instantly.

"On the record, I will take the stand that he is nothing more than the junior auxiliary bishop among five—"

"Damn it, Blackwood, six!"

I paused to consider that.

"Someone else is coming?"

"No, I'm merely hoping that for once you'll remember that you're a bishop. Maybe even dress like one for a change."

I sat down again. Idiot Quill could do a great deal of harm by undercutting the Cardinal's leadership and perhaps creating factions among the clergy. I ignored his unfair comment about my clerical dress. I often wore my bishop suit and would have worn it more if I could have found my pectoral cross and episcopal ring.

"Off the record, I will point out that Bishop Augustus Quill had the second-lowest grades in our class, has often been the victim of delusions, and was in fact bounced from Rome because he had been an embarrassment."

Cardinal Cronin leaned his chin on tented fingers. "That's pretty strong stuff, Blackwood."

"I won't say it that way."

My private phone rang. Doubtless Mary Jane McGurn.

"Father Ryan."

"Mary Jane."

I flipped on the switch for the speaker phone.

"Ah!"

"Blackie, what the hell is going on over there! There's a rumor that someone named Idiot Quill has been sent to Chicago to replace Sean. It's supposed to be announced by the Nuncio tomorrow morning at seven. Is it true?"

The Cardinal winced.

"You can say, Mary Jane, that a spokesman for Cardinal Sean Cronin denied these rumors categorically. Bishop Quill will merely be the junior auxiliary bishop. He will have no more powers than any of the others. The Cardinal, of course, welcomes his appointment. He feels that he needs all the help he can get."

The Cardinal, pleased at my skills in mediaspeak, beamed happily.

"Are you sure, Blackie?"

"Absolutely."

"The guy apparently thinks he's going to clean up the mess in Chicago."

"The Cardinal's spokesman said that there is no mess in Chicago."

"This guy is not, what do you call it, some kind of coadjutor?"

"Certainly not."

"Even you outrank him?"

Sean Cronin grinned fiendishly.

"Though not for attribution, you say that even Bishop John Blackwood Ryan will have more seniority."

"O.K. . . . Now, why do they call him Idiot?"

The Cardinal grimaced. It would not help matters for the people to know that a new bishop had such a nickname.

"On the deepest of background, his seminary classmates called him that because they thought the name fit."

"Wow! You guys are going to have fun with him! . . . You think he's crazy?"

I hesitated. We would be asked that often, almost always off the record.

"Bishop Augustus Quill is a dedicated, devout, sincere, and industrious man. The Holy Father must think that his many long years of work for the Sacred Rota have earned him the right to be a bishop. Now I go into background. He is perfectly sane but sometimes he misreads reality."

The Cardinal nodded approvingly.

"Delusional?"

"Your word."

"They got rid of him in Rome and dumped him on you and Cardinal Sean?"

"Arguably that is the case. That comment also is deep background."

"O.K. Great. I have my story for the ten o'clock news." She hung up.

Milord shook his head in mock dismay. "I'm glad you're on my side, Blackwood."

"Oh, yes."

"Where did she get the nickname?" he asked with a frown.

"Doubtless from a fellow priest, not encumbered by loyalty."

I fielded several more calls before the ten o'clock

newscasts.

I also placed one—to my illustrious sibling Dr. Mary Kathleen Ryan Murphy.

"Watch Channel Six if you can. Both of you. Then call me. O.K.?"

"O.K."

Mary Jane began with Augustus O'Sullivan Quill in front of a very expensive house in Forest Hills.

M.J.: Bishop Quill, what will your role be in the Archdiocese of Chicago?

(The Bishop is a large man, not so much fat as fleshy. His round face frequently lapses into a genial smile that does not always fit the words he is speaking. His forehead is high and is often creased with lines of surprise. He is wearing French cuffs—part of the uniform—a black clerical vest, an elaborate jeweled pectoral cross, and a sapphire ring that makes Sean Cronin's ruby seem small. He laughs intermittently, especially before he answers a question. It is a superior giggle that a pastor might use when asked a silly question by a second-grader.)

A.Q.: I really can't answer that quite yet. I must wait for Our Holy Father to announce it tomorrow morning at seven.

M.J.: It is safe to say, however, that you will be working in Chicago and with Cardinal Cronin?

A.Q.: I will not deny that.

M.J.: When the Cardinal retires in five years, will you replace him?

A.Q.: Oh my, that's a premature question. I am completely at the disposal of the Holy Father. I will do whatever he asks of me. For the moment I am merely eager to integrate my work with that of Cardinal Cronin.

M.J.: You've been away from Chicago for many years, Bishop. What qualifies you to become involved in the governance of the Archdiocese?

A.Q.: Prayer most of all. I spend an hour every morning on my knees in front of the Blessed Sacrament in fervent prayer. I like to think that during that hour I learn from God what he wants me to do that day. I also rely very much on my loyalty to the Most Holy Father, who is the vicar of Christ here on earth. With God and the Most Holy Father on my side, I don't see how I can fail. The Pope has been very good to me. When he ordained me a bishop in Rome—personally and with his own hands—he told me that I would do great things for the Church back in America. I am content to leave the future to God and to the Most Holy Father.

M.J. *(Eager to cut off this flow of piety)*: Isn't it true that you reversed every annulment case on which you were a judge in Rome?

A.Q.: The collapse of the family is the greatest single threat to American society. The family is the basic unit of society. Too-easy divorce and the promiscuous use of contraceptives are destroying the country. The Church must resist these tendencies with all its power and challenge the faithful to do the same.

M.J.: You disapprove of annulments?

A.Q.: Except in rare cases.

M.J.: You will work with the matrimonial court in the Archdiocese?

A.Q.: I assume so. All my experience and qualifications

are in that field.

M.J.: And you will clean up the mess there?

A.Q.: I will do whatever I can.

M.J.: Is it not true that if indeed you are appointed auxiliary bishop tomorrow you will be the most junior of them?

A.Q.: Ah, I don't believe that term has any canonical validity.

M.J.: Why is your nickname Idiot?

A.Q. *(Blandly)*: I don't believe I've ever heard that name.

M.J. *(To camera)*: This was the first interview with Bishop Augustus O'Sullivan Quill, rumored to be a replacement for Chicago's Sean Cardinal Cronin. If this is true, Chicago's two and a half million Catholics are in for some major changes. A spokesman for Cardinal Sean Cronin denied these rumors categorically. Channel Six was told that the Cardinal, of course, welcomes Bishop Quill's appointment. He feels that he needs all the help he can get. Nevertheless, Bishop Quill will merely be the junior auxiliary bishop. He will have no more powers than any of the others. Bishop Quill has called a press conference at the Chancery office tomorrow at ten-thirty. This is Mary Jane McGurn in Forest Hills.

ANCHOR: Mary Jane, does it look like Cardinal Cronin will lose some of his powers in the Archdiocese?

M.J.: He won't give them up without a fight.

Milord Cronin beamed happily at Mary Jane's last comment. His smile was quickly replaced by the worried frown that had taken possession of his face throughout the interview. I noted that someone else in the Archdiocese had also briefed her.

"He touched all the bases, Blackwood. Humility, prayer, Holy Father, experience in Rome, protecting family life—"

"*Most* Holy Father a couple of times."

"The faithful will rally to those themes."

"What faithful! He's thirty years too late with that approach."

"You think so? Well, maybe . . ."

"Those who will rally to him are those that don't like you anyway."

"Judging by my mail that will be a lot of them."

"How many times have I argued," I said with some asperity, "that crank mail is not representative?"

"I know. . . . Still, he'll be trouble."

"Oh, yes," I agreed.

The phone rang.

"Bishop Ryan."

It was my aforementioned sibling. "Hi, Punk. Hey, you and Sean have yourselves one big, fat, oily problem on your hands. . . . Is Sean there? Turn on the speaker phone! Hi, Sean."

"Hi, Mary Kathleen," the Cardinal said with a broad smile, a smile reserved for beautiful women.

"My Jungian consort is here too."

"Hi, Dr. Murphy," he said with a grin.

"Hi, Cardinal."

My sibling Mary Kathleen Ryan Murphy and her husband Joe are both psychiatrists, she a heterodox Freudian, he an eclectic Jungian. Ever since she had seduced him (not too strong a word, I believe) during a psychiatric clerkship at Little Company of Mary Hospital, the pre-

53

tense, shared by all, was that she was the better clinician of the two. Everyone, including Mary Kate, knew that the pretense wasn't true.

"How are all the kids and grandkids?"

"Flourishing. Chantal's oldest is a senior in high school. Petey's wife Cindasue is expecting her first. Didn't waste any time. I think your new bishop might like that."

"Diagnosis?" I said impatiently.

"Pretty easy. Borderline personality. Unusual type. Not very bright. Passive-aggressive. Little sexual energy. Delusional. Manipulative. Probably learned from his mother to control his father that way. Becomes the poor, innocent, sincere child to get what he wants. Then turns officious with subordinates. Will have to be slapped down hard, but even then won't get it."

"He'll mess up everything he touches," the other Dr. Murphy warned, "all in the name of God and the Holy Father—"

"Most Holy Father," I corrected him.

"PUNK," Mary Kate interjected, "stop interrupting!"

"Punk" is the mostly affectionate diminutive my siblings use for me. And their children—as in "Uncle Punk"!

"It's a well-structured complex, Cardinal. Impermeable, I'd say. He's built it over time to protect a fragile ego. Take it away and he's nothing."

I had suspected a diagnosis of that sort. There would be trouble right here in Athens on the Lake, Richard M. Daley, Mayor.

"What do we do?" the Cardinal asked weakly.

"Hit him with reality," my sibling replied. "Slap him down every time he misbehaves."

"Do not yield an inch," her husband agreed. "Ever."

"Sounds grim. . . . No cure? No treatment?"

"Only if some extraneous event shatters the system. Then he'll probably go into a sustained psychotic interlude."

"What," I demanded, "might we do to generate such an extraneous event?"

Silence from my sibling and sibling-in-law.

"Maybe," Mary Kate said carefully, "catch him making love to a mother superior on the altar during Mass."

JENNY

5

The man stares at me. His spirit comes out of his body and embraces me, caresses me, undresses me, plays with me. I should be offended, perhaps, but I am not. There is no cruelty in his gaze. It is always respectful. I am afraid of it, but I enjoy it. My mind and body go limp. I cannot think. I cannot concentrate on my work. It must stop.

If I were to target a man, it would be someone like him—attractive, gentle, intelligent. And wealthy. I do not want a man. I have not targeted him. I have done nothing to win his attention. I am precise and prim when we are at meetings and he is inspecting my work. If anything, I am shy and tongue-tied.

My friends tell me that I should remarry. They say that the reason I have put so much energy and effort into reshaping my body is that I want a man. They say men drool over me. I don't want that. I wanted to rebuild my self-respect after the divorce and the annulment fights. I've had enough of men. I want to avoid them for the rest of my life.

Yet, the first time I saw this man, who is the president of our firm, my knees became weak. I had thought that my sexual feelings had been forever extinguished. I guess I was wrong. I would like to sleep with him just to see what he is like. That's the first time I have admitted that to myself. I do not want to become involved with him or anyone else. Why did God make us with sexual feelings that continue long after we are capable of bearing children? Why did he make us so that we would be lonely when we lie in bed by ourselves? I do not want to need a man. But without one I will be lonely. I must make up my mind to be lonely.

He is still staring at me. He pretends to be working, but his eyes never leave me. Once more his spirit slips away from his body and comes to me. He covers me with his kisses. I melt.

I must stop that.

I ask one of my colleagues if I have ever seemed to hit on the boss.

She says of course not, I'm as prim as a fundamentalist teenage virgin. I should hit on him, she says. He lost his wife two years ago. He is lonely. Look at the sadness in his eyes. He's a wonderful man. You're gorgeous and the kind of woman he'd fall for. I'm not that kind of woman, I say. She replies, I mean the kind of woman who could make him happy. Just send up a signal and he'll come running.

I'm accused of doing just that, I tell her. By Donnie? Yes. She's a bitch. She thinks she owns him. She figures that she's indispensable to the firm and she ought to be indispensable to him too. He is barely aware of her existence.

She wants to get rid of me. I need the job. She'll never be able to do that. He likes you too much even from a distance to do that. You're too good at what you do.

Why must I have this sense of someone's spirit coming out to me? It's much more seductive than the first clumsy caresses. When did my husband lose interest in me? I wonder.

I am at a large dinner party in Forest Hills. I do not want to go, but the woman who invited me insists that I must get out of my house. There are several men who tried to "hit" on me, all but one of them married. I dismiss them with practiced ease. Bishop Quill is at the party. I ignore him as much as possible because I hate him so. In person he is a fat, soupy worm.

They put him next to me at the table. How could they? Have they forgotten what he did to me? He pays little attention to me. I don't think he likes women very much, especially a woman with a touch of décolletage.

"I'm surprised you don't remember my name, Bishop," I say. I know I have crossed the line and I'm going to explode.

"How would I know you?" he asks.

"You tried to ruin my life."

He looks puzzled.

"You reversed my annulment even though my husband had already married his mistress. You gave an adulterer power over my marriage."

"I do not remember the case, madam," he says coolly.

"My husband hated me. He wasn't interested in protecting the marriage bond. He wanted to punish me. That's why he appealed the annulment decision. You went along with him. I hate you. I wish you were dead."

"Although I do not recall the case, your husband had the right to appeal. You, of course, had the right to appeal." He went back to shoving tiny bits of meat into his mouth. Everyone in the room is quiet.

"I did appeal," I shout, "and they reversed you."

"That does happen," he says calmly, wiping his greasy mouth with a napkin.

I'm screaming now. "They tore your decision to shreds." I run from the table sobbing.

The hostess comes after me. She apologizes. "I didn't know he was the one. He is a bit of a drip, isn't he?"

I apologize too. I hadn't wanted an annulment. Father Dribben said I should. It seemed so easy until Ben appealed. Then it dragged on. One more way for Ben to punish me. Father Dribben finally got the reversal reversed, I explain to her. And now he's taken poor Father Dribben's place.

I drive back down to my apartment, furious at myself. I dream about him at night—I mean my boss. We are making love. He is so sweet and kind. And so passionate. Then Bishop Quill is on top of me. I scream with terror and wake up. I am aroused and cannot go back to sleep.

My shrink listens to my story. Why are you so hard on yourself? she asks again. He is a vile little man and you told him so. You never did that to Ben. You're getting better. I'm sure everyone in the room was on your side. You wanted the annulment, she tells me. You wanted to marry again in your church. Someone better. Father Dribben knew that.

You of course understood the dream? No, I didn't, I insist. Yes, you do. All right, I do. He stands for a new life and the Bishop stands for my old life. They both want me. Brilliant, she says. You could do my job, better perhaps than I do it. I don't want to marry again. I'm just lonely, so lonely. I begin to cry. The shrink is pleased. You are, Jenny, a healthy woman with thirty perhaps forty years of life ahead of you. Of course you want a man. You are not fated to make the same mistake again. You deceive yourself when you say that you wanted to recapture your beauty merely for your self-respect. You also deceive yourself when you say you come here to straighten out your emotions, which, in fact, are healthy. Your anger and your fears are both appropriate. You are here to be sure you don't make a mistake in your quest for another man. I do not mind that. You are very wise to have a counselor in this difficult but exciting time. I am not a teenager, I tell her. I went through this once and I won't go through it again. It is time, she says.

I work hard at the office and catch up on my work. He's not here. I am not distracted. Then he comes in. There is a look of terrible pain in his eyes. I am shattered. I want to wipe the pain out of his eyes and make them glow with joy. Now it seems that my spirit goes out to him. That has never happened before. It has always been that I perceive the man thinking about me. Even Ben, before the children came. Before he thought that they and I were an obstacle to the Nobel Prize he was destined to win.

Now I envelop him without even looking at him. I run my fingers through his curly hair. I cover his beautiful face with my kisses. I unbutton my blouse and lay his head against my breasts. He sighs deeply, content with me, for a moment healed with pain. My body is aroused again, ready for lovemaking. I drive the thoughts away. This is absurd. I glance towards his office. He is looking out the window towards the lake, a faint smile on his face. I force myself to go back to work. Perhaps I should look for a new job. I say that once to my therapist. She says there will be another man there. She asks why I will not let myself be brave enough to send this man a signal. My colleague says the same thing. I must send a signal. I won't send a signal.

He calls me into his office to discuss the revisions I've made on my design. I can feel Donnie's eyes like knives in my back. He stands up, as he always does for a woman, and tells me that my dress is pretty, as he always does. We discuss the design. He compliments me on it. Tells me I have a rare talent and that I am getting better every time. This one is just about perfect. I don't think he tells everyone that. I blush and thank him for the compliment. It's not a compliment, he says, flushing slightly. Well, it is that too. But it's the truth. Suddenly the erotic vibrations in the room are strong. My body betrays me and begins to prepare for intercourse. This is absurd. We successfully pretend that we are professionals, that there is nothing between us except my graphic. We finish quickly. I accept his suggestions. He's the boss. Besides, they're good suggestions. I promise him that I'll have the changes by tomorrow morning. My body feels so heavy that I can hardly walk out of the office.

Donnie strides over to my desk. What were you doing in there? she demands. He asked me to discuss my design. Let me see it she says, pulling it out of my hand. This is shit, she tells me. It's no good. We'll never use it. I think it's rather good, I reply. She tears it. I think it's terrible and I'm the one who makes the decisions around here, she states.

Fortunately the graphic is still in my computer and I can remember the changes he suggested. I see over her shoulder that he is watching us from the office. He winces when she tears the proof into little pieces and throws it in the wastebasket. You're not very good, she tells me. I don't think you have much of a future here. You ought to find yourself a new job before we get rid of you. I don't say anything.

You're trying to seduce him, aren't you? she sneers at me. I am not, I reply calmly, and think to myself, Not yet anyway. I warn you, she says, I'm not going to let you get away with that. You try one more of your fancy moves and I'll fire you myself. Now get to work on this graph I want. It's simple enough and I don't want anything fancy. I say yes, ma'am. She storms away.

I put her algorithm aside and call up my design. Perhaps because I'm so angry I find myself on a run. It flows. I incorporate his suggestions and build on them in a way I know he'll like. I glance towards his office. Donnie is in there. She is very angry. If he is, he does not show it, self-contained as always. Did he call her in after she tore up my work, or did she charge into the office to tell him she was going to fire me? Donnie has been with the firm for a long time. Everyone says that even if she is so obnoxious, she is

61

indispensable. Has she told him it's her or me? Perhaps. I'll know soon enough. She storms out of the office, her face bright red, but she does not come in my direction. Maybe I've won. I finish my revisions. I could bring the final version into him now, but that will make more trouble. I'll put it on his desk when I arrive in the morning. No, I won't do that. She might see it and destroy. I'll give it to him myself.

You must give up your illusions, my shrink tells me. What illusions? I ask her. Your illusions that you are a failure as a woman. You believed the verbal abuse from Ben. You got him through graduate school. You typed his dissertation. You kept his house neat. You raised his children. He was so inferior as a man that he had to blame you for everything that went wrong in his career, especially the loss of the Nobel Prize. What if he is right? I ask her. What if I never was any good in bed? Do you think he was right? No, I say. I think he was wrong about everything. Do you think you were good in bed until he lost interest? I hesitate. Of course. Then why do you hide behind your illusions of inadequacy? I don't know. Yes you do. I know what she wants me to say. I don't want to say it, even if it is true. It is too dangerous, Jenny? she demands. Hiding is safe. If I am an adequate woman I'll have to take risks. She sighs with relief. Can you seduce this man if you want to? Yes. Will he marry you? Yes. Will you be happy together? Happier than most. Then what are you waiting for? I'm afraid.

I knock lightly on the doorjamb of his office. He glances away from his computer. His eyes light up. Jenny! he says. I blush. I must put an end to his ogling me in the office. He shouldn't be looking at me the way he does even now. I am not a heifer to be evaluated by a cattle buyer. I have the revised design, I say. Let's see it. He stands up courteously as he always does. As I join him at his desk, he takes in every inch of me, stripping away my clothes with his eyes. This has to stop. I am not a slave on the auction block. He turns his eyes to my design. Sit down, please, Jenny. I do, anxious that he won't like it. You've built on my suggestions, I see. He frowns. I don't like it when my employees improve on my recommendations. He's grinning. I relax. No, sir, I say. He sits down. So do I. How much are we paying you? I tell him. Not nearly enough, he says, making a note. When people in the trade find out who did this, they'll swarm all over you. Thank you, sir, I say meekly, an innocent peasant virgin in the presence of her feudal lord. It's perfect as it is, he says. We'll put it into production at once. Give this to Donnie on the way out and tell her I said to put it in the process.

There's one more thing, sir. He raises an eyebrow. I charge ahead. I'm not a naked slave matron on the auction block, but you stare at me like I am. He gulps and turns red. My face is very warm. I don't mean to offend you, Jenny, he stumbles, or to harass you. I'm very sorry. I don't feel either offended or harassed, sir, I say smoothly. In fact, I feel flattered. However, people in the office might misunderstand. They might indeed, he replies, his smile returning. I shall do my best to be more discreet. Thank you, sir, I say rising to flee. Jenny, he says as I reach the door. Yes, sir? You must not be shocked that men stare at you. You are a startlingly attractive woman. So long as they do it discreetly, I say with a smile and a toss of my head.

Donnie glares at me when I give her the design and the disk on which it resides. He says to put it in the process.

She looks at the design and turns up her nose in disgust. Back at my desk. I sigh with relief. Everything is settled. There'll be no more troubling stares in the office. Thank God, I had the courage to be blunt about it. Blunt but not bitchy. At the end of the day he tries to enter the elevator just as the door closes. I hold it open for him. Thank you, Jenny. You're welcome, I say meekly. Would you feel sexually harassed, Jenny, he blurts out, if I invited you to dinner tomorrow night. He was supposed to say that, but not so soon. I don't think I ought to, I begin. Then the crazy woman inside me takes over. That would be very nice, I say. That night Bishop Quill rapes me. In my dreams.

I show the shrink my graphic of "Jenny on the Auction Block." Very interesting, she says. Not quite pornographic. You have covered yourself modestly but inadequately. I see that you are now able to accept your physical beauty. That is considerable progress. You will give this to the man? Oh, no, I say blushing, not at all. At least not now. I wonder who the slave will really be? she muses.

BLACKIE

6

It's ten-fifteen," the Lord Cardinal said nervously. "We have to get over there before he does."

I was searching for my pectoral cross, a silver form of the Brigid cross that my cousin Catherine Curran had designed. I had already found the plain gold band that she had also produced.

"You are the Cardinal Archbishop," I reminded him. "It

would be most unseemly if you rushed over there just to head him off at the pass."

"We should tell the staff not to let him start."

"I have already suggested that strategy to them. It will be a good test of whether he can manipulate your staff to violate a direct order from you."

"From you."

"I told them I was speaking in your name."

I found the cross and stuffed it into the pocket of my Chicago Bulls jacket, a memorial to a happier year.

The Cardinal did not approve of my informal dress, though he understood the reason for it. But long ago he had sworn the most solemn oath that he would pay no attention to what manner of dress a priest might affect.

"What do you think they will do?"

"Like accomplished bureaucrats, they will stall him."

My prediction turned out to be correct.

Milord Cronin, unlike most princes of the Church, values punctuality. Even if he knows everyone is going to be late to some function, he arrives on time. And then glares at his watch as others straggle in. This time, I explained to him, he must arrive fifteen minutes late to convey the impression that he had other and better things to do besides attending this press conference, which in fact he had not called.

The Chancery auditorium was filled with the media, cameras and microphones at the ready. Chancery office clergy were milling around uneasily. The four auxiliary bishops, looking like pallbearers, waited grimly.

Augustus O'Sullivan Quill was near the podium, waiting for an opportunity to seize the mike. He was dressed in full robes, a cassock with purple buttons and purple trim, purple zucchetto, a purple cummerbund, and purple socks inside shoes with silver clasps.

"Sean, Blackie," Kas Piowar rushed to greet us. "Where have you been? We had to pull the mike away from this guy. What the hell is going on?"

"Oh you of little faith," Sean Cronin said, now in his happy Irish gallowglass mode, his blue eyes flashing dangerously. He strode briskly up to the podium. The other bishops rallied behind him, like commissars supporting a marshal of the Soviet Union. The Cardinal grasped Gus Quill's hand in a warm greeting and bathed him in his very best smile—as he eased him away from the mike.

I melted into invisibility.

I must gloss this assertion. I am the most unimpressive of humans. You'd hardly notice me if you got on an elevator on which I was riding. I'm not really invisible, exactly, merely not worth noticing. I am the little man who wasn't there. But when I seriously make up my mind to blend into the environment, I really am not there. It is a very useful quality.

I realized that at some point I would have to put on my Brigid cross, lest Catherine Curran be offended should she see me on television without it.

Naturally, the Cardinal and I had decided what he would say.

"It's good to see all my friends from the media again," he began genially. "We haven't had one of these solemn high press conferences in a long time. This is the first one we've ever staged for the appointment of an auxiliary bishop. We should have done it for all the other five," he gestured at the pallbearers behind him. "They're key men in the Archdiocese; without them nothing much would happen. I am deeply grateful for their hardworking collaboration. Gentlemen, thank you!"

He turned and bowed to the four of them—black, Italian, Latino, and Polish. They smiled. The old man was still in charge!

"I want to welcome to their ranks today our newest and thus most junior auxiliary, Bishop Augustus O'Sullivan Quill. Bishop Quill has at last come home to Chicago from Rome. Gus, welcome home."

Applause from the clergy!

"He has returned to us after a long career at the Sacred Roman Rota, one of the Vatican law courts. Although we have a number of highly trained canonists in our diocese, including Monsignor Ted Coffey, who I see out there among you, one can never have too many good lawyers in the Church."

There was just enough irony in the Cardinal's patently false comment about lawyers to draw a titter from the crowd, just what we wanted and no more.

"I have often told the Pope that I need all the help I can get. I'm grateful for adding Bishop Quill to my staff of helpers. He was, by the way, ordained last month by the Pope himself, along with fifty or, Gus, was it a hundred other bishops?"

He paused to give Gus a chance to answer.

"Fifty-six, Your Eminence," he replied in a squeaky voice.

"Right, fifty-six. I bet that when the Pope saw him in line he said to himself, that man Cronin needs a junior auxiliary. Why don't I send him Gus Quill! So, Gus, welcome aboard. It's good to have you with us."

He had, on the whole, done well enough, I thought.

Gus Quill edged towards the mike.

"Are there any questions?" The Cardinal asked the representatives of the media.

"Cardinal, you said five auxiliaries, but there are only four up there. Is someone ill?"

My cover was about to be blown.

"Bishop Ryan is around here somewhere," he said with a wave of his hand. "As often is the case, he is in one of his invisible moods."

I barely had time to pull the Brigid cross out of my jacket and put it on. The light from the Channel Six camera, after wandering a bit, picked me out, creating a partial veil from the reflection of my Coke-bottle glasses (which were reserved for public occasions because I wear contact lenses at my siblings' insistence). I smiled weakly, which is also part of the persona.

"Cardinal, is it true that Bishop Quill has been sent here by the Pope to take over some of your powers?" a reporter asked.

"I'm not sure what my powers are worth any more, but the answer is no."

Dismissive grin. Nicely done.

"Has he been secretly appointed your successor?"

"I'm in good health and have five more years before retirement. No decisions will be made about a successor till then. But to be direct, because of the rumors that always arise, I inquired of the Secretariat of State in the Vatican and the answer was a flat no."

Gus Quill was sweating profusely.

The questions went on for a few more minutes. Milord handled them all nicely. Then Mary Anne McGurn intruded again.

"Bishop Ryan, do you consider Bishop Quill a rival for succession?"

Obnoxious young woman!

I chose to ignore the question.

"Bishop Ryan . . . ?" the Cardinal said, indicating I was to answer.

I remained stoic. There was no escape but I wished to register my conviction that the question was frivolous.

"Blackie . . . ?" The Cardinal shouted, as if to wake me up.

I ambled disconsolately to the podium and intruded myself between Gus and the Cardinal.

"Would you repeat the question, Ms. McGurn?"

"Do you consider Bishop Quill a rival to be the next cardinal?"

I blinked my eyes in bemusement, glanced at Sean Cronin, and then at Gus Quill, from whose face the sweat was now pouring more profusely.

"I think, Ms. McGurn, that my chances of becoming archbishop of Chicago are excellent, about the same, in fact, as those of Jerry Krause, the general manager of the late and much lamented Chicago Bulls!"

Laughter and applause. I remained at the podium, eyes still blinking rapidly, to fend Gus away from the mike.

"Arguably less so," said the Cardinal, stirring up more laughter and applause.

"On that happy note," he continued, "I think we can

adjourn this conference and Gus and his senior colleagues and I can go to my office and discuss his responsibilities in the Archdiocese."

The media people packed their bags and began to drift out. The Cardinal threw his arm around Gus and led the way, the other bishops closing in like jailers. I hung around to test the waters.

"Good answer, Blackie," Mary Jane informed me.

"Young woman, you are incorrigible."

"You guys really shut him down."

"For the moment."

"Our kind has a good slant on him. He'll have a hell of a time changing that."

"I shouldn't wonder."

Ted Coffey, who, like Gus Quill, had been my classmate in the seminary, was less optimistic.

"You guys did a great job, Blackie," he said, shaking hands with me. He was a tall, handsome black Irishman, with a square face and deep blue eyes, one of the most successful and popular pastors in the city. "Shut him down completely."

I sighed my patented West of Ireland sigh, which often sounds like the onslaught of a serious asthma attack. "We headed him off at the pass."

"This time. He'll be back. He's always back. He never lets up. I worked with him at the Tribunal and studied with him in Rome. It's a wonder he got the degree, he's so dumb. But he keeps plugging away with his phony piety and his worship of the Pope. You guys are going to have to slap him down hard every time he makes one of his moves, and he'll be making them all the time."

"Arguably."

"No arguably about it, Blackie. He's poison. Very dangerous."

Remembering the comments of Mary Kate and Joe from the night before, I sighed again. "Doubtless you're right."

A quarter of an hour later, the Cardinal and Gus appeared at the elevator door, surrounded by the gaggle of auxiliaries. The Cardinal conducted Gus to the waiting limo, which was indeed bigger than the Cardinal's own Lincoln Town Car, and waved him off. The others went their separate ways.

"Neatly done, Blackwood," young Kas Piowar said to me.

"Perhaps."

The Cardinal waved me outside.

"Well?" he asked as we began the walk down Superior Street towards the Cathedral.

I sighed yet again. "The general feeling is that the first round is ours, but that we will have to keep fighting, perhaps indefinitely. . . . What happened upstairs?"

"He doesn't listen, Blackwood. Or maybe he can't listen. He doesn't hear what we say. We talked about a lot of things he might do, all harmless. He simply said he wanted to serve in the Archdiocese in an important way. The conversation went over his head. He wants an important job and assumes he'll get it."

"Will he?"

"No way."

"Ah."

"He speaks of assuming responsibility for the Hispanic work, right in front of Ricardo, who is our Hispanic vicar and is doing a fine job in most difficult circumstances."

"Certainly. Does he speak the language?"

"Not much. Ricky came at him with a rapid flow of Spanish and Gus stared at him blankly. Then Ricky insulted him and Gus didn't understand a word. Ricky just rolled his eyes. Gus said he was still mastering the language."

"You're not going to let him near the Latino population just to get rid of him?"

"I'll get rid of him some way, but not that way."

"Hopefully. I'm sure he is where he is in the Church because a lot of other people up and down the line got rid of him."

"He's not a bad guy, actually," Sean Cronin continued, "sincere and diffident and pious. But he simply does not hear what you say to him."

"Or won't hear."

"All right, he won't hear or can't hear or whatever. Still, I think he means well."

"His meaning well and a dollar and a half will get you a ride on our mutual friend Rich Daley's subway."

In retrospect, that was a prophetic phrase.

"You're very harsh on him, Blackwood."

"You remember what my sib and sib-in-law told us last night?"

"I'm not likely to forget it."

"I have reason to believe that the secret of his success is that people shove him off to the margins to get rid of him and then he comes right back at them from another route."

"I suppose so."

"I have but one fear," I said.

"And what is that, Blackwood?"

"Your good-hearted generosity."

He was quiet for a minute.

"Nora says that's my tragic flaw."

"I defer to her superior experience."

He paused again.

"I think I can count on your South Side realism."

"Oh, yes."

Inside the Cathedral rectory he said, "There's one small thing. Gus will stay with us here for a while. Until we sort out what he's going to do."

"His idea?"

"I guess so," Sean Cronin said weakly.

"First mistake."

"I should have asked you first."

"No one has to ask me anything first," I insisted.

"I still should have. Two weeks?" he asked meekly.

"Not one day, not one second more, or you'll have to get a new Cathedral pastor."

"No fear of that."

I wasn't so sure.

7

At first Gus Quill was not a problem in our house. He was polite and affable, quiet at the dinner table but friendly, an amused audience to the banter between myself and other members of the staff, even if he did show up in a purple-buttoned cassock. He congratulated me on the excellent food, the fine conversation, and the warm spirit of the house.

"John, no one who knew you in the seminary would be at all surprised by your pastoral skills."

He even accompanied me on my hospital visits and took notes of what I said and what I did, because, as he said, he had almost no experience with this kind of ministry.

I should have been suspicious when he called me "John." No one calls me that, save for passive-aggressive nuns and fascistic RCIA (Rite of Christian Initiations for Adults) directors. As is patent, I am either "Blackie" (or occasionally "Blackwood") or, in the family, "Punk." My late father, Ned Ryan, called me Johnny, as in "We are the only sane ones in the family, Johnny. White sheep caught among the black sheep." Such an observation is arguably accurate.

Then one day Gus Quill decided that he had been named to replace me as rector of the Cathedral.

"John," he said one morning, halfway through the second week of his stay, "I just want you to know that I am in no hurry to take possession of this suite of rooms."

He took in with interest the mess of my room and the objets d'art on the walls—the three Johns of my childhood (pope, president, and quarterback of the hated Baltimore Colts); a print of a very bossy medieval Madonna, who was alleged to look like my mother, Catherine Collins Ryan; and Lisa Raffery, a maid of all work in a Prairie Avenue mansion a hundred years ago, whose diary had once protected me from a disastrous mistake. I had just returned from a session with the second-graders, one of the great joys of the week. I felt that the world was much like second grade, a crazy but rather benign place.

"Ah!" I said in some surprise.

"Whenever you have time to vacate it will be fine. I am content to stay in the guest room as long as it is necessary, though it's somewhat small and less than convenient."

For mostly genetic reasons, I am rarely at a loss for words. This was one of those rare times.

"By the way, John," he said in a man-to-man tone, "isn't that picture a little risqué for a bishop's study?"

He gestured at a painting my cousin Catherine Curran had given me. Like all her nudes, it was utterly chaste. In fact, it was a painting of the famous actress Lisa Malone, who had gone to grammar school with Catherine and me.

"I think it's quite chaste," I replied, "though perhaps, on occasion, distracting."

"Well, I would disagree. I'm sure Jesus wouldn't like it."

A thousand retorts formed on my lips, but I held them back.

"Perhaps."

"Anyway, I want to wish you all the best in your new assignment, whatever that may be."

He shook hands with me and departed with the confident air of a man who had just taken over.

I was so astonished that I didn't feel angry. It was most unlikely that Sean Cronin would send me out into the fabled world that existed beyond the boundaries of the Cathedral parish. At the minimum, he would never be able to steal my Irish whiskey and tell me to see to it, nor to seek my advice on how to deal with the media vultures.

It was also arguably the case that I would be better off somewhere else. One gets into a rut when one has been in the same place too long. Idiot Quill would be welcome to it. And the Cardinal to the chaos that would follow.

I was hardly the indispensable man, was I?

I realized that these largely self-serving reflections were probably unnecessary. I could pick up the phone, call the Chancery, where Milord Cronin was working this morning, and ask him what the new assignment was, thus unleashing the whirlwind.

That, however, would be inappropriate. I would bide my time and see what happened. I therefore departed the rectory for my pastoral rounds—the hospital, the dead, the dying, the sick, the troubled, the sad, the bereaved.

It was midafternoon when I returned to North Wabash. Despite considerable searching, I couldn't find the key, a not untypical occurrence, so I pushed the doorbell. No one came. I glanced at my watch. It was time for the Megan to be there. They were under strict orders to answer doorbells promptly. I had assured them that in years past many people had left the church in a rage because no one answered the doorbell.

I pushed the bell again. Still no response.

Thereupon I engaged in behavior that is politely called leaning on the doorbell. Megan O'Connor answered. Though her face was dark with anger, I knew that there was trouble because she was not supposed to be on duty. Megan Flores, the Mexican-American member of the team, was supposed to be our porter person.

"Bishop Blackie," she screamed, "we want to talk to you!"

I had a pretty good idea what the trouble was.

In their headquarters, I found Megan Flores in tears, Megan Kim solemn, and Megan Jefferson, like her Irish-American counterpart, ready to eat nails.

"Ah?"

"That terrible man made Megan Flower take down the cute posters she made!"

"He did?"

"Then he tore them up!"

"He didn't!"

Four torn posters were shoved in my face. Megan Flores, a.k.a. Flower, an ingenious graphic designer, had posted warnings that this was a NO SMOKING RECTORY, a NO FIREARMS RECTORY, a NO NUCLEAR RECTORY, and a NO DRINKING RECTORY.

I had always assumed that the last rule did not apply to the upper floors.

The posters caused laughter in all but the most reactionary visitors. Milord Cronin loved them, in part because he loved the vivacity and charm of my carefully chosen porter persons.

"Who is this iconoclast?" I demanded.

"Bishop Quill," they replied as one, each of them now crying.

"He came back from the church where he was praying for an hour," Megan Jefferson continued, "and said that God had told him those posters were not fitting. . . . What does he mean by fitting? Like a dress doesn't fit?"

"Arguably he means appropriate."

"Would God really tell him that?"

"I think that very unlikely. . . . I must report this defacement to the Cardinal," I said. "Bishop Quill is not my guest."

"And," Megan Jefferson said, "he told us God told him that we can't work here anymore after the end of the week!"

"We'll organize pickets," Megan O'Connor warned me. "We'll shut this place down, just like my great-grandfather did in the Great Depression!"

"I'll march with you! In the meantime, Megan Flores, you might begin to redo the posters."

The tears vanished.

"Even weirder than the last time!"

"Much weirder!"

Having thus reassured the troops, I ascended on our cranky and creaky elevator to the top floor of the rectory, where the Cardinal lived. I rarely bothered him up there, save on the house phone. A man is entitled to his privacy.

Conversation and laughter flowed out of the open door of the room. The Lady Nora, no doubt.

A long time ago she and her foster brother/brother-in-law had been lovers, for a very brief interlude, I suspected. Now they were good friends, a relationship of love that certainly was sexual but also chaste. Also none of my business, save that the Cardinal had once told me about it.

"Blackie," she said, "come in and have a cup of tea."

Even in her late sixties Nora Cronin's smile could melt all the ice on Lake Michigan in the middle of winter.

"I'd love to, but I fear that the natives are restless tonight."

"Which natives?" The Cardinal raised an eyebrow.

"The Megan are in open revolt."

"We can't have that!"

"It would appear that Bishop Augustus O'Sullivan Quill tore up Megan Flower's posters and informed her that the services of the whole Megan would not be required after the end of this week. He apparently came to these conclusions after an hour of prayer in church."

"What!"

"It would appear from other indications, which have come to my attention, that he believes that he has been appointed rector of the Cathedral, a task to which he is quite welcome."

"Shite!" He rose from his chair, spilling some of his tea. His face was locked in a grim frown—Phil Jackson finally driven to outrage by stupid refs.

"Sean," the Lady Nora murmured softly as she moved to sop up the spilled tea, "that man simply has to go. I don't like the way he looks at me when he sees me in the elevator."

"One or the other of us has to," I added, "before tomorrow night at the close of business."

The Cardinal sighed, imitating rather nicely my own West of Ireland sigh.

"Blackwood, sit down and drink a cup of tea with Nora. She will tell you that she wouldn't let me fire you even if I wanted to. She has the crazy idea that you're a good influence on me."

"Arguably," I agreed.

"Now I'll go down and apologize to the Megan."

"By your leave," I said to Nora Cronin, "I'll retrieve a tiny amount of Irish whiskey from my study. Milord will need it on his return."

"Bring some for me too, Blackie. We can all celebrate the departure of that terrible man. I'll brew a fresh pot of tea."

As sure as the sun would rise in the morning and as Rich Daley was mayor of Chicago, Gus Quill would have his marching orders within the hour.

However, we had not heard the last of him. At all, at all, as the Irish say.

TOMMY

8

I drifted back to the Hancock Center in a happy daze. We had covered a lot of preliminary material in forty-five minutes—material that normally would have required many dates with a woman who wasn't a young lioness. So far I was a man approved. "Weird" was not necessarily a negative word in the vocabulary of my generation. "Sweet" was definitely positive. I was definitely worth getting to know better.

And my reactions?

Who was I to resist the will of God?

Then I realized that God was playing with good odds. Christy Logan and I lived in the same neighborhood and went to the same church. We would have encountered each other anyway. Most likely. Bishop Blackie knew that too. Admittedly God had chosen a cool site for the drama to be worked out. I was a victim of a conspiracy. Not, however, at this point, an unhappy victim.

I spent the rest of the evening replaying our conversation. I had performed ably, like I normally did in the Eurodollar pit. She had found me not unacceptable. We were a long, long way from courtship. Yet it was legitimate to ask the question of whether, on the basis of what had happened in Ghirardelli's, I would, tentatively and speculatively, find Christy Logan an acceptable companion for the rest of our lives.

I remembered her enthusiastic lecture on *Finnegans Wake*. I could, I told myself, do worse.

Properly dressed in a dark gray suit and a Georgetown tie, I entered the lobby of the Water Tower apartments the following afternoon at 6:25. "Miss Logan, please," I told the doorman.

He smiled with infinite politeness. "I believe Miss Christina Logan is the only one home at present. Who should I say is calling?"

"Tommy."

He picked up a phone and pressed a button.

"Miss Logan, there is a very presentable young man named Tommy for you in the lobby. . . . Yes, Miss Logan, I'll tell him. She says, sir, that you are a few minutes early, but she'll be right down."

Promptly at 6:30—making the point that she was not uncontrollably eager?—Christy Logan appeared at an elevator door.

I gulped. "I was expecting a lioness and I encounter a goddess."

A shy goddess at that in a simple black shift with a touch of gold trim, black nylons, a pearl necklace, hair that was combed out and fell to her shoulders, a hint of make-up. I took both her hands in mine and drank her in.

"Tommy! You're embarrassing me!" she said, as a line of crimson spread down her face and over her neck.

"I'm sorry," I said quickly, letting go of her hands.

"I didn't say that you should stop embarrassing me!"

My fearsome young lioness actually wanted me to approve her appearance. Some men must have made fun of

81

her height and her strength. Tasteless jerks. A woman could be svelte without being skinny.

I linked my arm with hers. "For a soccer All-American you sure dress up stunning."

"Thank you." She beamed. "Let's walk around the block before we ride up to the Carlton Club. . . . Are you really a Hoya?"

"Can't you tell from my superior intelligence and cultivation?"

"I've never been out with a Georgetown boy before." She was giggling.

"Then you're in for a real treat." I giggled back.

"I mean, I saw that Georgetown tie and if it wasn't that I'd disappoint Mom and Dad, I would have turned around and went back into the elevator."

"Hey, it was hard for me even to talk to a Notre Dame woman."

"Pick her up."

"She invited me out and I didn't say no. I was picked up. You must have known I went to Georgetown, my manners were so superior."

"Well, at least you're not a slob."

She clung to my arm and huddled close to me. I was acutely aware of her intense, womanly warmth and her paralyzing scent. Careful, Tommy, or you'll lose it.

"You didn't invite me to come upstairs to meet your parents. Afraid they might not approve?"

"Afraid they *would* approve. . . . Such a nice Irish-Catholic boy!"

"Compared to whom?"

"Compared to no one. I don't bring many boys around.

Too many geeks out there."

"Maybe I'm a geek!"

"Maybe, but I don't think so. A little weird maybe . . ."

"But sweet."

"Moderately so." She squeezed my arm. "Hey, what's your name?"

"Tommy."

"Your *last* name. Even if I had brought you up to meet my parents, how could I introduce you? Hey, Mom and Dad, this is Tommy. I picked him up at Ghirardelli's. He's kind of cute, isn't he?"

"Moderately cute."

"A little less than that maybe, but we'll stop right here until you tell me your last name."

"Flynn. . . . I'm Amy's brother."

"Omigod! Why didn't I see that before! You have her black hair and white skin and neat teeth and twinkle in your eye and sculpted face! I must be blind! You are *really* Amy's brother!"

She touched my face as she made the comparison with Amy. Her fingers burned.

"Amy's my sister. And do me a favor—"

"I won't tell her that I picked you up in Ghirardelli's. Where we are now, we don't need that."

"Bought me with a second chocolate malt. . . . And where are we now?"

"Other than riding up to the ninth floor of the Ritz-Carlton, I haven't the slightest idea. We're not nowhere, but we're not much into somewhere either."

We laughed together.

"Do you go to church?" she asked, still clinging to my

arm as we walked across the lobby towards the Carlton Club.

"Of course I go to church."

"Really?"

"Every Sunday. Sometimes more often. I was away for a while, but Bishop Blackie wrestled me back in."

"You know Bishop Blackie! Isn't he cute?"

"The Megan are cuter."

"Aren't they adorable kids! You must be an active parishioner to know them."

"Not really."

As we walked to our table in the Carlton Club, every eye turned to take in my companion. She didn't seem to notice. The black shift, I saw, was made of clingy material that emphasized, subtly and discreetly, every curve in her wondrous body; it was an ostensibly modest garment that wasn't modest at all. In the presence of this warm, exciting, apparently fragile young woman, my temporarily captive lioness, my obsessive shower room fantasies seemed inappropriate and irrelevant.

You have to treasure your temporarily captive lionesses.

As we studied our menus—having both ordered Evian water on the rocks—I said, "Christy Logan, young lioness, you'll have to forgive me if I gawk at you. You're a resplendent woman, breathtaking, overwhelming, paralyzing!"

She put down her menu and looked like she was about to cry.

"There's a lot of me, I'm afraid."

"And every inch of you is beautiful."

How had I suddenly become skillful at complimenting

women? What was happening to me? I should not trust this one. She was too beautiful, too smart, too dangerous. Maybe I was the one trapped in the lion's den.

"Definitely sweet." She hid behind the menu. "Still weird. But definitely sweet."

"Moderately so."

"Maybe a little bit better than that."

"What happens after you graduate? More soccer?"

"Well I HAVE to go to the Olympics, but I'm not planning on a career as a soccer player. Maybe I'll retire as a lioness. . . . Grad school, naturally."

"In what?"

"Medical school, of course. Sports medicine."

"Where?"

"Northwestern. Where else?"

"You'll do your residency in Chicago too?"

"I'm a Chicagoan, Tommy Flynn, why should I want to go anywhere else? Have you read Alice McDermott's novels? And Anna Quindlen's?"

I admitted that I had.

"I think they're totally cool, but they're not Irish like we are."

"Totally cool"—she was still a child, Amy's age. Five, six years were a generation these days. I was robbing a cradle.

So we entered into a long discussion about whether you could tell where Irish novelists were from by how they wrote. I argued that she knew where Anna Quindlen and Alice McDermott were from because their stories were set in the New York area. She said she knew where they were from because they didn't have the same sense of parish community that we had. She also insisted that she'd known that Anne Rice was from New Orleans because her writing was so weird.

"Weird like I'm weird?"

"Totally different. Did you know she has returned to the Church? About time. Her images are all Catholic even when they're perverted."

"I see."

"You knew she was Irish?"

"I'm afraid not."

"Don't you ever look at copyrights, Tommy Flynn? It says Anne O'Brien Rice. Anyway, I'm glad she's back. Like Bishop Blackie says, "Once a Catholic always a Catholic.""

"Bishop Blackie is weird," I remarked.

"Of course he is. Wonderfully weird."

"I'm not wonderfully weird, however?"

"Well"—she paused to consider the issue—"not yet, but you might be."

"If I work at it!"

"Right . . . and, Tommy Flynn?"

"Yes, Christy Logan?"

"You are gawking at me an awful lot."

"I'm sorry."

"I don't mind. I just thought I'd tell you."

"Everyone in the dining room is gawking at you."

"Do I look that odd?"

"You do not look odd, you've never looked odd, you never will look odd, do you understand that?"

"Yes, sir, lion trainer!"

"You look beautiful. That's why they are gawking."

"Really?"

"Yes, really!"

"I had my chocolate fix yesterday."

A half-mad notion entered my head. I tried to fight it off. "I have a confession to make, Christy Logan."

"Oh?" Her faced twisted into a frown. "You're married?"

"No way."

"You're engaged?"

"Absolutely not."

"You're deeply in love . . . with someone else?"

"No way."

She paused, the frown easing.

"You're gay?"

"No, ma'am."

"Then, what?"

"Well, after watching you trample over the Lady Trojans and leave the field covered with mud and sweat and rain, I had a vivid and, I confess, delightful fantasy about you in the shower cleaning off all the muck."

"Really!" she brightened. "How wonderful! . . . Did you like me?"

"How could I not like you?"

"What's wrong with that?" she grinned. "People have fantasies, that's part of being human. I don't think anyone has had a fantasy like that about me before."

"I doubt that."

"Well, they haven't told me, anyway. When I'm in the shower from now on, I'll imagine you admiring me."

"Don't you think I was exploiting you?"

"Don't be silly, Tommy Flynn, you'd never exploit me. You were just admiring me, which I think is great!"

"Admiring you naked."

"Covered with suds and stuff. Men imagine women naked. That's why there are still humans around. I don't mind that, so long as they respect me."

"Sometimes they don't."

"I know that, but you do, so that's all that matters. . . . And after you'd seen me cavort around the soccer field like a demon."

"Lioness."

"And you still imagined that lioness without any clothes on!"

I wasn't getting anywhere.

"Would you be outraged if someone else imagined you naked?"

"Depends on who the someone else was." She shrugged at what she thought was a silly question. "Don't expect access to the real thing."

"I don't."

"At least not anytime soon."

I left that alone.

"I kind of want to know what you like about me—in your fantasy, I mean. Maybe I shouldn't ask."

"Everything!" I said as she signed the bill.

"Well, Tommy Flynn, would you like to take a walk around Streeterville with me?"

"It's probably a little chilly. You might need a sweater."

"I brought one down to the lobby earlier this afternoon, just in case I wanted to walk after dinner."

"I must have passed another test."

"I figured you would."

"Thank you very much for dinner."

"You're welcome. Daddy will pay for it, of course, and think himself lucky that his soccer star daughter has a date with a nice young man. I won't tell him you have neat fantasies about me."

"Don't," I begged her.

As we walked across the lobby towards the elevator she said, "I never asked a boy on a date before, except for high school proms. I never took one to dinner. It's kind of neat."

"Only a weird boy would accept such an invitation."

"Kind of weird?"

"Kind of."

"Moderately weird?"

"Wonderfully weird."

In the lobby I fitted the sweater around her shoulders. She glanced up at me with an appraising look. The young lioness was falling for me. Moreover, I didn't seem to mind. This was a very dangerous situation. If I let this crazy relationship go on much longer, I might have to spend the rest of my life in a lioness's den.

Perhaps she was having second thoughts herself. We hardly knew each other. Two hasty crushes. I would foul the relationship up if it went on much longer. She was a vulnerable young woman, at least when it came to men. Maybe I should end it after our walk.

Not a chance.

"I don't like to be pushy, Tommy Flynn."

"Sweetly pushy."

She laughed. Somehow we had taken each other's hand as we walked up the Magnificent Mile towards Oak Street. Why did my captive lioness have to be so fragile?

"ANYWAY, I have to drive back to the Dome tomorrow

before it gets dark. Could we meet over at the Cathedral tomorrow for Mass?"

"No way!"

"Why not?"

"Because I'll pick you up in your apartment lobby at twenty to ten."

"Great!" she squeezed my hand. "Then my mom and dad, who go to an earlier Mass, usually do brunch in the dining room at the Carlton. It's supposed to be the best brunch in Chicago."

"I have been there and it is. . . . Are you inviting me?"

We turned down Oak Street, the dark, silent lake on one side, and the Gold Coast of East Lake Shore Drive on the other.

"Well, if you don't think I'm pushing too hard."

"You're willing to let your parents get a look at me?"

"If you promise to behave."

"I'll try."

It would be easy to please her parents. I'm charming and respectable with adults. I mean real adults, not superannuated teenagers like myself. They'd have no idea how screwed up I was. They'd like me on sight.

"Then"—she drew a deep breath—"I have to exercise to rid myself of those Ghirardelli chocolate calories. We might swim in my pool."

My lioness in a swimsuit!

"I have a pool in my building too."

"Mine's nicer."

"It is that."

"Then you'll swim with me?"

"I'd love to."

"I mean *really* swim, not just fool around in the water."

"I *really* swim every day, Christy Logan."

"You sure I'm not pushing you too hard?"

"I feel charmed, not pushed."

Gosh, I was slick. Digging a big hole in the ground for myself too.

She squeezed my hand in gratitude.

"Tommy Flynn . . ."

"Yes, Christy Logan?"

"May I ask you a very personal question?"

"Sure."

"You may not like it. . . ."

"I may not, but I like the one who will ask it."

She took a deep breath.

"Why is there so much pain in you?"

Now who was naked?

"Pain?"

"In your pretty blue eyes, great sadness. Not all the time. Not even a lot of the time. But sometimes, especially when you look at me. Has someone broken your heart?"

"You really believe in taking a man's clothes off on a first date, don't you?"

"I didn't know it was a date. Maybe on a date I wouldn't have asked the question. I'm sorry. Please forgive me."

I put my arm around her shoulder.

"Nothing to forgive, Christy. You are, in addition to being smart and gorgeous and a soccer All-American, a remarkably sensitive and perceptive young woman."

"You don't have to tell me, Tommy."

"I want to. I've never told anyone but Bishop Blackie. It would be good to tell it to a sympathetic woman."

She put her arm around my shoulder, which was easy enough because, with her one-inch heels, she matched my five feet eleven inches.

"A woman did break my heart, Christy. It wasn't a girl-friend. It was my mother."

"Your *mother?* Beth?"

"Beth is our stepmother."

"She did seem kind of young. . . . Amy always calls her Mom."

"The girls all do. . . . I can remember back to when I was the only child around the house. My real mother was so young and so pretty and so loving. She must have adored me then. She sang to me and hugged me and laughed with me. Then when the girls came along, she changed. She wouldn't take care of us. Dad had to bring in a full-time nanny. She must have been lazy all her life. Indulged by her parents. Always a passive-aggressive person. She'd punish you by doing nothing. She'd go out to movies in the afternoon with her friends and to bars afterwards. She drank a lot and hit the girls, especially poor Amy."

"Amy seems fine now."

"She is, but it took a lot of therapy. My sisters turned out to be survivors. . . . Did Amy ever mention me to you?"

"Sure."

"What did she say?"

"She said that you were cute and rich and could be nice when you tried to, but that you were a recluse and were afraid of women."

"And you think now . . . ?"

"You don't act like a recluse or someone who is afraid of women."

"Don't be so sure. . . . Anyway, my mother would move away from the house for long periods of time to our house down at the Dunes, then to an apartment in Oak Brook. Sometimes she'd summon one of the girls, never me because she hated me so much by then, to wherever she was. The kids hated it. She'd hit them and make them cry and then send them home, saying they were spoiled brats."

"Your father picked up the bill for all of this?"

"He still loved her. He didn't know what to do. There were times when she was wonderful again, but they didn't last very long. Then when I was a senior at St. Ignatius, she summoned us all out to a restaurant in Oak Brook. There was another woman there. Mom told us that she had discovered she was a lesbian and this other woman was the love of her life and she wanted to share this good news with all of us!"

"Was she really?"

"I don't think so. She's back with a man now. . . . Amy vomited on the spot and then rushed off to the washroom. Lisa sobbed. Marie, the one most like me, sat and stared at her, just as I did. Finally I drove them home. Monsignor Coffey said that Dad should get a divorce and an annulment. Mom made the divorce proceedings as difficult as possible. I went off to college. All the girls went into therapy. The annulment went through without any trouble. Dad had been dating Beth. I think they were sleeping together. I sure hope so. They were about to be married when we learned that Mom was challenging the annulment. Some Franciscan named Father Innocent out in the suburbs helps people to do that. Monsignor Coffey, our pastor out in Oak Park, said to hell with it and married them anyhow. Then the annulment was reversed by that asshole new bishop. Someone ought to kill him. . . ."

"Tommy!"

"I usually keep the anger bottled up, Christy. I said that in back of the Cathedral last week."

"People heard you!"

"Sure, I didn't give a damn."

"Maybe you need a therapist, Tommy Flynn."

"I am seeing someone," I said, by which I meant that I would start seeing someone the first thing Monday morning.

"So you left the Church and Bishop Blackie wrestled you back?"

"It was really wrestling. I'm a lot happier now. He says that I have to rid myself of the illusion that I am a failure as a man because I am responsible for what happened to my mother."

"He's right, of course."

"As Cardinal Sean says, 'Blackie is occasionally in error but never in doubt.' "

"So you kind of half-like a woman, then you confuse her with your mother, and you get angry at her and screw up. So you tend to stay away from them."

"That's what Blackie says. It fits. I'm sure he's right."

"You don't seem afraid of me."

"You're different, Christy Logan. I don't want to mess up with you."

She was silent.

"I don't know whether there's anything really between us, Tommy. A pleasant weekend, forgotten by next weekend. However, if you think I would ever let you get away with doing that to me, you don't know what we young lionesses are like when we're really angry. Understand?"

"Yes, ma'am."

I was exhausted. I wanted to weep.

"You work this out with your shrink and don't ever try it on me. Understand?"

"Yes, ma'am."

"Even if tomorrow is the last day of our little romance, understand?"

"Yes, ma'am."

We were walking south on Lake Shore Drive.

"And tomorrow won't be the last day either. I won't let it be. Understand that?"

Instead of crying, I laughed. "I didn't expect you'd let it be."

Then we both laughed.

We stopped on the Drive and she pulled my head over to her breasts and let it rest there for a moment.

So we both wept.

"It was wonderful to be able to tell all of that to a woman," I said when she released me. "Thanks for listening. Sorry I had to dump it on you."

"You know damn well, Tommy Flynn, lion trainer, that your story binds us together. I think you're a hero. Silly Amy doesn't know that you're the one who held the family together. Someday I'm going to tell her."

"I didn't say that I held the family together."

"You did, though. I bet you were the one who eased Beth into the house."

"Maybe."

She was supposed to think I was a mess. Instead, she thought I was a hero. The lioness was trapping the lion tamer with sympathetic affection. I didn't mind.

We walked back along Pearson Street by that ugly museum of contemporary art that looks like a bunker that launches rockets and into the park, across from the Water Tower apartments. Christy led me into the park, which in daylight hours is flooded with rug rats and pretty young mothers.

"I always thought this would be a good place for kissing. There's no privacy over in the lobby. You're the first boy I've dragged in here. And since I paid the bill . . . well, my daddy will . . . I get to say whether there will be any kissing, right?"

"Right!"

"I'm thinking about it."

She brushed her lips against mine, cautiously, affectionately, generously.

"Nice," I murmured.

Then I put my hands on her solid rear end and drew her against me. I kissed her, not passionately, exactly, but still with some force.

"Very nice," she sighed. "Do it again?"

"You paid the bill."

I did it again, escalating a bit.

"Very, very nice."

"Thank you, ma'am."

"Take me home now, Tommy."

"It's just across the street."

"Really?"

I led her across the street, smiled at the doorman, and

watched as she entered the elevator. She turned towards me and waved and smiled as the elevator door closed.

The smile carried me all the way back to my apartment.

She's staying in Chicago, I thought. No reason why we could not be married after she graduates. The Olympics could be our honeymoon. I'll work on cleaning up my act with a shrink. Christy would never let me get away with old shit.

If she still wants me.

In the cold light of Sunday morning that all seemed absurd. Let her find her own way to Mass, I told myself, and rolled over in bed after the alarm. Then I popped out of bed. I'd have to find a corsage for her. The florist at the Drake, open doubtless for men like me, sold me a corsage of roses for a very high price. Worth it, I thought, at twice the price.

I arrived at the lobby of Water Tower apartments at eighteen minutes to ten. My lioness, robed in a mauve autumn dress with a short skirt, was tapping her foot impatiently. She looked at her watch as I charged in. Then she saw the flower box and melted.

"Tommy, you're so sweet. I won't say you shouldn't have because that's rude. Thank you very much."

And she kissed me, right in front of the doorman.

I helped her pin the roses on the dress, my hand brushing mostly without intent against her breast.

"How did you know what color I'd be wearing?" She kissed me again.

"I may have dirty thoughts about you all through the Eucharist, Christy Logan."

"For the last time, if you have thoughts about me, they

are not, I repeat not, dirty. Now is that settled?"

"Yes, ma'am."

I took her arm in mine and we walked over to the Cathedral. Bishop Blackie stood at the back of the church, vested for Mass.

"It's consoling to see two young parishioners coming into Mass together," he murmured, blinking through his thick glasses.

"See what he got me, Bishop Blackie, a corsage, real roses!"

For a moment she was a teen again, showing off to her favorite priest.

"I have always said that Tommy is a young man of impeccable taste, which today he proves in two ways."

She yelped happily. I felt my face grow warm.

"I'm going to phone that number tomorrow morning," I whispered to him. "I'll tell her you sent me."

"In the present set of circumstances, that phone call is mandatory."

I'm sure he changed the story for his sermon so it would be aimed at us. At me.

"Once upon a time there was this boy," he began, "a senior in college, who had a total crush on a young woman who was a junior. She was totally gorgeous and very smart and also very nice, like I mean she never got drunk, you know? She was so pretty and so popular and so cool that our hero couldn't believe that she even noticed his existence. A lot of his friends would go, 'That chick really is crazy about you,' but he thought they were just making fun of him. And some of her friends were like, 'She'd really enjoy going out with you.' But our hero, who was a very shy boy (all boys are shy even if they don't act that way, but he was very, very shy) thought that they were making fun of him too. His family had made a lot of fun of him when he was growing up, you see. Well, the young woman, whose name was Fiona, sat next to him in American Lit class and talked to him before and after class (about American Lit naturally) and stopped to talk to him when she met him on campus (about American Lit or about the women's basketball team on which she played), and about all he could do was reply with animal noises like he was a freshman in high school. You see, he thought she was like making fun of him too!

"Well, she kind of hung around his family at graduation and they thought she was totally cool. His mother was like, 'That young woman is in love with you and you're a total retard (that's the way people talked when his mother was in college) if you let her get away.' He thought his mother was making fun of him too. So he's like, 'She doesn't care about me at all.' And his mother goes, 'There's no one so blind as he who will not see.' My story has to end here, alas. Except I must tell you that Fiona represents God."

My lioness nudged me with one of her sharp elbows.

I was distracted through much of the Eucharist by the outline of her gorgeous breasts against her dress. She says they're not dirty thoughts, I explained to God.

"Great sermon, Bishop Blackie," she said enthusiastically as we left the Cathedral. "We both really liked it."

If I permitted this relationship to continue much longer, I would never escape from the woman.

Her parents were lovely people, both handsome cardiologists in their early sixties, the woman an older version of

Christina. Their other children were already married. These gentle folk clearly adored their All-American daughter. I understood why she was who she is. She had grown up in a climate of powerful and generous love. I envied her.

"Isn't this corsage lovely! I've never had a corsage for Mass before!"

Her parents smiled happily. I was clearly an acceptable date for their tomboy daughter.

"That was lovely of you, Thomas," Mrs. Dr. Logan said. Christy would look like her in forty years. I know when to go long on a future. Christy was a good future.

"Well," I said with my most charming smile, as we sat at a table and they brought us some champagne, "She paid for dinner last night, so I had to do something. I mean, she did pick me up and invite me out for dinner!"

"Tommy!" She blushed. "That's not true!"

"Let me tell you the story, Drs. Logan"—I turned on my most charming Irish political smile—"and I'll let you be the judges."

After we had collected our food from the array of tables—and I chose enough for lunch and supper—I told the story. But not before Christy Logan complained about my selections.

"Nothing but waffles and bacon, Tommy Flynn? That's not healthy!"

"I'll make up for it all week long. Now, as to the true story about what happened at the Ghirardelli chocolate shop on Friday last. . . ."

I told a true story, though not the whole truth, starting from my coming upon the Domer soccer team on TV. I left out my prurient fantasies after the game, my call to Bishop

Blackie, and Christy's crack about virgins' need for something sweet. However, I told the story with enough comic elaboration to keep the Logans, all three of them, laughing till the end.

"They love you," she whispered to me after brunch. "You pick up your swimsuit and I'll meet you in the club. It's right down that staircase."

"Yes, ma'am."

I grabbed my suit, which I had left at the desk of the Hancock Center, and rode back to the lobby floor of the Ritz, eager to see my young lioness in one or the other form of advanced undress.

She was back to jeans and sweatshirt when she met me at the door of the club.

"Promise you won't laugh at me?" she begged.

"Why would I do that?"

"I think I might have gone too far with my swimsuit."

"I doubt it."

"Mom and Dad thought you were wonderful. They said I showed excellent taste in the young men I pick up."

"No doubt about it."

I arrived in the empty pool area first and climbed into the spa. Christy emerged from the women's locker room a few minutes later, wrapped protectively in a towel.

"Promise you won't laugh?"

"I've already promised."

"Promise again?"

"I promise again."

She tossed aside the towel and jumped into the spa, as if to hide in its whirling waters.

"I'm gawking again, Christy, not laughing."

She snorted suspiciously and favored me with her warning frown.

Her modest two-piece swimsuit was not quite a bikini, but it did reveal a lot of my All-American soccer star, more than enough to deprive me temporarily of my power of speech.

She hunched her shoulders and cowered.

"I look ridiculous," she muttered darkly.

"You look like exactly what you are—a sumptuous young lioness, elegant, graceful, and so beautiful that I can hardly talk."

She looked up suspiciously, "I'm getting tired of that lioness metaphor."

I touched her belly with delicate fingers. Solid rock. She stiffened but didn't pull away from me.

"Young woman, listen to me."

"Yes, sir."

"Some idiot, probably a guy you wouldn't sleep with, caught you in a vulnerable moment and made fun of your height and strength, compared you, maybe, to those women who pump iron, and shattered your confidence in your loveliness."

"How do you know that?" she growled.

I moved my fingers along her belly. "Isn't it true?"

"Yes," she growled again.

"Two growls from Ms. Simba, better than a roar!"

She laughed and relaxed.

"I guess I still do like that metaphor."

"That miserable bastard lied. Now look into my eyes and see in their awe that he lied."

She carefully considered my eyes. "Pretty blue eyes . . .

hungry eyes . . . and, oh, yes, Tommy Flynn, adoring eyes!"

Then tears and her head on my shoulder. "You seem to like Ms. Simba's belly, Mr. Lion Tamer."

"Solid muscle."

She eased away. "Always will be. . . . Now, let's swim. We didn't come here to lollygag around in a whirlpool."

She moved to climb out of the spa. I took her hand and gently pulled her back in.

"There's no rush, Christy. I'm entitled to more gawking time."

She slipped back into the waters and continued to cling to my hand. We sat in silence, enjoying the warmth and each other's nearness. I did not want ever to leave the spa, so completely had I sunk into the swamp in the last forty-eight hours. This extraordinary young woman had captivated, enthralled, enchanted me. I was in love with her, already more involved with her than I had ever been before with a woman. I shouldn't be here holding her hand. Yet I was and I didn't want to let go. It would all disappear in the cold gray light of Monday morning. For the moment, I was in permanent paradise.

"Isn't my mom gorgeous?" she said suddenly. "I mean, for someone who is kind of old."

The blarney took command.

"Your mom is not kind of old," I insisted. "She is at the zenith of her life. Treat her with more respect."

"You're so sweet, Tommy," she sighed.

"Moreover, since you are a clone of your mother, a wise trader would go long on you as a commodity future."

She glared at me as she tried to figure it out. Then she got it.

"I'm not a commodity, Tommy Flynn," she retorted in mock anger. She pulled away from my grip and jumped gracefully into the pool. "Come on, I'll race you."

"No way."

Our swim, as she had promised, was hard work. Naturally, she swam an aggressive crawl that wore me out in five minutes. I didn't try to keep up with her. I'd never be able to keep up with her anyway.

Our lovely autumn day had turned to rain when I escorted her to her car in the bowels of Water Tower Place. We were quiet and thoughtful, she back in her uniform of jeans and sweatshirt and running shoes and "Captain Christy" jacket. Her hair back in its ponytail, she looked like a sixteen-year-old, though a very pretty sixteen-year-old.

"My e-mail address is easy to remember," she said with a giggle. "It's *Christy@soccer.ndu.edu.*"

"Not Captain Christy?"

"I thought about just "Captain," but I decided that would be arrogant. . . . What's yours?"

She opened the door of her aging Taurus and slung her shoulder bag into the back seat. I held the car door for her.

"*Gaylord123@aol.com,* as in Gaylord Ravenal, riverboat gambler. . . . Don't I get a good-bye kiss?"

She jumped out of the car, hugged me furiously, and kissed me long and hard. I had no choice but to respond.

"I love you, Tommy Flynn," she said as she jumped back into the car and turned over the ignition. She waved, backed the car out, and sped off, leaving me to hold up my hand in a dubious farewell. Such easy conquests are your young lionesses.

Or maybe so easily do they trap hunters.

Anyway, it had been a breathlessly romantic weekend. It was all over and that was that. But it had been fun, great fun.

I wandered disconsolately back to my apartment and turned on the TV. A golf tournament in the Sunbelt. I turned it off and picked up *Finnegans Wake*. I threw it aside. Someone had told me how it ended. I surveyed the rest of my books. A Laurie King mystery would have to do. Before I started it, however, I called Bishop Blackie and asked him for the phone number of the therapist I was supposed to see. He insisted that I mention his name. She owed him a favor.

In Chicago even psychiatrists owe favors.

BLACKIE

9

ANCHOR: A month ago, Bishop Augustus O'Sullivan Quill came to Chicago amid rumors that he was slated to replace Sean Cardinal Cronin. These rumors were promptly denied by the Chicago Chancery, although Bishop Quill has never denied them. Shortly after Bishop Quill's arrival, Cardinal Cronin dispatched him to Forty Holy Martyrs rectory in Forest Hills, about as far from the Chicago Chancery as one could go and still remain in the Archdiocese of Chicago. Channel Six has learned that not all is well in that parish. Our Mary Jane McGurn reports from Forest Hills.

(Ms. McGurn appears in front of a white stone gothic church.)

M.J.: That's right, Terri. If Bishop Quill should become Archbishop of Chicago, Catholics will not be happy campers if the reaction to him up here in Forest Hills is any indication. Bishop Quill succeeded Father Matt Dribben, who retired at the age of seventy. He promptly fired most of the parish staff—the director of religious education, the director of liturgy, two deacons, and the principal of Forty Holy Martyrs school.

(A smartly dressed and groomed matron appears on screen. The subtitle tells us that she is Ms. Loretta Heany, a former member of the Forty Holy Martyrs parish council.)

L.H.: He didn't consult with us about these dismissals. We met with him and asked why he had fired men and women who had done such fine work. He said he had prayed over the problem and concluded that they were not sufficiently loyal to the Holy Father and that it was his duty as a bishop to see that only those loyal to the Holy Father worked in our parish. We pointed out that several of these people had long-term contracts. He replied that he did not feel bound by the contracts his predecessor had entered into. We protested his arbitrary behavior and he dismissed us too. The next day he also fired the school board and the finance committee.

M.J.: What are the parishioners doing about this?

L.H.: They're attending Mass at other parishes. We have learned that the collection last Sunday was down eight thousand dollars.

M.J.: We also talked to the chairman of the parish athletic program. *(High-powered businessman on screen, John Creaghan by name.)*

M.J.: What happened to the athletic program, Mr. Creaghan?

J.C.: The Bishop phoned me one night to say that he was terminating the sports program, of which we are very proud of around here. He said that the Holy Father wanted us to help the poor and he could not approve of parish funds being spent on sports. I told him that the money was contributed privately at a dinner dance for the program. He said that didn't matter, it was still parish money. He also said he didn't approve of sports for young women.

M.J.: What will you do?

J.C.: We've scheduled another dinner dance. We'll go ahead without him. He probably won't let us use the gym. I like the Cardinal a lot. But he didn't consult with us before he sent Quill up here. If he doesn't take him back, this parish church will be empty in another month or two.

M.J.: Dissatisfaction is not limited to adults. We interviewed two students at Forty Holy Martyrs School. Their faces are obscured to protect them from reprisal. *(Two adorable sixth-graders. Names not given.)*

BOY: He comes around the school and tells us how much the Pope loves him. He's a creep!

GIRL: We young women have the right to a sports program of our own. I think he's disgusting!

M.J.: We asked the Chicago Chancery for a comment on the situation up here in Forest Hills. We were told that Cardinal Cronin has ordered Bishop Quill to rehire the staff members who were fired and to restore the athletic program. There's no sign of that happening up here, however.

ANCHOR: Were you able to talk to Bishop Quill himself, Mary Jane?

M.J. *(Who has been saving this up)*: We tried to, Terri.

(Screen shows Bishop—in full robes—scurrying out of church and trying to get to the rectory. M.J. interrupts him with her mike.)

M.J.: Bishop, do you have any comments on the unrest in Forty Holy Martyrs parish?

B.Q.: You should be home taking care of your children, young woman. *(Brushes mike away)*

M.J.: That about says it all. . . . This is Mary Jane McGurn reporting from Forty Holy Martyrs rectory in Forest Hills.

Mercifully I turned off the TV, after fumbling with the wrong buttons for a few moments. Sean Cardinal Cronin was slumped in my easy chair, his face buried in his hands.

I sighed loudly.

"All right, Blackwood, you said I should have sent him as chaplain to an old people's home. You were right."

"What happens if he refuses your orders?"

"Then I will remove him as pastor."

"There will be a canonical process over that. It will take time."

"I know, Blackwood, I know. However, I can appoint an administrator to the parish."

"The Vatican won't like the public scandal in a trial."

"I think you're wrong there. They'll agree that the guy is a public embarrassment."

"Perhaps."

He knew more about the Vatican than I did and was usually very canny in dealing with them. A tape of the broadcast would doubtless go to the Nunciature and to the Secretariat of State.

He sat up and removed his hands from his face.

"Even his brother can't stand him."

"Peter Quill? Unless I am mistaken, he is on your finance committee."

"You know damn well he is, Blackwood. . . . He says to me, 'Idiot is still an idiot and will never change.' He thinks I should get him the hell out of there."

"My—"

The phone rang. It was Ted Coffey, Gus's old colleague at the Tribunal. I gently touched the button on the speaker phone.

"I told you, Blackwood, that the guy was vicious. He's sick. Sean has to get him out of there."

"Ah!"

"He's never had much authority before. He tried to get himself appointed officialis here and that didn't work. So he went to Rome, where they called him Alpine Augustus at the Villa Stritch, where the American bureaucrats live. He tried for years to become chief of the Rota and they kept fending him off. I saw him around the Tribunal. He was oily with his superiors and his colleagues and terrorized the secretarial staff. He's a Nazi."

"Arguably."

"He belongs in the nuthouse."

"That's a point of view. You should write one of your stories about him."

"No one would believe it."

Having made his case, Ted hung up.

"Ted is a little strong, isn't he, Blackwood? The mess up in Forty Holy Martyrs doesn't affect him or his parish."

"So I observed."

"I didn't know he wrote stories, but then what do I know?"

"Fantasy stories for small fantasy magazines. Under the name of Burke T. Burke. He started writing, he says, to escape the horror of burying a teenager every week or two when he was in Hispanic work."

"You've read his stories?"

"Glanced at them. Unquestionably literate and intelligent. Too mannered for my taste, but then I don't particularly like fantasy. The real world is more than fantastical enough."

"We're going to have to do something about Gus."

"Oh, yes."

For weal or woe, someone else did something about him first.

JENNY

10

We eat at the new Chevarin's. He is polite and attentive. We waste little time before we become serious. The loneliness is terrible, he says. I agree and add, The embarrassment of becoming a teenager again wars with the loneliness. So much fear, he says. Fear of death. He smiles sadly. We didn't have that when we were teens. Is there any way, I say, to contend with loneliness besides sex? For some people, maybe. Then he adds, By the way, Jenny, the image of you as a naked slave matron on the auction block is utterly charming. My face becomes very warm. A chauvinist image, I say. *Playboy*. He sighs, not really. Someone to be rescued. I have to hold back my tears. Incorrigibly romantic, I say. That's me, he laughs. What will you do with the slave matron when you rescue her? Take her home, he replies promptly. And then? Love her and protect her for the rest of my life. I tell myself I wouldn't mind being taken home and loved and protected. You'd screw her long before you get her home. Only if she wanted me to and only tenderly. I snort skeptically. We're flirting. Dangerously. We turn quickly to lighter matters.

He touches my lips with his at the entrance of my apartment building. If this is the beginning of a courtship, it will be a long and leisurely one. I like that. I do not remember my dreams, but they are about him, sweet and reassuring dreams, just as he is a sweet and reassuring man. I wake up happy for the first time in a long time.

The man pursues me relentlessly. He is skillful and confident. He knows how to attract and arouse a woman. He senses my terror, which amuses him. Therefore, he will not take me. I will have to surrender myself. That seems to amuse him too. Everything about me amuses him. Yet I see the pain of memory in his eyes. He thinks he can slake the agony of loss with me. I am a replacement, an amusing, distracting replacement. I will never be more than that. My therapist is angry at me for framing the situation in that way. Why can't you be content with what is? she asks. Does he not ease the memories of your husband and your hatred for that terrible bishop whose life you threatened and on whom you still fixate? I can't help my dreams. She sighs. You can help the illusions you recall in your dreams. They are so real, I protest.

He sends me gifts almost every day. Flowers, candy, jewelry, shameless and expensive lingerie, which I eagerly put on. He writes me slightly erotic sonnets that tear at my heart. He briefly caresses my thigh in the darkness of the opera, which is probably my fault for wearing a skirt with a long slit. He touches my breasts, a touch that, despite the layers of clothes that protect me, sends an electric shock through my body. He does all the things a man would do who wants to seduce a woman so that he owns her, body and soul. Despite his delicacy and restraint, he is still an aroused animal who, when he does own me, will consume me with hungry fury. Sometimes I want to be consumed with such hungry fury. I know that when he is inside of me, he will be thinking of his wife. I will be little more than an obscene picture. My shrink says I should either end the relationship or surrender. I hate that bishop even more than I hate my husband. He is a gross, vulgar, evil man.

We meet each other's children. I am nervous. Children, even grown children, resent stepparents. Mine, however, promptly adore him. Mom, are you sleeping with him? my daughter asks. That's a terrible question to ask your mother. Yeah, but are you? Not yet, I say, my face hot. Well, don't let him get away. You're entitled to a lover like him. He certainly worships you. He can't take his eyes off you. His eyes won't leave my clothes on, I protest. So what's wrong with that, Mom?

The next day, his children are less obvious. They are polite and friendly but, I am afraid, sizing me up skeptically. Don't worry, one of his daughters whispers to me, we like you a lot. We're just dazed by how lovely you are. My face is hot again. Thank you, I say, close to tears. We're on your side, she adds. He'll be very good to you. She's close to tears too. Later, her brother says as we're leaving, we already love you, Jenny.

And you think you're not worth loving, Dr. Murphy says. I'm only a substitute for his wife. His children want to have a substitute for his wife to make him happy. His wife is dead, Jenny; you're not competing with her. Every minute I'm with him, I say, I feel she's haunting us. Sometimes, Jenny, despite your intelligence, you're a damn fool.

He takes me to his church, the Cathedral. There is a cute, funny little bishop greeting people as they go in. I think he may be Dr. Murphy's brother. I almost say something about the other bishop. I know he doesn't like him either. He preaches. He quotes from a book by Annie Dillard.

God is no more blinding people with glaucoma, or testing them with diabetes, or purifying them with spinal pain, or choreographing the seeding of tumor cells through lymph nodes, or fiddling chromosomes than he is jimmying floodwaters or pitching tornadoes at towns. God is no more cogitating which among us he plans to place here as bird-headed dwarfs or elephant men—or to kill by AIDS, kidney failure, heart disease, childhood leukemia, or sudden infant death syndrome—than he is pitching lightning bolts at pedestrians, triggering rock slides, or setting fires. The very least likely thing for which God might be responsible are what insurers call acts of God. . . .

God, he says, suffers when we suffer. Jesus reveals to us the suffering of God. He is always nailed to the cross. God is always suffering. For some reason these words sear my soul. I begin to weep, then to sob. The man puts his arm around me, not understanding yet understanding. At times like this, he really is like God for me. Now, he even suffers with me.

At brunch afterwards, he caresses my thigh. I almost invite him back to my apartment, but I don't. Like Dr. Murphy says, I am a damn fool.

RAMON AND LUIS

11

T he man is quite mad," Luis says.

"Dangerously mad," Ramon agrees.

"Is there any reason to think he has been promised he will succeed Cronin?"

"Our people in Rome, who would know, say that there are absolutely no grounds for that belief."

"Yet he has come much farther than his intelligence or ability warrants."

"So have many others."

"That is true."

"Nonetheless, it seems very unlikely. We must be cautious with him."

"We will not, however, provide the money for the television station he wants?"

"That is a quite absurd proposal. Yet he is very serious about it."

"I fear he took our reserve as agreement. His kind often does."

"That is true."

"It would seriously embarrass us."

"That is also true."

"We must distance ourselves from him."

"That may prove very difficult."

"One understands how Cronin must feel."

They both laugh wryly.

"It would be most useful if he could be discredited."

"Yes, it would."

"However, we must not appear to be involved."

JENNY

12

The pursuit must end. I am aroused all the time. We both must find release, if only for the sake of our sanity. I say to him at supper, I have a naked matron back at my apartment that I might raffle off tonight. He gulps, surprised and pleased. Maybe frightened too. Frightened? I ask him. His face colors. Naked matrons, he says, are glorious prizes, but they are also a serious challenge. They tend to surrender pretty quickly, I say. At the apartment I show him the painting I have developed from my graphic. I didn't know you painted, Jenny, he says. This is wonderful. So is she. You see yourself very clearly. We face each other, both of us frightened. He opens the first button on my blouse. I cringe with sweet terror. His fingers go to the second button.

Later, I am exhausted and content in his arms. He has been very good, overwhelming me with his savage hunger.

Ben was never savage, only mean. Perhaps I like savage men, who are not mean. He does not fall asleep. He continues to kiss and caress me. I feel like I am some kind of spoiled goddess. Naked matrons are a lot of fun, he says with a laugh as he tickles me. I think I'll keep this one. She amuses me. She didn't have much choice, I reply as I squirm.

Then his mood changes. He rolls over and pins me to the bed so I can't move. You belong to me now, woman, he says sternly. You're mine. I'll never let you go. That doesn't leave me much freedom, I say. All the freedom in the world to run away, he says. And I have all the freedom to chase you. Then he reaches over to his jacket pocket and removes a box. In it is a huge emerald ring. We usually brand our slave matrons before we take them away. This is your brand. He puts it on the ring finger of my left hand, a claim staked out. Then he takes me again. Spectacularly.

I wear the ring on a chain around my neck, between my boobs. My psychiatrist doesn't see it. You look very happy this morning, she says. I'm ecstatic. Will it last? I don't know. Probably not. And the man? Right now, he's like a god to me. Is it mostly up to you whether this lasts? That's not fair. I'm not talking fair. Yes, it's mostly up to me. Then I tell her he gave me a ring, an emerald. You're not wearing it? Around my neck. Does he consider it an engagement ring? More like a wedding ring. Ah, he plans to marry you? He's always planned that. I'd rather be his mistress than his second wife. Time, she says impatiently.

He knocks at the door to my apartment. I am wearing a terry-cloth robe. I have put a larger one on the table near the door. As soon as he enters, I begin to undress him, as though it were a businesslike procedure that I had done many times. He frowns, his modesty offended. Turnabout is fair play, I tell him. He smiles and relaxes. He has such a beautiful body, lean, hard, strong. You'll do till I find someone better, I say as I toss him the robe and lead him towards the bathroom. I can hardly believe I'm doing this. However, it is too late to stop.

I take off his robe and point to the shower. Reluctantly and awkwardly he enters. He doesn't like this. However, he's going along with me. He changes his mind when I join him and we lather and bathe and tickle and tease one another. We laugh and giggle and play. He now is enjoying the game enormously. I've never been in a shower with a woman, he says. It won't be the last time, I promise him. I hope not, he gasps, it beats taking one by yourself. Cheap erotic entertainment, I reply. Better than a porno flick and with a live actress. He moans with pleasure. I'm dizzy. He takes me into his arms in preparation for intercourse. I lightly push him away. Not yet, I say. Not till I'm ready and in the way I want. He bites his lip and nods his head. I hope this establishes, I say, that sometimes I will be the one in control of sexual matters—as well as others. Anytime you want, he gasps.

Later, I dry him off and take him to bed. We make love my way. He screams with pleasure and then falls asleep, utterly exhausted. I am greatly pleased with myself. Tonight I am the boss. He is my dear, beautiful slave. I dream of Bishop Quill being in the shower with me.

Proudly I tell Dr. Murphy about the interlude, without the details, the next day. So you think there was rich symbolism in taking sexual control away from him, she says skeptically. You think this signifies a change in the distribution of power in the relationship. Maybe, I say. He knows I'm more than just a receptacle. He did not know that before? she asks. I suppose he did. Now he knows it vividly. She nods and waits for me to say more, damn her. I never had the nerve to act like that before. For an amateur I think I was pretty good. Did he? His mind was blown. He'll never forget it. . . . The times I tried it with Ben, he slapped me. Slapped you! You never told me that he slapped you. Whenever he was impatient with me. Not hard; enough to hurt, not enough to leave a mark. We must ask later why you never told me. Now I want to know whether you have some confidence in your own sexual powers. I shrug. Enough to know I will do that again whenever I want to.

You ignore the most important part of the interlude, don't you? What's that? You know, tell me. No, I don't. Come on, Jenny, you know better than to play these games with me. I surprised him. No woman ever loved him that way before. Not even his sorely missed wife? Apparently not. Does it not occur to you that, for all her wonderful traits, she might not have been very good in bed? I wouldn't dare think that. The hell you wouldn't. Furthermore, does it not occur to you that your sexual skills, however recently acquired, might outshine hers? I have no way of knowing that. Is it just possible that you might be an utterly different sexual experience for him, one that he has only dreamed of and which surprises and overwhelms him? I hadn't thought that, maybe you're right. Maybe I can make him forget his wife. It would be wrong to forget her, she insists, a betrayal. My point is that he can value you for what you are without forgetting her. Do you know how many men his age in life yearn for a partner like you? So therapy has made me a pretty good whore. You're an asshole, Jenny, she says, and it's time.

She's right. If I admit it to her, there will be no running away. In the office, he sees me and rolls his eyes. We are very discreet there. However, everyone knows. They are silently cheering for us.

Another time, after Sunday brunch at his apartment, he is inside of me, just beginning to thrust. He pauses. You are astonishingly transparent, Jenny, he tells me. You have no defenses anymore. I can slip into the beautiful crystal waters of your soul just as easily as I slip into your body. Hardly a time for poetry, I think. You can slip into my body easily, I reply, because you have made me soaking wet with all the things you've done to me. I could spend the rest of our lives plumbing the depths of your astonishing mystery and only begin to know you. Still, the exploration will be pure joy.

This is all very lovely, I think. Maybe what's happened to me in the last few years have made me totally vulnerable. Maybe I've lost, or am losing, all my defenses. Why, however, does he pick this time when I'm already squirming with need to talk about it? I say to him, and while you're exploring these mysterious depths you can fuck me whenever you want. I use words like "fuck" and "screw," which I have never used before, and which he never uses because it shocks him. I enjoy that too. For the love of God, I cry, time-out's over! Let us get on with the game! Indeed, he says, as he begins to thrust again, for the love of God. I tell myself later, as I nap in his arms, that I guess I can put up with the poetry.

He tells me that I am losing my defenses, I tell Dr. Murphy. That I have become transparent. Do you think that's true, Jenny? I don't know. Maybe. Is it harder to hide? Physically, I can't hide at all. Emotionally . . . I don't know. Would you like it if most of your defenses vanished, at least with him, so that you became almost totally vulnerable in his presence? I'd be terrified. You know that's the price you will have to pay if you continue with him? I understand that, I say. In fact, I'd never quite understood it that way before. So? I don't know.

He drives me to a small home he owns on a lake to see the autumn leaves. It is a secluded spot in the woods, on the shore of a smooth, silver lake. Perfect for an assignation, I say. Is that what this is? he asks. Just a nice domestic weekend with some fucking thrown in for amusement.

We are very domestic. He lights a fire. I prepare the meals. I fear her presence in the house, but there are no traces of her. We walk in the woods and sing together. There is no strain between us. One weekend is not a true test. I am not surprised that we are compatible. That's not the problem.

I sketch a little. He tells me I'm astonishingly good and that I should do it more often. I know that. I've known it for years. Then I do him a little sketch of me peeling off his clothes. He is disconcerted but he loves it. I tell him that I may do a whole series on him as a lover. I can hardly wait, he says.

We attend Mass at a small local parish on Saturday afternoon. He drives the car with one hand and explores my thigh under my miniskirt with the other. I don't stop him. He reaches my most tender region and stops. I gasp. He laughs and continues. I am tumescent when we leave the car for Mass. Bastard, I tell him. He laughs. You'll have to wait till after supper. I'm not going to ruin my beef Stroganoff, just because you can't keep your hands to yourself. He laughs again. I do too.

The sermon is terrible. However, I pretend to listen intently. Since turnabout is fair play, I torment him on the way back to the cabin. The Stroganoff can keep. After dinner we sit on the porch and watch the sun set behind the pines and the lake turn black. We sip the port I had brought along. What are your imperfections, Jenny? You're the one who slips into the mystery of my soul. How do you see them? I have lots of imperfections, I tell him. The worst one is fear. You are afraid now? Yes. Of what? That I don't deserve the happiness I feel and that it will slip away. Odd, he says, I feel the same way.

The next morning we are like comfortable married people. We eat our breakfast—Belgian waffles with sausage and a fruit cocktail—in our robes and sip tea and read the papers as we watch the Sunday morning television. He calls me Maureen once and does not notice. I would never call him Ben. I let it go. The second time, I challenge him. I'm Jenny, I say firmly. Dear Lord, he says, shocked and embarrassed, I'm terribly, terribly sorry. I'm furious. I want to go home now. She is here after all, haunting me. Astonishing words come out of my mouth. No problem. I understand. It's all right. He holds my hand tightly. Thank you, he says. Don't worry about it, I say. I won't get angry when it happens. It's perfectly natural. I've turned on the spa, he says. It will warm up in a hurry. How warm is it outside? I ask. It will be in the seventies by noon. Have you ever made love outside? I ask him. No, he says. Neither have I, I admit. I suppose we will have to try it. This will show him that I am not angry, that I don't mind a competition that I am certain to win. He needs a little healing. Why not? He agrees. So we try it.

Late in the day, he became impatient with me when we were preparing to drive back to Chicago. Jenny, leave that stuff. We should be on the road. I cowered. Don't be angry at me, I begged. I'm sorry. His eyes were wide in surprise. I'm not going to hit you, Jenny. I'm sorry I was impatient. Your instinct to clean everything up was probably right. I stood in front of the sink, my head bowed. Here, let me help put things away. He wasn't much good at it, but I let him help.

Ben hit you, Jenny. Slapped me, enough to hurt, not enough to leave a mark. He was pretty good at it. How often? He stood transfixed, a platter in one hand, the other on a cabinet door. Hundreds of times, I suppose. Not much at all at the beginning. A lot later on, when he said it was my fault he lost the Nobel. You didn't use it in the divorce? Finally, we did. My daughter, who had seen him do it, threatened to testify. He and his lawyer backed off. I'll never hit you, Jenny. Never. I know that. I'm sorry I made a fuss.

You didn't get angry at him when he called you by his wife's name, Dr. Murphy says in some surprise. No. Well, yes. I was very angry, but I didn't want to hurt him, so I kept my loud, shanty Irish mouth shut. So now you will never be able to humiliate him again when he slips. I guess not. You are improving, Jenny. You realize that your competition model is not very useful. I don't know, Dr. Murphy. Can you imagine a woman with a man like that and a hidden place like that who never once screwed him, excuse me, made love to him outdoors? Do you think he would have asked her, Jenny? It should not be up to the man to ask, I insist, astonished at myself.

He and I are sitting on the couch in his apartment, partially undressed, cuddling together like two companionable married people, relaxed and content. My boobs are bare, my bra hanging on my arms. He likes me that way. I don't know why men like boobs so much. However, they do, and that's their privilege. He begins to talk about himself. I am amazed. His parents were immigrants. He lived in poverty as a child, worked his way through high school and college and graduate school. He's proud of what he's done, but not sure that it wasn't mostly luck. He worries about the company, though it's in good shape. He has enough money to retire tomorrow and wonders what he would do then.

He and his wife married young, high school sweethearts. She was pretty and vivacious, though her health had been poor even as a child. Her spirit was wonderful, but her poor body couldn't keep up with her. As the children came along, she experienced one health problem after another. Gradually, she became an invalid, brave, uncomplaining, and exhausted. He had become a caregiver, when he was not at the office. That was all right, he loved her. She was sad because she had become a burden. It wasn't a burden, but it was still difficult. She told him often during her final days that he should remarry quickly. He refused even to think of it. He had fallen out of the habit of sexual love and felt he could do without it. He dated only occasionally, afraid of that world at his age. After two years, however, the loneliness tore at him. It was all right during the day. At night here, in the apartment, it seemed like hell. Then they had hired me, as he saw it, a poised, intelligent, sexually appealing woman. He wanted me, all of me. He was frightened of the agonies of the pursuit until I gave him a sign that it would be all right. Even then he was terrified of a misstep—that he would, in his hunger and awkwardness, not respect me.

We are both weeping. I thought you were a skilled, polished seducer, I tell him. Your instincts were flawless. He is surprised. He says that he's probably a bad risk. I laugh and tell him that he's the best that's likely to come along. I draw him close and caress his face. He sighs contentedly. I tell myself that neither of us is what the other thought. That's all right. I now love him much more than I had before. I offer him a boob. He licks the nipple gently till it is ready. Then he draws on it with his lips. Fire rushes through me. He needs a wife and a mother and a mistress. What man doesn't? When we make love later, it is gentle and sweet, the best yet.

He is not the man you thought he was, Dr. Murphy tells me. He's better, I reply. More complicated, more problematic, more fragile, she says. More human, I say. Not the challenging sexual conquest you expected? Still that, and now a challenging human being. You can deal with that? Certainly, I tell her. I want to. I know I can. Why so much more confident? Because he gave himself to me last night. Then I add, besides, I told my husband, my ex-husband, to fuck off yesterday. What! He borrows money from me. Calls me and demands a couple of thousand dollars or he will try to reopen the divorce settlement. I know he won't be successful if he tries that. However, I want to avoid the hassle. Yesterday he was quite rude. You're sleeping with a rich man. You can afford to help. After all it's your fault that I didn't win the prize. You owe it to me. He is completely convinced that it is my fault because I distracted him from his work. It's none of your business whom I'm sleeping with, I tell him. How many times have you been unfaithful to your trophy wife? He warns me about going back to court. I tell him never to ask me for money again. He tells me that I will regret my refusal. Then I tell him to fuck off. I don't feel guilty either.

I put my head in my hands. The man and I are two flawed and wounded people, Dr. Murphy. Not as badly flawed and wounded as others, but still far from what we might have been and should be now. Still we can carve out some happiness together in whatever time we have left. I have no doubt of that anymore. You're becoming a dangerous woman, Jenny, she tells me. You like yourself that way. Now it's time.

I see him at the office and am sexually aroused. Tumescent all the time. I encounter him in a corridor. Free at lunchtime? I ask him. Yes, he says. Want to grab a bite to eat? No. No? Is the apartment the firm keeps for guests free? Yes, it is. Good, I'll see you there at noon. Oh, yes, Dr. Murphy, I've become a very dangerous woman.

PETER

13

I had lunch with my brother at the club today, Grace. It was a hellish experience. As soon as we walked in the place became as quiet as a funeral home. Some of my best friends turned their backs on me. Two women got up and walked out. Sure, I tried to point these things out to him. But you know Idiot. He only sees the things he wants to see.

" 'Do you realize what you are doing to me and my family?' I said to him when we were seated. 'We don't dare show our faces in public. They blame us for you.'

"He tucked his napkin into his Roman collar and dug into his salad. You know the way he eats, systematic, dogged, disgusting.

" 'I don't understand what you are talking about, Peter.'

" 'All the things you've done at the parish—firing those people, dismissing the parish council, closing down the sports program. People hate you and they hate me because I'm your brother.'

" 'I'm doing only what the Holy Father wants me to do,' he said calmly. 'I became convinced that those men and women were not teaching sound Catholic doctrine and morality. If I am to be true to my mission as a bishop, I must dismiss them.'

" 'And insulting that young reporter on camera . . . Now you'll have the media against you all the time.'

"He kept munching away at his salad like a self-satisfied

little rabbit.

"'Someone needed to speak the truth to her. The Holy Father tells us that mothers of young children should not work unless they absolutely have to.'

"'My wife Grace works, Gus.'

"The main course arrived. He began to cut the beef into tiny bite-size pieces like he always does.

"'But she opened her store only after the children were raised. The Holy Father does not object to that.'

"'Don't you have any thoughts of your own? Does the Pope do all your thinking for you?'

"'The Pope is the Vicar of Christ. He tells us what Christ wants us to think.'

"'Are you going to follow Cronin's orders about restoring jobs to those people you fired?'

"'I will have to pray over it, Peter. It would not be wise at this time to risk an open fight with him, even though I believe he is close to heresy.'

"'For the love of heaven, don't say that on television!'

"'I do not intend to say anything on television. The media are the enemies of the Church. I plan, with the help of the Legion of Corpus Christi, to open my own television station here to preach true Catholic doctrine to all the faithful.'

"'Those creeps.'

"'They are loyal to the Most Holy Father.'

"I was so disgusted by the way he ate the meat that I couldn't touch my own food.

"'When are you going to launch your TV station?'

"'In God's own good time.'

"'Are you really going to be the next archbishop of

Chicago, Idiot?'

" 'I have been given reason to believe that, Peter. Yes, I have.'

" 'When?'

" 'Whenever the Most Holy Father directs me to assume control.'

"He's shrewd, Grace, not nearly as dumb as he sometimes sounds. He realizes now that he can't afford to get into an open fight with Cronin, who has plenty of friends in Rome. . . .

"Do I think the Pope really sent him to Chicago to straighten out the mess? I'm not sure. He sincerely believes it, no doubt about it. But you know how he is, he misreads what people say to fit his own fantasies. I kind of doubt it. Cronin doesn't seem worried. He chatted with me at the last finance committee meeting when some of the other guys wouldn't look me in the eye. . . .

"Sure I talked to Idiot about your shop. Over dessert— well, his dessert. He slogged down a huge helping of chocolate ice cream, smeared his napkin.

"I said to him, 'Idiot, do you know what this is doing to my business? I lost five big accounts in the last two days. One man said to me that he wanted no part of a relative of yours.'

" 'That is unjust,' he said calmly.

" 'No one comes into Grace's shop anymore. She has the reputation of selling the finest dresses in Forest Hills. Now her clients are going to the mall instead.'

" 'That, too, is unjust,' he says, wiping chocolate off his mouth, 'and I regret your difficulties. But I must follow God's will and do what I have been sent to Chicago to do.

This is only the first phase. When people see that this is how the Most Holy Father wants a bishop in Chicago to act, they will respond with enthusiastic faith.'

" 'And we may be broke.'

" 'Surely, Peter, you exaggerate,' he said. . . .

"Will he obey Cronin? I think he will. Sean is one tough son of a bitch when he has to be. Just like his old man. If I had to bet, I'd bet on Sean. But Idiot is tough in his own sloppy, goofy way too. . . .

"What do you mean, Grace? Well, yes, I agree with you, it would be helpful if we could find some way to take the wind out of his sails."

TOMMY

14

The first sessions with the therapist, a handsome woman in her early sixties with probing gray eyes, were hellish.

"Why will you not admit that you have incestuous feelings about your stepmother?"

"I have admitted it, Dr. Ward. She's a knockout. I admire her. She's been wonderful for the family. I don't feel guilty for finding her sexually attractive."

"And she finds you sexually attractive?"

"I don't know. She likes me. I've been an ally. I think she finds me amusing."

"An ally? You did not resent her when she replaced your mother?"

"Resent her? I urged Dad to marry her. He needed a wife,

the kids needed a mother."

"You did not resent her replacing your mother?"

I considered that.

"Not much to tell you the truth. My sisters did at first. I was happy that Mom was out of our hair."

"Once, however, you loved your mother very much."

"When I was a little boy and she sang and laughed and told me stories."

"When did you start to hate her?"

"It's hard to say. Probably when she started to hit my sisters."

"Hit them?"

"Mostly when she was drunk and they were unruly, as little kids are. They were too much for her."

"She had no help?"

"Dad hired a full-time nanny to do all the work. Still Mom could not stand them. That's when she moved out on us."

"So you have a very strong love-hate fixation on your mother?"

"Not much of anything anymore. I feel sorry for her. I don't think of her much. You're right, memories of love from early childhood, then anger afterwards."

I noticed that my hands were clenched and that my shirt was wet. I was fortunate that these sessions were after my morning at the Exchange, not before.

"Then you transferred these feelings to your step-mother?"

"And maybe to every other woman too?"

"You go too fast."

"I suppose I do. . . . You could say I love Beth. She's

brought peace to the family. My sisters are making it into adulthood all right. I remember the first time I met her. . . ."

"And your reaction?"

"I was surprised that Dad had found such an attractive woman."

"You wanted her for yourself?"

I laughed.

"I don't deny it. . . . To be more specific, I hoped I could find someone like her—good-looking, smart, tough."

"And her reaction to you?"

"She was frightened, of course. She saw me as a potential enemy."

"And you reacted?"

"You wouldn't believe it, but even at sixteen I could be a charming, genial Irishman. I turned on all my charm. I think she began to see me as an ally."

"I can believe it. Here was a mother figure you could desire safely."

"Hey, I'm not denying it. She decided that I was a potential ally. Which I was. Most of what she did with the girls, she did on her own. They identify with her totally. She asked me occasionally for suggestions and I made some on my own. It was a kind of professional relationship."

"You never felt any resentment towards her?"

I paused to examine my reactions.

"I went off to Georgetown when they were married. I suppose that if I had lived at home, something might have gone wrong. I'm not sure. I never had time to feel that she was getting too close and then push her away."

"Which is how you deal with other women?"

"That's my record so far."

"You do not live at home?"

"No. I felt it was better to stay out of their way. I wanted to feel I was independent, I guess."

"And the alluring presence of your stepmother would have been disturbing?"

Did Beth disturb me? You bet your life she did. Why hadn't I perceived that before?

"I didn't think of that then, but you're right. Neither of them needed me, except as an advisor on the telephone."

"You resented that?"

"I didn't think so then. Maybe I did. I just wanted to get out of the house."

"And this soccer person, is she like Beth?"

An obvious question. Had I fallen in love, if I had fallen in love, with a replica of my stepmother?

"Let me think about that. Neither of them is passive-aggressive like my mother. Both are strong women. Christy . . . she's a lioness. I wouldn't call Beth a lioness."

"What would you call her?"

"I'm not sure. . . . My point is that she's not as . . ."

"As what?"

"As fearsome as Christy."

"Fearsome? You fear the soccer girl?"

"Soccer woman."

"Of course." Dr. Ward permitted herself a small smile.

"No, I admire her courage and her strength and her determination."

"Domineering?"

"Doesn't need to be."

"Aha, that is very important. However, we are out of time."

I walked back to my apartment, feeling worn and discouraged. On the one hand, I hadn't learned anything I didn't already know. On the other hand, it all seemed new and vivid and deeply troubling. My thought at the end, that Christy didn't need to be domineering, was brand new. Like the shrink, I thought that was very important.

In the apartment I ate two cartons of yogurt, hardly a balanced lunch, and compensated for that by sinking my teeth into an apple.

I turned on my Dell Latitude LT and checked my e-mail. The top message was from a certain *Christy@soccer.ndu.edu*. About time she wrote. Why should I take the first step, right?

Hi Tommy,

I'm so embarrassed. It's been hard to write this e-mail because I'm ashamed of my behavior over the weekend. You were very tolerant of me and I have to apologize to you. I have the biggest crush I've ever had in all my life on you. I threw myself at you like a silly fourteen-year-old. I was shameless. I don't know what happened. Maybe it was the mixture of laughter and pain in your pretty blue eyes. Anyway, I'm sorry I was such a geek. I don't blame you for not writing to me. You don't have to answer this letter.

Christy Anne Logan☹

I turned off the computer. She was as flaky as the rest of

them. Stupid kid with no sense at all. I was free of her. It would be easy. Just take her advice and not reply. I wouldn't even have to go back to my shrink.

I threw myself in my recliner chair and turned on the television. ESPN.

God intervened again. We were back on the muddy pitch in South Bend. The Fighting Irish were taking on the Lady Huskies, a deadly serious foe and a serious competitor for the national championship. They had not one but two potential All-Americans.

Why do you do these things to me, God?

You don't have to watch her, asshole, God replied.

I know.

Naturally, I did watch her.

At the end of the game, er, match, I was drained. I remained in my recliner, exhausted, collapsed, wiped out. Not so beat, however, that I didn't permit myself a brief visit to her shower room. She was counting on me being there, wasn't she?

I called up her letter from the "Old Mail" file and fashioned a reply.

Dear Christy Anne Logan,

God played another one of her tricks on me this afternoon. I came home after a heavy session with my shrink, feeling rotten and disgusted with myself and the world. I turned on the TV, which happened to be on ESPN, where it usually is. I found I was back on the same swamp that you Domers call a soccer pitch and that the Irish were fighting the dreaded Lady Huskies.

Well, there was one big difference between the match

and the one last week against the Lady Trojans—besides the fact that the Lady Huskies are a dangerous rival. The difference for me was that I was no longer a mildly interested spectator, indulging in spectator sport. The beautiful blonde lioness rushing down the field was now a woman I knew. She was, you should excuse the expression, which is not intended to be possessive, my Christy.

Why, I wondered, does this lovely young woman, with whom I'm thoroughly besotted, play such a rough game? Why does she have to roll over in the mud like she's a two-year-old? Why does she lie there in the mud after one particularly obnoxious Lady Husky knocks her down like she's unconscious? Why do even the Lady Huskies seem concerned about her? Do they think she is indispensable for their Olympic trip? Will she ever get up? Then she bounds up with a crazy grin, wipes the mud off her face with her shirtsleeve, and keeps on playing. On the bench, the coach of the Fighting Irish looks worried, but she knows better than to pull Captain Christy Anne off the pitch unless a stretcher is needed.

I perceive that my Christy Anne is the strongest, fiercest, most determined woman on the pitch. I realize that I had better act right with her all the time, or I'll be clubbed like an unruly cub. I'll never dare to act like fat, old, lazy Simba.

The Lady Huskies are game, but they don't quite have it. They keep the score tied at 1-1 until the last five minutes of the second period. Then my fearsome lioness streaks among them and, with a mighty boot from her gorgeous leg, puts the Fighting Irish ahead. I note that she is limping. What's happened? Why doesn't the coach take her out? Probably because it would be worth her life if she tried!

Then to sew things up, she sets up one of her wings (is that the right word?) for a final score. Fighting Irish 3, Lady Huskies 1. Naturally! Even then the coach doesn't pull her out. When the ref blows her whistle, the defeated Huskies swarm around her to embrace her. They know who the champ is. Then she limps towards the locker room, chatting merrily with her teammates. I am reluctant to violate her privacy by joining her in the shower. I know, however, she will be disappointed if I'm not there. So I enter, respectfully, of course, and watch her wipe off all the mud, an awful lot of mud, if I may say so.

Now as for your confession of a crush? Tell me about it! I've never been so smitten in all my life! We'll just have to see how it works out and not run because it's all kind of scary.

Anyway, I'm sorry for not writing before today. Congratulations on your mighty victory. And take care of that ankle.

Love,
Tommy☺

Well, that was that. We were into the second phase of our love affair. Exploration, I suppose one could call it. "Getting to know you." Here was where I usually goofed up. If I survived through that . . .

My fantasy of her naked body in the shower was now so

intense and so sweet that sometime we'd have to consider—ugly word—commitment. We were too young. She was too young, and as Megan at the Cathedral said, I was certainly too young.

After supper I turned on the Dell again. As I expected, there was another e-mail.

Tommy, Tommy, dearest Tommy,

I'm sitting here in front of my screen sobbing my heart out. My ankle really hurts and I'm on codeine and Empirin or something like that and am totally flaked out. I'm feeling real sorry for myself, so I try my e-mail, though I know you wouldn't answer and there was your wonderful and funny and loving letter.

Yes, we'll just have to see how it works out. I promise I'll never lose my nerve again.

I'm too filled up with emotion to say anything else.
All my love,
Christy

PETER

15

Have you heard the TV, Grace? . . . I know the store is open. This is important. The Idiot has disappeared. Perhaps we are rid of him. On an L train. After his Spanish lesson. He rides it part of the way back to Forest Hills and then his driver brings him back to the rectory. . . . Sure it's an affectation. And last night he wasn't on the usual train. They say that the train has disappeared too. . . .

"I know L trains don't disappear, Grace, though you've never been on one, so how would you know? . . . Yes, he's not at the rectory and he's not at the parish where they've been trying to teach him Spanish. . . .

"Of course the police know about it. It's on television. Maybe they won't find him. . . .

"I know it's one more disgrace for us, but after it's over they'll forget about him. . . .

"Yes, I hope so too.

"I have to go, Grace. The police are here to question me."

LUIS AND RAMON

16

So matters arrange themselves well at last."

"I wonder if that is so."

"Why is that?"

"The fool had publicly aligned himself with our work. We may be blamed for his disappearance."

"That is possible."

"He may also reappear. We have no idea what condition he will be in or whom he might blame."

"With all the lies that are told about us, we may be suspected."

"What should we do."

"We must inform our superiors, of course."

"Naturally."

"We must also see whether any of our contacts in the police force can tell us anything."

"If he is dead, it is a great scandal, though possibly a relief for us."

"And if he is alive, his career will be finished. It will be very difficult for the fools who sent him here."

"Our friends in Rome will make that point."

BLACKIE

17

My candy bar in one hand and my Diet Coke in the other, I drifted out of the terminal and into Albany Park. The streets were lined with vast apartment buildings, with twenty or thirty apartments around large courtyards. When they were built, before the Great Depression, they would have been considered moderately luxurious, their face brick colorful, their windows large, their rooms spacious. They appeared at the end of the L line because they were only a half-hour from the Loop and what was still in the countryside in those days. Jews, with a long tradition of apartment-house living behind them in Europe, had moved into the neighborhood after the First War—or to put it better, perhaps, after the first phase of the thirty-year war from 1914 to 1945. They left behind much less attractive immigrant neighborhoods in Rogers Park and Douglas Park. Synagogues, temples, community stores, and delicatessens sprang up on the main streets, especially on Lawrence Avenue. One could walk the streets of Albany Park in those days (I am told) and think one was in Brooklyn or Queens instead of Chicago.

Then, with changing times in the late forties and fifties,

many of the Jewish residents made the pilgrimage, like other Americans, to the suburbs and their single-family homes, especially to Skokie. Some Jews remained in Albany Park, especially in newer single-family homes at the north end of the neighborhood. After them came families of almost every nation under heaven—Japanese, Indians, Pakistanis, Palestinians, Filipinos, Thais, Laotians, Vietnamese, Afghans, and especially Koreans. Most of these groups had strong family cultures and a work ethic that made white Americans look lazy. While there were troubles among teenagers and some gangs, the family ties were strong and Lawrence Avenue, while run down, was more cosmopolitan than it had ever been. Albany Park was the American melting pot of the 1990s.

I noted that a Jewish delicatessen on the corner of Lawrence and Kimball promised deluxe pastrami sandwiches, which meant pastrami with coleslaw in the sandwich. I resolved that I would stop there on the way back. I wandered down a couple of alleys off streets near Kimball. Three-story back porches had seen better days, perhaps, and the backyards were gravel instead of lawn, but the alleys were neat and orderly.

Did I know what I was looking for? Certainly. I was looking for Idiot Quill, who I was now convinced was not dead but, like the unfortunate motorman, uh, driver, lying somewhere in an alley, waiting to be found. Not necessarily in an alley close to the L terminal, but perhaps.

Why was I convinced? It would take me a long time to figure that out. An unconscionably long time, I might add.

I was about to give up my perhaps quixotic quest in an alley behind apartment buildings in the fifty-one-hundred block of North Central Park. I noticed at the far end of the alley an irregular object against an old garage, one that, like most of the others, was far too small for contemporary cars, save the VW. The object looked like a roll of old tarpaulin, something that should not exist in this spotlessly clean alley.

I bent over the tarp and pulled it back. Indeed, it was Augustus O'Sullivan "Idiot" Quill in his shorts, which to my surprise were not purple. He was warm and there was a pulse in this throat—alive and moderately well and a problem for all kinds of folk, myself included.

Patently he had overdosed on some kind of narcotic—or more likely had been overdosed. I sighed, searched in my various pockets for my phone, feared that I had lost it back at the terminal, then discovered that some malicious leprechaun had hidden it in the pocket of my obsolete Bulls jacket.

I was lucky enough to punch Mike the Cop's number the first try.

"Reilly Gallery, Annie Reilly."

"Truly," I said.

"Yes, of course, who else . . . Is that you, Blackie? I have a huge collection of oatmeal-raisin cookies for you when you get a chance, and apple-cinnamon tea to go along with them."

"I can resist anything but temptation, especially by such delights, as you well know."

"You're on the Bishop Quill case? You want to speak to Mike?"

"Alas for my fading gallantry, yes."

"Blackie . . . Find anything?"

"Oh, yes. In point of fact, I found the pastor of Forty Holy Martyrs Church in Forest Hills."

"I figured you would. Alive?"

"It would seem so. . . . My problem is that I have no direct link to the ingenious John Culhane. Perhaps you could seek him out and tell him he can find two bishops, one as conscious as he usually is, which may not be very conscious, and the other OD'd on, if I am not mistaken, some variety of heroin."

"And where can he find these prelates?"

"In an alley behind the fifty-one-hundred block on North Central Park."

"I'll call him. Be careful, Blackie."

I then pushed the "1" button.

"Cronin."

"Blackie . . . We have one live but badly drugged bishop. I have summoned the Chicago Police Department. Doubtless they will transport him to Augustana Hospital."

For a moment, no sound at the other end. Milord Cronin was doubtless sizing up the appropriate reactions of calls to Rome and the Nunciature.

"Where did you find him?"

"In an alley . . ."

"In an alley?"

"Precisely. In fact, in an alley behind the fifty-one-hundred block of North Central Park."

"Any other details I should know?"

"He was clad only in his shorts, which, you will be relieved to hear, are not purple. I am no expert in such matters, but I would venture that someone has injected him with a massive dose of heroin."

"Heroin?"

"Heroin."

"You found him yourself?"

"Naturally."

"I won't ask how."

"Don't. Trade secret."

Called a hunch.

"All right, Blackwood, I'll make the calls. Someone should be around the proper congregation in Rome. . . . Go over to Augustana with him and see that they treat him right."

"No."

That stopped Milord Cronin cold. Almost never did he hear that word from me.

"NO?"

"Am I the Cardinal Archbishop of Chicago? Is Idiot Quill my auxiliary? Will the Chicago media wonder where the Ordinary of the Chicago Archdiocese is when all they see is the easily missed auxiliary?"

He laughed, his most unrestrained laugh.

"Easily missed and very dangerous . . . Where should I pick you up?"

"At the Kimball and Lawrence terminal."

"See you soon."

A blue-and-white squad car, blue light whirling frantically, turned down the alley, followed by a police ambulance with an even more frantic light. I knelt next to my brother bishop to say a prayer for him and to give him conditional absolution before he faced the hospital and the end of his career.

18

You knew that this guy would hide the L train in the last place the CTA would look for it?" John Culhane asked me as he drove me back to the terminal and my rendezvous with Milord Cronin.

"Moreover, since the Brown Line goes around the Loop, it would easily have access to the Green Line, as the Lake Street L is now called, much to the delight of the West Side Irish."

"Why the hell would he go to all that trouble?"

"Doubtless for the same reason computer hackers create viruses. It pleases his ego to outsmart everyone and in a spectacular way. He is arrogant. He intends to flummox all of us."

"He won't get away with it."

"Arguably."

"And when you learned that he had dumped the driver in an alley near the terminal, you figured he would dump the bishop in the area too. So you went out and found him just as I had figured that out."

"You had many other things on your mind."

John Culhane grunted. "The driver is in and out of consciousness," he continued. "He has no recollection of what happened. The medics say he may never remember, unless he lets us hypnotize him."

"Even then you will learn little," I pointed out. "A car across the tracks. Several masked men force their way into the train. A couple of them hold him and another injects him. He loses consciousness. Perhaps the men are Hispanics."

"A drug gang moonlighting and paid enough not to brag about what they did?"

"The man is a monster," I sighed. "He is, however, vain. Therefore, he is likely to take a chance that will undo him."

"Tell me more about this annulment stuff. I don't understand it at all."

I sigh my loudest sigh. "Few do. We have failed to explain what the sacraments are and hence the faithful don't understand what it means when we talk about marriage as a sacrament."

"An outward sign instituted by Christ to give grace," he recited the Baltimore catechism answer.

"Not inaccurate, but hopelessly inadequate. A sacrament is designed to reveal something about God, and in that revelation grace, God's love, is communicated. Thus, the Eucharist reveals the God who gives us food and drink and Jesus to sustain our faith. In marriage, the union between man and woman, pace Saint Paul, discloses that God loves us with a passion that exceeds, but is not totally unlike, the passion between man and woman."

"Why have I never heard this before?"

"Because we've been too stupid to put it that way. In any event, it is patent that a certain amount of maturity is required for a marital union to reflect the implacability of God's love. Church law has recognized for some time that there are impediments to the reception of the sacrament, such as physical incapacity, meaning inability to consummate the marriage, and the intention to exclude a permanent union or childbearing. In the 1960s, the American hierarchy, concerned about the pastoral problems of divorced and remarried Catholics, persuaded Rome to expand these impediments to include psychic incapacity, which has come to mean the lack at the time of marriage of sufficient emotional maturity to form a union which reflects that which exists between God and his people."

"At that age who is mature?"

"Arguably. My own conviction is that such maturity is reached only when the couple surmount some critical situation. At that point, divorce becomes unthinkable."

"So almost any divorce could justify an annulment? Catholic divorce?"

"De facto, that would seem to be the case, though piously our matrimonial tribunals would deny it. Thus we have a solution to the pastoral problem of divorced and remarried Catholics, but one that causes some scandal because perhaps nine out of ten annulments in the world are granted in America and because the arguments I have just detailed are too subtle for many, especially those who do not want to understand them."

"So there's some kind of hearing?"

"And then a pro forma review. Given the pain and the anger and the trauma that accompany divorce, an ecclesiastical annulment often aggravates the tensions between husband and wife. Thus they have one more situation in which to hurt each other. However, when it is over they are free to try again, or at least to start receiving the sacraments again."

We had parked by the Kimball and Lawrence terminal. Cops were still swarming around.

"Wouldn't it be easier simply to let them receive the sacraments?"

"Oh, yes. Then the annulment courts would have to close

down. . . . The German bishops proposed this to Rome on the grounds that God wants everyone around the banquet table and were promptly slapped down. In this country, many priests do that in the rectory office."

"Including you?"

I was not about to go on the record on that one.

"There is another loophole, called the 'internal forum' solution. If a person who wishes to remarry for one reason or another is unable to obtain an annulment, she or he may still argue that there was never a real sacramental marriage. When that argument is presented to a priest, he may say that if such be the case, then that person has the right in the natural law to contract a new marriage and continue to receive the sacraments. This is called 'internal forum,' which means that it is a private, almost secret, decision, valid but not publicly ratified by the Church."

"A lot of priests do this sort of thing?"

"Actually the priest has no authority, he is merely a consultant. The person makes a decision in conscience and in theory could do so without a priest. The Vatican would like to have the priest act as a kind of judge, imposing conditions and perhaps arguing against the act of conscience. But it is a long way from Rome to most rectories."

"I see."

I doubted that he did. However, bright man that he was, he would be able to explain it to others.

"The parish priest's concern is with the spiritual welfare of his people. He can be quite creative in getting around those rules which he finds impede that welfare. Sometimes his attitude leads to abuse, sometimes not."

"Where does Bishop Quill fit into the picture?"

"Normally both the husband and wife are delighted to have some sort of closure to their failed marriage. However, a few are unable to comprehend the enormous change in the Church's attitude towards divorce that is latent in annulments. Some feel that the Church is taking away their marriage. Some argue that their children are made illegitimate—though the annulment decree legitimates them in that is the real worry. Some say, I know I had a real marriage—though the argument is that it was real but no sacramental. Finally, some are so angry at their sometime spouse that they want to prolong the agony to punish the spouse and perhaps the replacement spouse. There is a retired Franciscan named Father Innocent—really—in the western suburbs who directs such aggrieved parties in the appeal procedures. So they choose to appeal the decision to Rome, to the Sacred Roman Rota, on which Bishop Quill served with notoriety, if not with distinction."

"Oh?"

"He reversed with gusto, if not convincing arguments every case that crossed his desk. One can imagine how the other party and possible substitute spouse reacted to that. They had thought it was all over and they are back to ground zero. Some just walk out on the Church, arguably not without reason."

"No appeal?"

"There's always the possibility of an appeal to the Apostolic Signatura, which is the church's Supreme Court, or to another tumulus of the Rota, if anyone wants to bother. In fact, I understand that on every appeal Bishop Quill was reversed, which is perhaps why he was sent to Chicago."

"What a mess . . . Why is the Church in the legal business anyway?"

"For a long time it was the only legal force in Europe. For a couple of centuries all the popes were canon lawyers. We remain in it from force of habit. The Greeks are much more tidy about these matters. Decisions about remarriage are made in the local parish."

"The implications here are that someone whom Bishop Quill hurt by his decisions might have set up this plot to discredit him."

"That might be the case. In truth, however, it is an extraordinarily baroque form of revenge."

"We should find out who in Chicago suffered from his reversals?"

"That would be one way of proceeding. I cannot promise that the results of such a quest would be successful. It is one thing to hate a man and to want revenge and quite another to elaborate such a twisted mechanism for discrediting him."

"Maybe the guy is a computer hacker."

"Or woman."

"How could a woman think up something like this?"

"How could a human think up something like this?"

At that point a sergeant approached the Commander's unmarked car with some more news. Having ascertained it was not relevant, I disembarked from it and proceeded across Kimball Avenue to the delicatessen, where I purchased two deluxe pastrami sandwiches and two iced teas. I had just returned with these treasures in hand when the Cardinal's black Lincoln Town Car pulled up.

"What do you have there, Blackwood?"

"Lunch, two deluxe pastrami sandwiches of the sort that

one can find only in the few remaining authentic Jewish delicatessens in this city. Enjoy, it's good for you."

"No chicken soup? Hey, this is good. Don't tell Nora that I'm eating it."

"The protein is also good for you."

We had just finished this gourmet meal when the driver pulled into the emergency entrance of Augustana Hospital. The media folk were placed to prevent our entrance. Milord Cronin, with his ruby ring and his emerald pectoral cross, waved aside their questions and slipped through them. Invisible as always, I ambled along in his crimson wake, though the only cardinalatial sign he wore was a red thread around the gap that revealed his Roman collar. It was enough.

"You stay here, Blackwood," he said to me in the lobby, "and sniff around."

It was an accurate, if unflattering, description of my work.

19

M.J.: Cardinal Cronin, what is Bishop Quill's present condition?

S.C.: He's intermittently conscious. He recognized me. He, ah, kissed my ring.

OTHER JOURNALIST: What happened to him, Cardinal?

S.C.: Someone injected a very large dose of heroin into his veins, almost enough to kill him.

M.J.: Will that have a permanent effect on him?

S.C.: We hardly think so. In the short term, he is likely to be disoriented and confused.

O.J.: Has he taken heroin long, Cardinal?

S.C. *(Controlling impatience)*: Anyone who knows Bishop Quill knows that he does not use drugs. He hardly even drinks. This event is part of an attempt to discredit him. We do not propose to let that happen.

M.J.: Why would someone want to discredit him, Cardinal? Might it be because of the unrest in his parish?

S.C.: I hardly think so, Mary Jane. It's much too violent an assault to be the result of a parish feud.

O.J.: Have you informed the Pope?

S.C.: I was in touch with the Nunciature and the Congregation of Bishops this morning. It's too late in the evening to call them again. I'll report tomorrow.

O.J.: Will the Vatican remove him because of this incident?

S.C.: That would be most unfair.

O.J.: How soon will he return to his parish, Cardinal?

S.C.: The doctors say it may take some weeks. I called Father Matt Dribben, the retired pastor of Forty Holy Martyrs, and asked him to become temporary administrator.

M.J.: How did all this happen? I mean the L train and the bishop and everything?

S.C. *(Thin smile)*: I think I'll leave that to the police, Mary Jane.

M.J.: What sort of man would create such a plot, Cardinal?

S.C.: Person, Mary Jane.

M.J. *(Embarrassed)*: Yes, Cardinal.

S.C.: The same kind of person who makes computer viruses.

O.J.: Will you remain here with the Bishop?

S.C.: Of course. Thank you all very much.

20

How did I do?" the Cardinal asked me in the lobby of the hospital.

"I could not have done better myself."

"I must really be getting sneaky, huh?"

"Arguably."

"Did they believe me?"

"Up to a point. The possibility that a bishop of the Holy Roman Catholic Church is a drug addict is too good a story for them to give up completely."

"Do they believe that the Vatican will not dump him?"

"We Americans," I observed, "have the innocent notion that a person is innocent till proven guilty. From their years of wisdom with human depravity, not excluding some of their own, the Curia Romana believe that an accused man is guilty till proven innocent and he really can't prove himself innocent."

"You're right, Blackwood. He's burnt flesh. . . . Look I'm going to stay here for awhile. I'll have my driver take you back to the Cathedral, where you can man the fort."

"I can easily ride back on the Brown Line."

"As the Megan would say, NO WAY. I don't want to lose two bishops in the same day."

Back at the Cathedral, Megan Jefferson yelled at me as soon as I came in the door, "Is that you, Bishop Blackie?"

"No, it's the prophet Elijah," I murmured.

"There's this funny man who can't really talk English on the phone. He says he's the Pope and wants Cardinal Sean!"

"I'll take it." I walked into the office the Megan had appropriated for themselves and took the phone from her hand. I will not attempt to replicate the Nuncio's broken English.

"Bishop John B. Ryan," I said curtly.

Only when speaking to representatives of the Holy See do I so identify myself.

"Where is the Cardinal?" he demanded.

"He's at the hospital with Bishop Quill."

"What have you done to this poor man? Why have you killed him?"

"To whom am I speaking?"

"I am the Nuncio!"

"Ah, good afternoon, Your Excellency. This is Bishop John Blackwood Ryan. As I said, His Eminence is at the hospital with Bishop Quill."

"This is terrible, what you have done to him. A bishop murdered in Al Capone's city. There will be serious repercussions in the Holy See."

"Actually, Your Excellency, it is Michael Jordan's city. And if you would do me the honor of listening to me, you would realize that Bishop Quill is not dead. He is in the hospital and, at the risk of repeating myself for the third time, His Eminence is with him."

"He is not dead?"

"No, Your Excellency."

Intelligence is hardly required to be a successful papal diplomat.

"What happened to him?"

Now the fun starts.

"He was kidnapped. Someone injected him with a near

153

lethal dose of heroin. He is presently recovering."

The cry of horror at the other end of the line could not have been louder if I had told him that Gus Quill had been found making love with a mother superior on the high altar of the Cathedral during solemn Mass.

"You must keep it out of the media!"

"I'm sure that Your Excellency is sophisticated enough to realize that nothing is kept out of the media in this country."

"Why does Cronin do these things? They will be unhappy in the Vatican with him."

"I assure Your Excellency that the Cardinal had nothing to do with it."

"You must find out who did this terrible thing!"

"The Chicago police are currently investigating."

"The police!" he wailed again. "The police must be kept out of it. Speak to the authorities!"

"The authorities in our city, Your Excellency, as you surely realize, are mostly Catholic. They will therefore avoid any hint of covering up for the Church."

As time would tell, that was not a fully adequate statement of what would happen.

"I want Cronin to call me at once."

"I will relay that message to His Eminence."

"They will be very angry with him in Rome."

"As is his custom, Excellency, he will quiver with fear at the prospect."

"Is that man real?" Megan Jefferson, who had been listening wide-eyed, asked.

"No, Megan, he is not real."

It might be thought that this exchange proves beyond all

doubt that I'm innocent of ecclesiastical ambitions. Alas, it does not. I was talking bishop-speak to him and he had not the slightest notion that I was pulling his leg. It did not matter, however, because, as I had explained to Megan Jefferson, he was not real. No way.

I retired to my quarters to ponder the events of the day. I still had to make my visits to the hospital, but they could wait till I heard from the Cardinal. I had no intention of phoning him to tell him that the Nuncio had demanded that he call to report his reasons for introducing heroin into the bloodstream of Augustus O'Sullivan Quill.

The issue, I told myself, as I turned on my e-mail, was not who might have wanted to make trouble for Bishop Quill. There were legions of people who did not like him, including most of the parishioners of Forty Holy Martyrs. But among these myriad suspects, who would want to put out a contract on him? Even if we had a list of those who hated him that much, who among those might have had the resources and the imagination to put out the contract? Perhaps, when the police assembled such a list, a name would appear that made sense. I thought that, however, to be unlikely. Our friend was clever enough to not be on one of those lists. The police would search diligently. There would be media stories with veiled hints—in Chicago, very veiled—that the Church was covering up again with the help of the authorities. It could get messy.

Our friend was very vain, however. He would want to show off his cleverness. Then, perhaps, we would have him.

It could take a long time.

My personal line rang.

"Punk? Your sister."

"Eileen? I did not leave a message when I mistakenly called your number this morning."

"No, Mary Kate!"

"Ah, the famous Mary Kathleen Ryan Murphy!"

"You're baiting me, Punk!"

"Would I do that?"

"Yes, you would, and I'm one of the few who catch it. You and Sean have a real load of shit on your hands now!"

"That thought has not escaped me."

"He's going to come apart at the seams, really go psychotic. What will Rome do?"

"Try to put him in a monastery somewhere?"

"He hasn't done anything wrong!"

"The Vatican will assume that if a bishop's bloodstream is filled with heroin, he wanted it there."

"He may never recover, you understand that?"

"I had not thought it would be that bad."

"It might not, but it easily could be. You and Sean should get him out of Augustana—a good place, but not for him—and get him into a private room at St. Joseph's. Get him a first-rate psychiatrist, I can make referrals if you want, and round-the-clock psychiatric nurses. And keep a close eye on him."

"Of what gender should these respected colleagues be?"

"Women, of course. His problem was clearly with his mother."

She gave me three names, all presumably Catholic.

"Mind you, Punk, you may have to warehouse him for the rest of his life. His ego simply cannot stand this kind of trauma."

"He will not be the first Chicago bishop to whom this has happened."

"If you don't slow down, the same thing will happen to you."

"Is that the clinician talking or a concerned sib?"

"Punk, you're no good, you never have been! Tell Sean to give me a ring."

No reason that the Cardinal should take my word for it. I sighed.

I did not ask her what the symptoms of my imminent psychic collapse might be. She would doubtless describe behavior in which I had engaged since childhood, behavior that led the women in the family to conclude, not unreasonably, that I was a changeling.

The phone rang again. It was the Cardinal.

"Blackie! What the hell have you been doing on the phone? I've been trying to get you!"

"Talking to my sib, who proffers psychiatric advice free of charge."

"Good, I'll have to talk to her. I'm on the way back. We have a gosh-awful mess on our hands. I'll be there in about ten minutes. Don't go away."

"I had not planned to. . . . The Nuncio was on the phone . . ."

"To hell with him!"

That was, I felt sure, not his considered opinion. However, even when he considered it, Milord Cronin was not likely to change his mind.

Again the phone rang.

"Blackie, Nora."

"Indeed."

"How's Sean taking it?"

That's what a lover always wants to know.

"Wonderfully well! He's at his manic best!"

" 'See to it, Blackwood,' you mean."

"Oh, yes."

"None of that weltschmerz stuff he does sometimes?"

"Not yet."

"You'll let me know?"

"Bank on it."

How many Irish Catholic matrons in Chicago, I wondered, knew what weltschmerz was?

Milord Cronin, on rare occasion, becomes weary of life and dubious about his efforts through his life. That happens to men in their early seventies, I have been led to believe. But then, at what age after twenty-five does it not happen?

He thereupon strode into my room, roman collar pulled out of his clerical shirt—none of these vests that other bishops affect for Sean Cronin—and hovered over me like a caged black leopard with his forelegs against the bars of his cage.

"He's geeked out, Blackwood. Totally. Out of his mind."

Thus had the Megan jargon influenced him.

"Predictably."

"Hysterical! Shouts prayers! Begs the Pope to help him! The good Swedish people at Augustana don't know what to do with him. . . . What did Mary Kate say?"

"She recommended that we move him to St. Joseph's, put him in a private psychiatric room, and assign a first-rate woman shrink, excluding herself, by the way, to take care of him. She thought it possible that he might not recover. Incidentally, she predicted the psychotic symptoms you described."

"I'll phone her."

Naturally. Two celebrities do not trust a mere sweeper bishop to be an adequate intermediary.

"She gave me this list of names."

He glanced at the list as he sank into my easy chair, which I had thoughtfully cleared in anticipation of his arrival.

"All Catholics, I see."

"Arguably."

"Why women?"

"She remarked something about the problem being his mother."

He nodded as he put the list in the breast pocket of his jacket.

I prepared him a libation of the very best Bushmill's Green Label single malt Irish whiskey. Normally, he steals it himself. Today, however, had been a very bad day.

" 'Tis yourself that has the heavy hand! . . . Don't tell Nora!"

"My lips are sealed."

"Sometimes I think you work for her instead of me."

"Which would display excellent taste on my part."

He sipped the Bushmill's, of which it can be said, without any fear or hesitation, that it surely does clear the sinuses.

"Good stuff. . . . What do we do now, Blackwood?"

"We continue our existing posture. Bishop Quill was mugged by person or persons unknown. We have full confidence in the ability of the CPD to resolve the matter satisfactorily. It is absurd to think that Bishop Quill was a heroin addict or ever used narcotics of any kind. He is recovering from the incident, but it has been a brutal blow to his, ah, health. . . . No, that won't do. Let us say, to his organism."

He inclined his head in agreement and continued to sip his whiskey in slow and thoughtful quantities. "That makes sense. We will not tell them that Bishop Ryan is continuing his own inquiries."

"What does *he* know about such matters? I should think it would be wise to wait till the waters settle down. This one will take time."

He inclined his head again. "Any hunches?"

"Someone monstrously clever. Vain, unbearably vain. That will finally do him in, I believe."

"Gus is finished, you know, even if he recovers."

"It would seem so. However, he was probably finished anyway when they shipped him out to us. I would imagine those behind such a deployment will scurry for cover."

"He had his illusions. Now they have become delusions, perhaps permanent."

"Solves a lot of our problems. Admittedly it creates some new ones, but they will pass. As you doubtless recall, one of your predecessors spent thirty years or so in an asylum quietly passing his time in prayer and good works."

"Bishop Duggan . . . and everyone soon forgot about him."

"We all have illusions. We cannot survive without them.'

"Like your delusion that you are my éminence grise?"

"Arguably. The path of wisdom is to discern which are harmless and which are deadly. Usually the latter are ones that involve a lower estimation of oneself than is appropriate. In this matter, I believe that both Bishop Gus and his tormentor have the same problem."

"Gus's delusion is that he's going to be archbishop of Chicago!"

"He needed that delusion to escape from the truth that he was perfectly capable, upon ordination, of being a kindly parish priest—a truth that still survives in his quixotic attempts to identify with the Hispanic poor. He ran to escape mediocrity, failing to realize that what he was escaping wasn't mediocrity at all but his low estimate of himself."

"Sounds like you picked that up from the good Mary Kathleen."

"It is but common sense."

"And his enemy?"

"A person of monumental illusions, which he has doubtless reinforced this day."

He drained his glass with a single swallow, a blasphemy that made me cringe. Then he jumped up, took my list of possible therapists from his pocket, and said, "I'll call Mary Kate now. She's at home?"

"Indeed."

"Meantime, you start thinking about who the enemy is. See to it, Blackwood!"

Invigorated by the water of life, he ventured forth like the USS *Langley*, a ship with which I am familiar, moving at flank speed.

An image of the enemy flickered in my preconscious, danced for a moment, and then slipped away.

He would be back. Or she.

TOMMY

21

The soccer person really said that to you?" the shrink says when I tell her about the fantasy bit— mostly to get her reaction.

"Yes, ma'am."

"She has had a lot of experience with men?"

"I don't think so. She says she's a virgin."

"Where would she get such an attitude?"

"She reads a lot."

"Such as?"

"She explained *Finnegans Wake* to me the other day."

"And she plays soccer? Like Mia and Brandi and that bunch?"

"Yes, ma'am. . . . Do you think she needs to see a psychiatrist?"

The doctor snorted. "That one? About that, you should not worry. . . . Now, tell me about your father."

So she didn't think Christy was weird. Well, she wasn't.

"He's a great man, Doctor. A brilliant lawyer, witty, charming, generous, kind. Everyone loves him."

"Yet he could not keep your mother in line?"

"He did everything he could. He let her have her freedom. He found a nanny for the kids. He paid her bills. He asked for a divorce only after the lesbian thing, and then only because Monsignor Coffey—that's our pastor out in Oak Park—told him it was time. He couldn't have done anything more."

"I see . . . But never once did he tell her to stop this foolishness and see a therapist or he would end the marriage?"

"Oh, no. Dad could never do anything that cruel."

"Would it have been cruel, especially in the early days?"

"Terribly cruel."

"What would your mother have done if he had delivered that ultimatum?"

"I don't know."

"Was there a chance she might have done what he demanded?"

"I suppose so."

"Then was it not cruel for him to have remained silent?"

"I don't see why!" I said hotly.

"Was it not the only chance the poor woman had?"

"Dad could never have done that! He loved her too much!"

"Or perhaps not enough."

"I don't get it, Doctor. He was wonderful to her."

"Was he? Did he not in fact subsidize her neuroses, whatever they were?"

"You don't know my father!" I said furiously.

"You are right, Thomas, I do not know him. But I do know that in intimate relationships one must sometimes be firm with the partner. Not to be firm is unfair and cruel. To withhold firmness is not a sign of love, but of a failure of love."

"But . . ."

"Those who love are firm all the time, every day. It usually is easy and routine, though sometimes it has to be more forceful. Without it love is impossible. Do you not understand this?"

My stomach tightened.

"Yeah. I guess . . . but I love my father!"

"Of course you do, Tommy. One can love another very much and yet harbor resentments against that person. I suggest that all through those years when your mother misbehaved, you were deeply angry at him for not intervening on your behalf and that of your sisters to make her stop. You resented the fact that he did not make her return to the lovely woman who sang songs to you when you were a child?"

"I can't remember ever feeling that way!"

A great, yawning hole opened up under me.

"It does not follow that you did not feel that way—and in your unconscious you still do. How could it have been otherwise?"

"There was nothing he could have done!"

"That you say now. You couldn't have known that then."

"You mean I have to work all that out with Dad now?"

"Did I say that, Thomas?"

"No."

"Does your father ever argue with your stepmother?"

"With Beth? . . . I don't know. I don't think so."

"Probably he doesn't have to. Every intimate couple has to draw limits."

"Beth would be a lot easier. . . . Maybe they do it in lawyer talk."

"Probably they do. Your mother was a serious problem. She would frighten many men. I do not blame your father. I merely suggest to you that his reaction was not adequate. You were furious with him because, among other things, you had to protect your sisters when he did not."

"O.K., but if you're right, what's the point of that now?"

"I suggest, Thomas, that your problems with women are not the result of your resentment towards your mother but of your resentment towards your father."

"That's silly!"

"Hear me out. In your early relationship with a young woman, you are charming and she becomes fond of you. Then she does something that strikes you as irresponsible. You both underreact and overreact. Thus you confuse the young woman and drive her away. You don't complain about something that bothers you, habitual tardiness, for example, and then you lose your temper."

Ouch.

"That's a pretty fair description," I admitted.

"The problem is that you have no good model for how to draw the line when a line must be drawn, gently, lovingly, but firmly without putting the relationship in jeopardy."

"Oh."

"With the soccer person, that may not be a problem. It is altogether possible that she would simply refuse to let you put the relationship in jeopardy. Nonetheless, it might not be a risk you want to take."

"I certainly wouldn't, but how do I learn at this stage of life?"

"You watch how others do it. When there is a problem, however mild, with the soccer woman, you deal with it immediately, waiting for the proper moment, of course, instead of putting it off."

"I don't want to hurt her feelings. . . . Damn, I sound like your description of my father!"

"It is time, Thomas. Think about our conversation."

In the harsh grayness of a Chicago autumn, I looked around, not sure where I was or what I should do next. My emotions were in a jumble, like the pit on a witching day. I could not figure out what emotion to concentrate on. No, there was one that was paramount. My psychiatrist thought that my lioness was a remarkable young woman. Of course she was. Worth going through all this hell for?

Silly question.

I walked home briskly, determined to think through what we had said to one another instead of watching television.

First I sent an e-mail to *Christy@soccer.ndu.edu*.

Christy my love,

Another bad session with the shrink. I think I'm digging pretty deep and learning a lot about myself. But that's not your problem. What I wanted to say is that on the basis of what I say about you, she thinks you're remarkable. I knew that all along, but it's nice to have a very wise woman confirm it. I suppose you won't like me talking to her about you. If you do mind, I'm sorry.

All my love,
Tommy

A reply came back while I was changing my clothes to go down to the exercise room.

Dearest Tommy,

Sometimes for a sweet, wonderful boy, you have the strangest ideas. Why would I object to you talking to your shrink about me? I'd be offended if you didn't tell her about me. If I'm important to you, why would you not talk about me?

What does she like about me?

I wish you were here, or I was there, so I could kiss you.

Christy ☹ ☺

I thought I'd better reply right away.

Captain Christy,

She is impressed with your reaction to my shower-room fantasies.

Confused,

Tommy

I had hardly finished when she fired back.

Tommy,

WELL, I don't know what's so unusual. I'm, after all, a healthy young woman, with all the hormones that come with that. But if it makes her like me, I'm impressed. One thing, however, in some locker rooms, there are other girls in the shower with me. You are NOT, I repeat ABSOLUTELY not, to have fantasies about any of them. Is that clear?

Jealous lioness ☹

I threw back my head and laughed. Vintage Christy.

Dear Lioness,

I wouldn't dare. Besides, unlike Simba, I'm monogamous. Finally, those other young women couldn't possibly compare with you.

I'm going to my workout now.
Love,
Simba (human variety) ☺

22

Let us return to your stepmother," my shrink said, confusing me once again by changing the subject at the beginning of a session. "Do you have fantasies about her like you do about the soccer woman?"

"You mean about playing with her boobs in the shower?"

She shrugged, as though that were an acceptable male description of fantasies.

"Not as vivid or as sustained."

"But naked?"

"Yes, I guess so."

"Would she be as pleased as your friend at Notre Dame?"

"I would hardly think so. I could never ask her."

"Why would she not be pleased?"

"She's married, to begin with, and she's my stepmother."

"But you don't call her Mom, do you?"

"No."

"Your sisters do?"

"Sure."

"She would like it?"

"I think she'd be very pleased."

"But you don't?"

"Well, we're both adults, equals, kind of."

"In fact, you are not. She is married to your father. You

cannot be her equal."

"I suppose that's right."

"So by not calling her Mom, at least on occasion, you preserve the illusion that she is, in some remote sense, sexually available to you."

"You have a dirty mind, Dr. Ward," I said with my most charming Irish grin.

"We all do, Thomas."

"So if I call her Mom, the incest taboo will eliminate my fantasies about her boobs?"

"Minimize and contain them," she said evenly. "After all, you are not an archangel."

"Christy says that if we didn't have fantasies there wouldn't be any humans left."

"She is quite right. Now, I want to ask you a question about Christy."

"Shoot."

"Do you intend to marry her?"

"It's early days, as the Brits say."

"Granted."

"I don't want to answer that question."

"Yet you will."

"Doctor, I am here struggling with this stuff because I don't want to foul up with her."

"It is time."

A couple of Rubicons challenged me the following weekend.

Beth phoned me while I was reading.

"Tommy, it's Amy's birthday this coming week. I thought we'd have one of our little family parties for her on

Sunday. Do you think you would be free to come?"

Such a timid question. Was Beth afraid of me? Hadn't I been an ally?

"Great idea, Beth. Sure, I'll be there. What time?"

"Say, noon. She'll have to drive back to the Dome."

University of Chicago graduate. We had socialized her to the proper word.

"Sure, it'll be fun."

"It will be good to have you."

"Beth . . . don't hang up. Would it be all right if I brought a girl, uh, I mean, a young woman?"

"A WHAT?" She was genuinely shocked.

"Er, a young woman?"

"A DATE?"

"I don't know if you could call her that. I think you will all like her."

"I'm sure we will. We'll be looking forward to meeting her."

Smooth, counselor.

As soon as we ended that conversation, I phoned a certain number at Notre Dame.

"Christy?"

"I thought this was an e-mail romance. They're more sexy."

Impossible young woman.

"Your friend Amy has a birthday next week."

"I know THAT," she said impatiently.

I had interrupted serious study.

"They're having a party for her."

"I know THAT too. A private family party."

"I have permission to bring a date."

"Where are you going to find a date?"

The young lioness was making fun of me.

"I tried three or four and they said they were busy. I thought you might want to join us."

"Oh, Tommy, I'd love to. . . . Amy will just about freak out. How formal is it?"

"Clean jeans, nice blouse."

"Got it. I won't tell her a word. We'll have a ball. . . . Will your parents like me? I mean as your friend and not just as Amy's classmate."

"They'll about geek out."

"Tommy, I keep saying it, but it's true. You're the sweetest boy in all the world. Don't forget to buy her a present."

Sweetest boys in all the world need to be reminded to act right.

"Why don't you buy for me a totally sexy gown and robe!"

"Great! She'll really geek out."

"Why am I nervous?" she asked me as we pulled up to our house on Oak Park Avenue. "What a wonderfully funny old house!"

"You're nervous because you're now not Amy's classmate, but my, er, date."

"Girlfriend."

"Woman friend."

"Friend."

"All RIGHT."

We got out of the car and walked up the creaky old steps. She held my hand. Nothing like making things explicit.

Amy threw open the door.

"Christy, you are totally NOT his date!"

"Friend," I said.

Amy threw her arms around Christy, then around me, and then around Christy again. She thinks she's going to be a bridesmaid and godmother, I thought.

"How long have you been dating?" She screeched.

"I wouldn't call it dating," Christy said thoughtfully. "How long would you say, my love?"

The "my love" was part of the act.

"It seems like forever," I said.

Amy screamed and hugged us both again.

She certainly approved of the relationship.

Inside the house. Time for introductions.

"Mom," I said to Beth, "I think you've met Christina Anne before, though in perhaps a different context. Christy, this is my father, Thomas Patrick Flynn, always called Thomas to distinguish him from his son. Dad, this is Christina Anne Logan, All-American soccer player from your alma mater."

Dad rose to the occasion, as I knew he would.

"Christy, I've read a lot about you and heard even more from my daughter. I'm delighted to meet you . . . and astonished that you are in the company of my son. Astonished and delighted."

"He's a soccer fan," Christy said, her eyes gleaming wickedly.

Already she had made common cause.

"Why didn't you tell me, Christy?" Amy, still hysterical, demanded.

"Had to protect my reputation."

Then I saw the tears in Mom's eyes. If I had known it would mean that much to her, I would have used the word long ago. Tommy Flynn, you're a jerk.

There was much hugging and kissing.

"Thank you, Tommy," Mom whispered as she kissed me.

"Long overdue," I replied, close to tears myself.

Thus a whole class of minor fantasies slipped out of my life. My shrink had been right.

It was a festive afternoon. Amy was "totally geeked out" by my present.

"Even if you picked it out, Christy, I never expected him to buy me anything like this."

"He really has very good taste," my love insisted, "for a man."

We had to break up early because both the Domers had to return to school. It was agreed that Amy would ride down with us and then back to Notre Dame with Christy. After some discussion, I was permitted to sit in the front seat with Christy. No heavy kissing at the door of the Hancock Center.

Why the hell not?

So, I kissed her quite passionately before I climbed out. She responded in kind. I'm sure Amy's eyes bulged.

"Love you, dear," I said.

"Love you too," Christy gasped. "Write me a nice e-mail, would you?"

Amy would be certain that the two of us were in love.

Well, weren't we?

So I sent her an e-mail.

Dear young lioness,

You certainly did embarrass me in front of my sister in the car with that wild lioness kiss. I felt very awkward. Amy is probably convinced that we'll marry right after you graduate. It was a very nice kiss, by the way, but you caught me completely off guard.

I know now that you're back there under the shadow of the Golden Dome, you'll settle down and concentrate on your school work.

Love,
Tommy

The next morning, there was a reply waiting for me.

Tommy, you geek! If you think I'm going to play the game you play with your poor sisters, you're even weirder than I think you are. I agree that it was a nice kiss. Makes me shiver to think about it.

Love,
Christy Anne

We saw each other several times in the next few weeks. She would drive into town at the end of the day for a movie or a concert or an opera, always dressed smartly, as though she were an accomplished, professional woman instead of an adolescent hoyden.

"What time is this opera over? I have to drive back to the Dome."

"Eleven-thirty. And you won't drive back to the Dome."

"Whadayamean?" She twisted her face into her patented frown.

The hoyden, cum lioness, reappeared.

"I mean, it's better if you stay at your parents' house."

"I don't want to stay there. They don't know I'm in town. What will they say?"

"You'll tell them you were at the opera with Tommy, and they'll be pleased. You can even tell them that Tommy made you stay at home."

"No. I can do what I want!"

"Not on my time."

"Whadayamean, your time?"

"I invited you to drive in for the opera. You're my responsibility. I don't want you driving home in the small hours of the morning without any sleep."

"I've done it before!"

"Regardless."

"You sound just like my parents."

"That's because I'm so old."

She thought about it and then reluctantly agreed.

"Well, at least you didn't threaten never to take me out again."

"No, but you have to stay at their house every time you come in for a date."

"You think you can run my life?"

Was I doing this right, I wondered.

"I wouldn't dream of that, Christy. I'm just trying to protect my sleep."

The frown disappeared and was replaced by her radiant smile.

"You're weird, Tommy, but I still love you. . . . Thank you for being concerned about me. You're right."

It was that easy. No evidence of any improvement in my skills. She was capable of docility on certain occasions, that was all.

We would kiss after such dates and engage in mild caresses. Nothing serious. I insisted to myself that this was still a remote courtship. Nothing would be serious for a long time.

I watched the games on TV. Notre Dame was sweeping through the season. However, in the ratings they were number two or three behind Stanford. The Cardinal, I was informed, were very good and very stuck-up and played very dirty.

My heart was in my throat during every game. My lioness never let up, not even when the team was a couple of goals ahead.

BLACKIE

23

That the Church of the Forty Holy Martyrs in Forest Hills would be a late Renaissance baroque edifice was most appropriate, it had always seemed to me. Not that the suburb itself looked like a Renaissance town. Far from it; if anything, the community looked like someone had designed the homes to be eighteenth-century Tudor, not so large as the Tudor castles in Britain and Ireland, but far warmer (or cooler, in the summer), better lit, and with infinitely more convenient conveniences. It was far and away the wealthiest parish in the city, a fact of which its members were fully aware and very proud. That Matt Dribben, Canaryville Irish, should be pastor there seemed at first to be one of Sean Cronin's little jokes, though his name was on the personnel board's list, which went to the Cardinal. The good burghers of Forest Hills were skeptical about the appointment. How could a man who had worked among African Americans (some of the parishioners said "blacks," or even "Negroes," since being politically correct was hardly on their agenda) most of his priestly life possibly understand their spiritual needs? They reckoned without Matt's South Side Irish political instincts and his utter innocence of every kind of ideology.

The rectory, in which I sat eating lunch with Matt, was utterly inappropriate for such a parish—an old farmhouse that had stood for more than a century on the land the Archdiocese had bought long ago for a parish in Forest Hills. A succession of pastors had remodeled it, but they resolutely refused to demolish it, despite the claim of many of the parishioners that it was an eyesore that had a negative impact on property values.

"So, are you here, Blackie, to investigate the harm that poor Gus did to his parish, or to look for suspects?"

Matt had just celebrated his seventieth birthday and retired as pastor. He was tall and skinny, with a few thin strands of hair plastered neatly on the top of his head. His brown eyes were pleasant and very shrewd and his grin charming, till you realized how shrewd he really was.

"Are they not the same question?"

He clapped his hands enthusiastically.

"No wonder Sean made you a bishop! You learn quickly!"

"Ah, no, Matthew. I was born with that knowledge!"

He applauded again.

"Well, if you want to know how important a pastor is to

a parish, I can answer that for you. It takes him years to accomplish any good, and then his successor can destroy it overnight. Your good friend Gus Quill wiped this place out overnight. I could hardly believe the devastation. The poor man had no sense of people at all."

Which was one good way to describe a borderline personality.

"Usually reliable sources, however, tell me that peace and tranquillity have returned."

"Yeah," he sighed, "just when I was looking forward to some peace and an improved golf game in retirement." His eyes narrowed. "Sean is not thinking of sending you up here, is he?"

"Not very likely, Matthew, since he knows full well I would retire the next day."

"You're welcome to it, you know."

"You will be here as an administrator indefinitely, Matthew. Perhaps, when you are satisfied that Gus's mess has been swept away, he would accept a plea for retirement. However, I would not count on that."

"It is kind of good to get back here. I hoped the new pastor would let me stay in the rectory. I didn't think I'd be responsible for the place."

After a three-month postretirement vacation, Matt Dribben was delighted to be home again.

"You have succeeded in restoring tranquillity to the people of God in Forty Holy Martyrs?"

"Tranquillity is not something they are very good at. They'll complain about poor Gus for years. Still, the worst is over, except for the staff. They're a harder nut to crack."

"Indeed."

"Dessert . . . maybe a dish of chocolate ice cream?"

My bad habits had traveled before me.

"Only a small dish."

Matt grinned, infinitely pleased with himself.

"You never put on any weight do you, just like me?"

"I am forever doomed to be pudgy. . . . Now tell me, Matthew . . . which of your parish staff is most likely to have connived a plot against Augustus O'Sullivan Quill?"

"Aha! Now we get down to cases! I figured you'd ask that question!"

"Indeed."

"I don't have to tell you, Blackie, that since Rome won't ordain women or married men, we have a priest shortage. So we fill up the vacancies with laypeople and an occasional permanent deacon. Good staff are hard to come by, even if you pay them well. Who wants to be a second-rate priest!"

In fact, I paid the Megan three times the going rate for baby-sitters and counted myself lucky. I was reasonably satisfied with my lay staff too, and paid them accordingly. However, no one was more important than the ones who answered the rectory doorbell.

"So, you make do with what you can get . . . former priests, former nuns, folks that like to hang around church, those who want in on the church power action. Some are good at what they do, others not so good. Some are kind and gracious, others are bossy, still others are neurotic. The pastor has to warn and cajole, encourage and restrain, particularly those who want to deny sacraments at every turn of the corner. Especially he must realize that he is dealing with fragile egos. On the whole, my crowd is pretty good, though it will be a while before they recover from poor Gus. He kind of stood for everything they hate and fear in the Church."

"I understand," I said with my most sympathetic sigh.

"Take Orlando Carlin, for example. He has a Ph.D. from Harvard in education. He was a Jesuit with an eye for the ladies. One of his pretty students twenty years ago was Sister Joel Reed. Enough said. He could do much better, so could she. However, they never got over being a priest and nun, even if they were keeping house. So they're here waiting for the Church to change its mind on them. She's become a kind of an angry ideologue and he's, well, he's still got an eye for the ladies."

"Here in the parish?"

"I don't think so. I warned him once. He still flirts a little. . . . My point is that she's a fine director of religion education and RCIA and he's a brilliant adult educator Could they have connived to poison poor Gus with heroin? Sure, they could have. They're both angry enough and smart enough. Did they? I kind of doubt it."

"Why?"

"They're too full of themselves to bother with revenge But what do I know? Judge for yourself."

"Hmm . . ."

"Then there's poor Herman Crawford, our organist and music director. Good music doesn't come cheap anymore Herman is neurotic as all hell. Requires constant reassurance. Wants to sing 'Palestrina' every Sunday. Afraid no one likes him. Actually does a damn good job. Probably gay, not active as far as I know. I figure that's none of my business as long as he doesn't take up with a kid from the parish, which the poor guy would never do."

And it used to be fun to be a pastor!

"I can see why Joel Reed and Orlando Carlin would have a grudge against Gus Quill, but why your presumably gay music director?"

"Someone whispered into Gus's ear that Herman was gay after the choir Mass on Sunday. Gus went up to the choir loft and fired him on the spot in front of the choir. Said that he wanted no perverts working in his parish. Poor Herman has been brooding ever since. There's a lot of rage in the man."

"Gus didn't even bother to spend an hour in prayer before he did it?"

"Huh? Oh yeah, I see what you mean. They tell me that was his standard line whenever he dismissed someone. He would not reconsider the decision because he had prayed for an hour over it before he decided. That was the line when he fired the whole parish council in one fell swoop."

"Ah?"

"Do you have a parish council?"

"Doesn't everyone?"

"Do they try to tell you how to run the parish?"

"Not twice."

"A lot of people around here, who have nothing much else to do, like to meddle. My father wasn't a precinct captain for nothing. I kid them along and it works out. They come up with a lot of good ideas. . . . Anyway, I've set you up for an interview with Larry Henning, the chairman of the parish council. As long as he thinks he's my right-hand man, he does a fine job with them. Gus said he couldn't be his right-hand man anymore. Broke the poor guy's heart."

"He is your right-hand man, Matthew?"

"Course not. I have a dozen or so around the parish who think that. Maybe two or three really are, including Crystal Lane, our youth minister, who is a saint."

"I don't get to see her?"

"She's not on the list of people. Believe me, Blackie, she likes teenagers, she's gotta be a saint."

I like teenagers too, and I'm not a saint, but that didn't prove anything.

"Ms. Reed and Dr. Harmon will be in their offices now. They insist on seeing you together. Incidentally, she's not 'Joel' anymore but 'Joe,' with an *e* on Joe."

"Indeed."

None of the interviews were especially pleasant or informative, not that I had expected them to be.

"The first thing we want to know, John," Ms. Reed charged in, "is whether that fucking bastard will be back here."

Arguably she had once been a pretty young nun. Now she was an older woman whose face and soul had been twisted with free-floating rage. I knew her kind well. While I did not like them, I sympathized with their plight.

"He is recovering slowly," I temporized. "It will be a long time, if ever, before he is ready for arduous ministry."

"Typical bishop shit. I want a straight answer."

Her husband, still handsome with iron gray hair and shifty eyes, smiled tolerantly.

"That was a straight answer," I replied.

"I say that whoever kidnapped him did the goddamn Church a big favor. I wish I had thought of it."

"Indeed."

"What my wife means," Orlando Carlin drawled, still very much a New England Jesuit, "is that many of us work here at considerable financial sacrifice because we still have the dream of a Church renewed according to the spirit of the Second Vatican Council. We don't think it was right for the Cardinal to send a man like Idiot Quill up here."

The point was well taken. What could I say?

"The Cardinal was taken aback by his actions. As you know, he ordered Bishop Quill to rehire everyone he had fired."

"He should have apologized to us," Joe snarled at me.

"I think his reassignment of Father Dribben was an act of good faith and good will to everyone in the parish."

"Old Matthew is all right," Orlando conceded. "Perhaps a bit too clever by half, but basically a good heart."

"Now, you really want to know whether we had any part in kidnapping him and shooting him full of heroin, don't you?" his wife barked at me.

"My goals are more modest. I'm trying to learn if anyone has any ideas who might have committed the crime."

"Crime! I'd say it was an act of heroic virtue! We didn't do it. We're both sorry we didn't think of something like that. If we knew who did, we wouldn't tell you."

Poor woman. The trauma of change in the Church had ruined her life.

"The thing is, Blackie—I may call you that, may I not?"

"Everyone does."

"The point is that on occasion revolutionary political action is not inappropriate. Poor Idiot pushed his community in the direction of valid revolutionary action. I can tell you without violating any confidences that there was considerable discussion about what course of action we as the oppressed should take. I can also assure you that no one shed any tears over his fate. . . . Is he really a vegetable?"

Ah, the clichés of the 1960s! How nostalgic.

"He is suffering from an acute psychotic interlude," I said. "The doctors hope for a recovery."

"You understand that we must be silent about what conversations our colleagues may have had with us. This was an oppressed community, as I'm sure you realize. We were entitled to seek liberation."

Forest Hills victimized by oppression, indeed. Not to put too fine an edge on the matter, this was bullshit, playacting revolution. Yet it was possible that there had been some kind of conspiracy in the parish.

I approached Herman Crawford with delicacy. Since Milord Cronin's brother, Cardinal Prince Josef Ratzinger, described gay people as "fundamentally disordered" there has been no other way.

"Father Dribben," I told him, "reports that you have a great love of Giovanni Pierluigi."

His soft gray eyes lit up, "No one has ever written religious music like the maestro of 'Palestrina,' " he said. "Not even Byrd or Lassus. You have a polyphonic Mass at the Cathedral, don't you, Bishop?"

"We have a folk choir, a Gregorian scola cantorum, a polyphonic choir, a Celtic choir, and several children's choirs. It seems reasonable to assume that such is the obligation of a cathedral."

Herman, in a tiny office next to the choir loft, surrounded by piles of musical scores, was a trim, nice-looking young man with rimless spectacles and a high forehead.

"Do you think God hates me because he made me gay, Bishop?"

"I think God loves us all, as a parent loves a child. He doesn't hate anyone."

"Is it God's will that I'm gay; is it part of His plan?"

"God works with everything that happens and draws us to Herself by Her own ways. In that sense, surely it is God's will. However, it is not God's will that we suffer for what we are. When we do suffer, God suffers with us."

He sighed sadly. "I try my best, Bishop. I do what I can."

"I'm sure you do."

"Bishop Quill said that I was objectively evil. In front of the whole choir. He is the one who is objectively evil, isn't he, Bishop Ryan?"

"It was a terribly un-Christian thing to say."

"If I had a gun or knife, I would have killed him. He deserved to die."

"Ah?"

"I don't know whether I mean that. I was beside myself with rage. I couldn't speak. I rushed out of the choir loft screaming."

"And the choir?"

"Oh, they came after me. What else could they do?"

No homophobes in that choir.

"So there are many people here in the parish who are not unhappy at Bishop Quill's sickness?"

"Everyone is happy about it, except some old fuddy-duddy reactionaries and Crystal, of course, but she's a saint."

"I have heard of the young woman. Did not the bishop fire her?"

"He didn't notice her. She's sweet and pretty and kind of tiny and no one notices her at first. He banned all teenagers. However, he didn't realize that he had a youth minister. Even if he fired her, she still wouldn't hate him. Like I say, Crystal is a saint."

Or perhaps, the only forgiving Christian in the parish.

"Was there discussion of getting rid of Bishop Quill?"

"Sure there was. Everyone wanted to get rid of him. I'm glad he's gone crazy. If you ask me, he was always crazy. I hope they keep him in the loony bin for the rest of his life. I hate him."

"Do you think that anyone in the parish might have been involved in his kidnapping?"

"I don't know and I don't care," he shouted hysterically. "He got what he deserved!"

The atmosphere of hatred for Gus Quill in the parish was intense and dangerous. Still. I must tread carefully.

"I can understand the feelings."

"I didn't do anything to him, Bishop. I didn't. I couldn't. I wouldn't want to hurt anyone."

"I would not think so," I reassured him.

"This is a wonderful parish. I don't ever want to leave here. Is he coming back?"

"I don't think you have to worry about having to leave here."

"Thank you, Bishop, thank you very much. I didn't have anything to do with what happened. I really didn't."

I gently disengaged from this tormented man. We had done terrible things to him. As Matt Dribben had said, Gus didn't know people. Rather, more clinically, other people barely existed for him.

As I waited in the rectory office for the arrival of Larry Henning, the chairman of the parish council, I reviewed the bidding. Parish staff often confuse how they feel with how the parish feels. That there was a poisonous attitude towards Bishop Quill on the staff was beyond question. In the rest of the parish, there was doubtless general dislike, but hardly a will to get rid of him. Not so soon anyway. Yet there were certainly groups of parishioners, especially those who most closely identified with the parish, who shared the staff's nearly irrational hatred. It would take more resources than I had to investigate the whole parish.

Much to my surprise, I found my cell phone in the pocket of my now sadly obsolete Bulls jacket. Even more to my surprise, I pushed the right button the first time.

"Reliable Security, Casey speaking."

"Indeed!"

"Blackie! What mischief are you up to now?"

"I am exploring the community of the People of God in Forest Hills, also known as Forty Holy Martyrs parish. I think there is need of a much more intensive investigation."

"You want us to poke around? Reliably?"

"And discreetly. There may have been an organized conspiracy up here. I am skeptical of the hints I hear, but we cannot exclude them. In a community with this much talent and this much money, there are surely individuals who could be our mastermind."

"No doubt about that. . . . Any ideas about where to start?"

"The usual spots, commuter stations, beauty salons, barber-shops, the places where people talk."

"We'll have a go at it, Blackie. No promises."

"I expect none."

Lawrence T. Henning, as he introduced himself, was a cautious and careful man, from his expensive navy blue Italian suit to his carefully groomed widow's peak hair. He carried, not too lightly, the aura of a major corporation executive, which he surely was not. His dark eyes were expressionless, and not once in our conversation did he smile. In an earlier era in the Church, he would have been the all-powerful head usher, truly the pastor's right-hand man. Now he was a figurehead who took himself very, very seriously.

"I'm happy to meet you, Bishop Ryan," he said with a firm handshake. "There have been bad times here. In all candor, the parish needs healing."

"Father Dribben seems to be doing his best."

"Father is a wonderful priest. The former pastor left a lot of wreckage behind."

"So I understand . . . and not a little anger?"

"That is to be expected. A parish is not quite like an accounting firm. The ties are fragile. They can be destroyed very quickly, more quickly than I would have expected. It will require a long time to restore them."

"Like Humpty Dumpty?"

"I beg your pardon?"

"All the king's men couldn't put him back together again."

"In all candor, I doubt that the parish will ever be restored to its previous condition. Father and I are trying our best."

"I'm sure you are. . . . Is it true that Bishop Quill swept out the whole parish council at his first meeting with them?"

"In the first five minutes."

"How did it happen?"

"We meet regularly on the first and third Mondays of each month. The Bishop came into the conference room in his full robes. He informed us that he had just come from church, where he had prayed for a solid hour about the meeting. Ms. Mary O'Hanlon—her husband is O'Hanlon Industries, I'm sure you know—asked whether the contracts with the parish staff would be honored. He told her that such a question was no one's business but his own. Then Joseph Toliver, the commodity trader who I'm sure you've heard of, said that since the parish was liable for a suit, it was indeed our business. Then the Bishop stood up and ordered us out of the rectory. I tried to reason with him. He told us that we had no canonical powers and no right to meet except at his request. He warned us to leave or he would call the police. We left."

"And went not gently into that good night?"

"I beg pardon?"

"You all were quite angry and so you raged against the failing of the light?"

"What could you expect, Bishop? Many of us have put enormous time and energy into the parish. It is an important part of our lives, of our very identities. As the kids say, 'Martyrs! The biggest and the best!'"

Would, I wondered, the forty holy martyrs, had they ever existed, have approved this class-based cry? I rather doubted it.

"Down in the city there are rumors that the kidnapping of the Bishop, and the injection of heroin into his bloodstream, were somehow devised up here."

"How could there not be such rumors? Personally, I don't

credit them. We are not that kind of people. On the other hand, one can never be sure. The Chicago police, I am told, discount such a possibility. Nonetheless, I certainly feel safe in saying that there were few regrets up here at the Bishop's misfortune. Moreover, there was great joy when Father Dribben returned. People said that the Cardinal had redeemed himself."

"I'm sure he will be delighted with that vote of confidence. . . . And your own personal feelings?"

"Personal? I don't think they matter. However, since you ask and in all candor, I was not disappointed to learn what happened to him. He had it coming."

The man paused, as if trying to control himself within his image of the corporate executive.

"In all candor, Bishop," he continued, his thin lips tight, "if I had learned of a conspiracy to destroy him without killing him, I would have joined it."

"I see."

"However"—he relaxed, having recaptured the mask that went with his role—"there was no such conspiracy that I know of. That is not to say that there might not have been one. If there were, it was carried out with the utmost secrecy."

"It was," I sighed, "a very professional operation, the sort I would expect from this community."

"Exactly."

When he left, I sneaked into the kitchen to make myself a cup of tea and perhaps exorcise the headache that these worthy Christians had produced. A small, waiflike girl child appeared.

"Father Matt said you'd like some tea before you left,

Bishop. I'll make it for you. I might even find some cookies for you."

"Wondrous. . . . You would be Crystal?"

She giggled. "How did you know that? Oh, well, everyone seems to know who I am."

The young woman's smile was arguably the most radiant currently to be found on the planet. In an earlier age, she would have been a novice in a religious order. Now she was a youth minister who looked younger than most of her charges.

We sat at a booth in the kitchen to drink our tea and eat our cookies.

"I hope you don't think me forward, Bishop Ryan." She grinned at me over the rim of her teacup. "Father Matt said I could talk to you."

"Father Matt is patently the boss."

She giggled again, then tried to become serious.

"I'm going back to school next autumn to study for my doctorate in psychology at Loyola."

Saint Thérèse went to the Carmel in Lisieux. This counterpart a century later would go to Loyola for a doctorate in psychology. Thus God plans the lives of bewitching young women for every era.

"Admirable."

"My contract here will be over and I really couldn't commute downtown, so Father Matt said that I should talk to you about—"

"You're hired," I said.

"Oh, Bishop!" She jumped up and clapped her hands. 'I'm so happy. I promise you that I will do a good job."

"Somewhere here I have a card," I said searching

through my pockets. Naturally, I didn't have a card.

"I know where the Cathedral is, Bishop."

Who didn't?

So it was arranged that she would stop by the Cathedral and we would talk about her employment. I assured her that the fact of such employment was a settled matter. How else do you deal with a saint when you find one?

"Tell me about Bishop Quill," I said.

Her face clouded.

"Poor, dear man, there was so much good in him, Bishop Blackie. No matter how hard he tried, he just couldn't get the good out."

So quickly I had become Bishop Blackie. She would, upon arrival, make common cause with the Megan against me.

"Why do you think that was?"

"I suppose his poor mother isolated him from everyone else." She shrugged. "The goodness is still there. I could see it sometimes in his eyes."

It was a diagnosis that my far more sophisticated sibling could but endorse.

"You're not angry at him?"

"Why should I be angry at him? . . . Will he recover?"

"Perhaps. The doctors are very cautious."

"I will keep praying for him."

Matt walked to the car with me.

"A fifty-five black Thunderbird. Appropriate. . . . So you talked to Crystal and hired her on the spot?"

"What more could one do?"

He laughed.

"She's no fool, Blackie."

"I noticed that."

I also noticed that she was the only one in the whole parish who had some sympathy for Gus Quill.

"You're planning to visit those gombeen men down the street, from the Legion of Corpus Christi?"

"Arguably."

"Today?"

"I must return to my hospital calls at the Cathedral. Later in the week."

"Giving the illusion of not being in a rush."

"Perhaps."

"They're a sneaky bunch. Watch out for them."

TOMMY

24

Finally, it was time for the national championship—the Irish against the Lady Cardinal at the Florida State pitch in Tallahassee. What would the Irish do on a pitch that wasn't mud-soaked?

"Will you beat them?" I asked Christy on the phone.

"That's a silly question, certainly we'll beat them."

"That's what I like from my young lionesses—fierce confidence."

"They're very good, Tommy. Very stuck-up, but very good."

She had learned the sports lingo. Before a big game, you are both very confident and very respectful of the tough opponent.

I decided that I would fly to Tallahassee to see the match.

Why not? I would not, however, warn her beforehand. She didn't need to know that I was in the stands for the first time.

The Florida panhandle at that time of the year was like a South Sea Islands paradise compared to the City of Chicago, Richard M. Daley, Mayor. The temperature on the field at game time, the media predicted, would be in the middle nineties.

The local papers were filled with news of the game. Even the *New York Times* had a moderately long story. It was all Stanford. Multicultural team, great talent, maybe the best women's college soccer team ever. Gifted players, a musician, an actress, and an artist. Young African-American coach. Number one all season. Undefeated. Their adversary? Plucky young women from a school more famous for its men's football team. All-American captain Christy Logan was probably no match for the faster All-Americans on Stanford's team.

Well, we would see.

There has been little love lost between Notre Dame and Leland Stanford Jr. Memorial University since the notorious incident at Stanford when their band ridiculed Catholicism at half-time. The University, a model of political correctness in all other matters, argued that the band was an independent organization and the University was not responsible for what it did. The argument, need I say, cut no ice either at South Bend or among the Irish alumni, real and imagined, around the country.

As a Hoya I was strictly neutral. I didn't like either of them.

The sun shone brightly over Tallahassee that afternoon, a

bad sign, I thought, for the Irish, who were mudders. The small stadium around the pitch was almost filled. I saw the Drs. Logan at a distance, but did not want to bother them.

The warm-ups struck me as ominous. The Lady Cardinals, in bright red uniforms, seemed bored and sullen, as if they felt it was a disgrace that they had to play against a patently inferior team. They also looked mean, very mean. That judgment, however, was from a prejudiced perspective. Christy's young women in dark blue and white with gold trim acted like the playful pride of lionesses they were. Christy had them smiling and laughing. Certainly not intimidated, but perhaps too loose.

For the first part of the first half, under the searing sun, the Cardinals ran all over the Irish. They were indeed lightning fast and very physical. One of them knocked my young heroine on her butt several times. The officials had apparently decided that they were going to let the young women play soccer and not interfere with the game.

Stanford scored early on an easy goal when the Irish defense collapsed. They swaggered around like they were South American male soccer players. It was all over.

However, Christy, shouting orders, warnings, and encouragement, rallied the pride, which settled down to a grueling defensive game. They held the Cardinals to nothing more than a few ineffectual shots at the goal. Finally, as the half wound down to this last minute, the chief lioness broke through, raced towards the goal, faked a shot that drew the Cardinals goalie (one of their All-Americans) in her direction, and then rifled the ball across the pitch to a wing, who easily drove it in.

It was 1-1 at half-time. A wise gambler, quite apart from

his loyalties, would have gone long on the Irish, despite the fact that the Irish walked off the field sweating profusely and the Cardinals seemed unperturbed by heat. The bay area was much warmer than late autumn Chicago, I realized. The Cardinal had the weather on their side.

Stanford came out in the second half with renewed fury, fast, brutally rough, and grimly determined. This time, however, Notre Dame was ready for them. They withstood the onslaught. My Christy was all over the pitch, stealing the ball from their allegedly faster and better All-American strikers. The crowd, which had been pro-Cardinal at the beginning, was now on the Irish side. Someone struck up the notorious (to a Hoya like me) victory song. I sang it, God help me, at the top of my voice.

> *Rally sons of Notre Dame,*
> *Sing her glory, and sound her fame*
> *Raise her Gold and Blue,*
> *And cheer with voices true,*
> *Rah! Rah! for Notre Dame.*
>
> *We will fight in every game*
> *Strong of heart and true to her name.*
> *We will ne'er forget her*
> *And we'll cheer her ever,*
> *Loyal to Notre Dame.*
>
> *Cheer, cheer for Old Notre Dame*
> *Wake up the echoes cheering her name,*
> *Send the volley cheer on high,*
> *Shake down the thunder from the sky,*

What tho the odds be great or small
Old Notre Dame will win over all,
While her daughters are marching
Onward to Victory.

Christy shook her fist and grinned at the crowd.

"You from Notre Dame?" a young woman with a thick southern accent next to me asked.

"Nope," I said. "One of them is a friend of mine."

"The big blonde?"

"As a matter of fact, yes."

"No doubt who the best All-American out there really is."

It turned out she was on the Florida State University team. She also admitted that the chief lioness was totally beautiful.

"I hadn't noticed."

The match ebbed and flowed up and down the pitch. Near misses for both sides. Superb defensive play. I still would have gone long on the Irish, though they were clearly exhausted. Christy loved last-minute victories, didn't she?

Then, with only three of the forty-five minutes left, one of Stanford's All-American strikers broke free and dribbled down the pitch. The Notre Dame defense was momentarily disorganized. The Cardinal bench shouted, "Sonia! Sonia!" There was no one between her and the goal.

Then, almost out of nowhere raced the top lioness. As she had done all afternoon, she deftly booted the ball away from Sonia without hitting her. Then she charged back up the pitch through both disorganized and exhausted teams,

Sonia in hot pursuit.

Christy broke free from the swirling masses of red and dark blue jerseys and dashed towards the goal. She was going to drive all the way in so the goalie wouldn't have a chance to block the shot.

Then Sonia caught up. She stuck out her foot and tripped Christy before she could kick the goal. The crowd gasped as Christy landed face down on the turf. There was dead silence for a moment as she struggled to her feet and shook her fist again. Loud applause from the crowd. This time I started the singing of the victory march.

The ref appeared with a red card. Sonia was banished from the game. No replacement permitted. Sonia shouted obscenities. The Stanford team rallied around her. The Stanford coach went crazy. The crowd booed. The ref was not impressed. She pointed towards the locker room and banished both Sonia and the coach.

The official ruled that there would be a penalty kick. She waved both teams away from the goal. The Cardinals screamed again. Christy limped towards the line. One on one, I thought, Christy and the goalie.

Christy faked with her shoulders, then booted the ball by the goalie, who fell on her face as she dove to stop it.

Christy jammed her finger against the sky. Notre Dame was number one! I had won my imaginary bet.

Then she waved off the coach. She was just fine. She continued to hobble, however.

The last two and a half minutes were brutal. The Cardinal abandoned all restraint and turned the match into wild melee. Restrained by Christy's stern warnings, the Irish hung back and let Stanford destroy themselves. The crowd sang the victory march over and over again, albeit only the last stanza.

I mean, who knows the other verses?

I worried about my brave lioness. She was limping badly. The match ended. The Cardinal stalked off the field without a word of congratulations. Christy collapsed on the bench, obviously in great pain. I rushed down the steps, past a startled state cop to whom I shouted, "My girl is hurt," and over to the bench. The Drs. Logan had beat me to it. The rest of the Domers stood by in frightened silence.

Tentatively, Mary Logan ran her finger down her daughter's left leg. Christy screamed.

Mary looked at her husband. "Fibula! If we're lucky, it's only a hairline."

"My leg is not broken!" Christy yelled, wincing with pain. "We have to celebrate!"

"The first thing to do is to immobilize the leg," John Logan said to the trainer. "Do you have a gurney?"

Someone had rolled one out.

"I don't need a gurney!" Christy protested. "I'm fine!"

"And call an ambulance."

"Yes, doctor. Tallahassee Memorial?"

"Of course."

"No ambulance!" Christy cried.

I interjected myself into the dialogue.

"Christy Anne," I said gently, "Please grow up for a few moments. Your parents are doctors. If they say your leg is broken, it's broken. They want to fix you up so you can go to the Olympic tryouts. Now don't make matters worse than they already are."

She glared at me. "What are you doing here?"

"Came to cheer for the Irish lionesses."

"Well, since you're here, the least you can do is to hold my hand. It hurts!"

I held her hand, my heart breaking at her pain.

Mary Logan, fitting the temporary splint in place, looked up at me and smiled.

"Thank God you're here, Tommy Flynn."

"Ouch!" Christy wailed as the splint was slipped into place. "Tommy, where are you! Tighter!"

I squeezed as tight as I could.

An ambulance rolled onto the pitch. A crowd had gathered, Notre Dame players, fans, and interested observers. A TV camera was grinding away. Christy waved as they rolled her onto the ambulance. Her parents climbed in. Somehow or the other I did too. Then, just as the door closed, Christy raised her hand and finger. NUMBER ONE.

"She played for two and a half minutes with a broken leg?" I asked John Logan.

"And kicked the winning goal. . . . Tommy, we never had anyone like her in our family. She's a throwback!"

Apparently the ambulance driver had radioed to the hospital. A young resident was waiting for us outside the door of the emergency room.

"Real fighting Irish," he said as they rolled Christy down to ground level. "I'm John Peters. I went there too."

"John Logan, Doctor. I'm Christy's father. Mary Logan, her mother. We're also alumni."

Doctors recognize other doctors. I don't know how. Same with priests.

"Let's all sing the alma mater song," Christy suggested

through gritted teeth.

"St. Mary's, in my day," Mary Logan set the record straight.

They wheeled my wounded lioness into an emergency room.

"We'll have you fixed up in a few minutes, Ms. Logan. We'll take some X rays first. . . . What is your diagnosis, Dr. Logan?"

"Call me Christy. . . . Where are you, Tommy Flynn? Why aren't you holding my hand?"

I recaptured the hand from which I had been detached when they were wheeling her into the hospital.

"If we're lucky, a hairline fracture of the lower fibula."

Very gently the doctor ran his finger along her lower leg. Christy yelled in protest.

"Right there, Christy?"

"Yes, Doctor," she said. "Make it go away. That's what doctors are for."

"We'll give you a shot and take you down to X ray. I'll call Dr. O'Halloran, our orthopedic person. She's a Domer too."

"Just so long as there's no one from Stanford!"

"What's that noise?" Dr. Peters said, startled by a roar from the lobby.

"Christy's teammates," I suggested.

"Tommy Flynn," the lion queen ordered, "go out there and tell those geeks to chill out. This is a hospital. There's sick people here."

"Yes, ma'am."

"Then come back and hold my hand."

"Yes, ma'am."

The lobby was in chaos. Two outnumbered security guards were trying to restrain a group of noisy, smelly young women in blue-and-white soccer uniforms, a couple of them waving unopened bottles of champagne. There were also some adults—coaches, trainers, hangers-on, and one tall priest.

"All right you geeks," I yelled. "Christy says you should chill out."

Instant silence. Even in absentia, she was in charge.

"First of all, she's all right. It's probably a hairline fracture of the lower fibula, which, if you have to break your leg, is the best way to do it. They're taking X rays and the orthopedic specialist is on her way. They're giving her a shot now to ease the pain—that's medication, not gin!"

Laughter.

"The resident in charge is Dr. John Peters. The orthopedic specialist is Dr. O'Halloran, first name unknown, gender female. They're both Domers. I think Christy will get the red carpet treatment she deserves and expects. . . . Now if you geeks keep quiet, I'll see if I can arrange a little celebration."

"Are you Christy's boyfriend?" a child, no taller than five-two, asked me.

"No, ma'am. I'm her lion trainer."

The security guards continued to struggle to ease the crowd out of the lobby.

I dashed down a corridor, asked a nurse where Public Relations was, and ran down another corridor. The sign on the door said LORETTA CLIFFORD, COMMUNITY RELATIONS.

I brushed by the secretary.

"Ms. Clifford, we have a situation down in the lobby. The

captain of the Notre Dame soccer team is in emergency with a broken leg—"

"Did we win?"

Another one of them. Figured.

"You did. The team is in the lobby wanting to celebrate with their heroine. The security people, understandably, are trying to get rid of them. . . ."

Ms. Clifford knew her work. She picked up a phone and gave a few terse orders to Security.

"I think we can control the situation if we permit them to talk to Christy after her splint is applied and to have a few sips of champagne."

"You can deal with them for that?"

"They'll do whatever Christy says."

"Right! It's a deal."

She was on the phone again as I left the office.

Back in the lobby, there was a truce between the Domers and the cops.

"I'll be right back," I shouted. "Cool it!"

Inside, Dr. Peters and the Logans were looking at X rays.

"What's your guess, Dr. Logan?"

"Your call, Dr. Peters," Mary Logan said, peering intently at the X rays.

"Lemme see," Christy demanded. "It's my leg."

"There's a crack in the front bone of your lower leg right here, Christy. We may not have to set it."

The orthopedist arrived in T-shirt and shorts, called away perhaps from a pool side. Gorgeous. She was African American.

"You poor child, what did they do to you!"

"She like totally tripped me!"

"I saw it. . . ." She looked at the X ray. "I'm Jean O'Hal-loran, by the way."

"These are my parents, they're doctors too, but they're no good unless I have a heart attack. The lug is Tommy Flynn. He holds my hand, which he isn't doing right now."

I returned to my duty.

"You played on this for three minutes?"

"Two and a half."

"Did you know it was broken?"

"I'm like, now you've done it, Christy, but you totally can't quit now."

"Child, as a Domer I applaud your courage," she continued to peer intently at the negatives. "As a doctor and a parent, I think you're crazy."

"That's the kind of things lionesses do," I observed.

"Will I be able to play in the Olympics?"

"Well"—Dr. O'Halloran pondered—"maybe. If you're very, very careful and do exactly what I tell you to do and what the orthopedists in Chicago say. . . . What hospital, Dr. Logan?"

"Northwestern."

"Alf Hightower? The best."

"I'm going to medical school next year," Christy informed her. "And I'm going to specialize in sports medicine."

The painkiller was beginning to have an effect.

"Fine, but even then you don't diagnose yourself, right?"

"Yes, ma'am."

"Now we're going to put a splint and a brace on this leg, give you another shot, keep you here overnight, and let you go home to Chicago maybe on Monday. It's crutches for two weeks at least, understand?"

"Yes, ma'am."

"Dr. O'Halloran . . . ," I intruded.

"Yes, Tommy Flynn, hand-holder."

"You may not have noticed, but the lobby is filled with Domers, the team mostly. They want a brief celebration with Christy. I cut a deal with Loretta Clifford that if it was all right, one small sip of champagne for everyone and they'll go home."

"After we get the splint on. You a precinct captain or something, Tommy Flynn?"

"Not yet."

I grabbed a stack of paper cups from a supply cart that had been left unguarded. In the lobby, Loretta Clifford, standing with the security people, looked amused.

"All right, geeks!" I shouted. "Another message from herself!"

Silence.

"She says you're making too much noise. When she tells you to chill out, you should chill out, right?"

They chilled out.

"Now, here's the deal. Dr. Jean O'Halloran says that it is indeed a hairline fracture. They're putting a splint and a brace on it, giving her another shot, and keeping her in till tomorrow. She'll come out here and you can open two—count 'em, two—bottles of champagne. Everyone gets a small drink, Christy only a sip. Then you leave quietly and Christy has a long night's sleep. Got it?"

They nodded solemnly.

"You," I said to the small girl child who was a fearsome striker on the pitch, "pass around the paper cups. One to a customer. Christy has this painkiller stuff in her, so she may be a little more geeky than usual. But I'm not sure that we'll be able to tell the difference."

More laughter.

I went back to Christy's room. Dr. O'Halloran was carefully adjusting a splint.

"Hurt, child?"

"No, Jean, but Tommy Flynn should be holding my hand just the same. That's all he's good for, you know?"

They all laughed. Tommy Flynn as milady's fool.

"What do you think, Dr. Logan?"

"As Christy says"—it was Mary Logan's turn to speak for the family—"we'd only be a help if she had a heart attack or needed heart surgery. It looks fine to me."

With infinite delicacy, Dr. O'Halloran locked the brace in place.

"No messing with this child, hear?"

"Yes, ma'am."

"Now you go out there and have your little celebration. Then we'll take some more X rays and put you to bed."

"Tommy Flynn, you push this wheelchair."

"Yes, milady."

So we entered the lobby with all four medical doctors in tow. The media were there already. Two TV cameras.

The waiting Domers broke into cheers. Someone gave Christy the championship cup, which she shook triumphantly. They opened the two bottles of champagne, poured a little into every paper cup, and gave a cup to Christy. As I had ordered, it contained only a sip.

"To Christy!" the small girl child shouted.

"Christy!" They all bellowed.

Then someone, surely not I, did the inevitable.

" 'Cheer, cheer for old Notre Dame'—let's have all three stanzas!"

Hoya or not, I sang along with them.

"Chill out!" the lion queen ordered.

They did.

"Dr. O'Halloran says that if I keep all the rules, my leg will be fine for the Olympics. You geeks know how good I am at keeping rules, right?"

Derisive laughter.

"So I expect you all to make sure I do, right?"

Universal agreement.

"I'm fading fast," she admitted. "I want to thank all of you for winning and for putting up with me all season long. You're the greatest! And we're number ONE!"

They had to sing the victory song again.

Two TV reporters pushed their way through the crowd.

"Christy, do you think Sonia tripped you deliberately?"

"No way," she said firmly. "In the heat of the game, we all do things that we wouldn't do normally."

"How do you feel now, Christy?"

"Happy . . . and very sleepy."

Then they left quietly. Mary Logan wheeled her back into the emergency room.

"What's your name, son?" the tall priest asked me.

"Tommy Flynn, Father."

"You a senior?"

"I was five years ago—at Georgetown!"

He shook hands with me. "Even Hoyas have souls. That was a superb performance."

"Thank you, Father."

"Are you, uh, Christy's . . ."

"Not yet."

He shook hands again.

"She'll be a fortunate young woman when you are."

Gulp.

In the emergency room, they were inspecting another set of X ray negatives. The lioness was pretty well tranquilized.

"Looks good," Dr. O'Halloran said. "We'll do another set tomorrow, Dr. Logan. Four sets to bring home to Dr Hightower."

"I think my hand-holding services are no longer required," I said.

I leaned over and rested my lips against hers.

"Be good, Christy Logan, national champ."

"I will, Tommy Flynn, hand-holder." Then her voice sank to a whisper. "Would you smuggle a malted milk into this place for me?"

"Sure."

John Logan walked me to main entrance of the hospital

"Are you staying at the FSU Marriott, Tommy?"

"Yes, sir."

"We are too. Maybe we can have supper tomorrow night when we get herself out of here."

"Sounds great."

"She is the most unusual of our children," he began tentatively.

"I can believe that."

"She has never paid the slightest attention to us. She doesn't do bad things, drugs or drink or boys, and she's always respectful."

"I don't doubt it."

"However, we have absolutely no control over her."

"I don't doubt that either."

"You tell her what to do and she goes along."

"Sometimes."

He sighed. "I don't know what your secret is, young man, but more power to you."

"Thank you, sir. I may need it."

I did smuggle the malted milk back into the hospital later. It was easy. The security folk thought I was one of their guys.

Christy's room was semidark. Wearing a hospital gown, she was lying on a bed with her leg suspended in the air. She looked like a sixteen-year-old again. Mary Logan was sitting in a chair next to the bed saying the rosary.

"Hi," I whispered. "I was told to smuggle in three malted milks, one for you, one for Christina Anne, and one for myself."

"Thank you, Tommy. She's dozed off. But I'm sure she'll wake up for you."

"I don't want to bother her."

"No bother. She'll go right back to sleep."

"How's she doing?"

"Fine. She's a strong and healthy young woman. The leg will heal quickly. She may feel twinges occasionally on cold and rainy days. They'll remind her of her great triumph. It really was great, wasn't it, Tommy Flynn?"

"The greatest!"

"Bishop Blackie called. He said that it was arguably the greatest victory in the whole history of the Fighting Irish."

That sounded like Bishop Blackie.

"Christina dear, that nice young Tommy Flynn is here with a treat."

Her eyes opened wide.

"WELL, it's about time."

We consumed our three malted milks, I kissed her good night, and slipped away.

No doubt that the Logans were on my side.

The papers the next day were filled with the story. Stanford's formal protest was the main topic. They had complained that as important a game as the national championship should not be decided by an official's mistake. Sonia was quoted as saying, "I never touched her. It was definitely a fake. We shouldn't lose because the ref was too dumb to spot a fake." Their coach insisted that it was a blatant misjudgment that "cannot be permitted to deny our young women a national championship which is rightly theirs." The Notre Dame coach had only two words to say: "Sour grapes." Unnamed experts argued that the soccer federation would most likely reject the protest since there was no precedent for such a reversal of a ref's decision. There were rumors that Sonia would be banned from soccer for a year, and thus precluded from trying out for the United States Olympic team.

Somehow it was not so newsworthy that a young woman with a broken left leg (admittedly only a hairline fracture) had won the game.

The most powerful element in the rehash, however, was a *New York Times* spread of frames from the TV tape. It showed Christy deftly stealing Sonia's dribble without touching her, skirting around the Cardinal player, and dribbling down the pitch, and next Sonia sticking out her foot, and then the actual contact, and finally Christy tumbling to the grass. There was no doubt that she had been tripped.

The *Times* headed the story: TRIP, REAL OR FAKE?

I spent the day in the FSU bookstore and reading beside the hotel pool.

Pale and subdued, Christy hobbled into the restaurant of the FSU Marriott that night on crutches. She was wearing a gray pant-suit with white trim at the neck and cuffs, and her pearl necklace and earrings. Wounded lionesses have to look chic.

I made a big fuss of helping her into her chair.

"How you doing?"

"I ache everywhere. Otherwise, I'm fine. I can't even swim for two weeks. I'll be like, totally fat."

"No more secret malted milks!"

Her eyes widened in feigned innocence.

"I'd never do that. Some weird boy might try to pick me up."

She was on her way back.

"The media were waiting for us when we came downstairs," John Logan said with a sigh. "Those Stanford people are real geeks."

"Totally," his daughter agreed. "Like, they go, what would we do if the USSF told us to give the trophy back, and I'm like, Stanford would have to come to Notre Dame to get it and bring their geeky band along with them."

"I thought you hit just the right note, dear, when they asked you whether you thought the USSF would suspend Sonia, and you said if they did, you'd write a letter asking them to change their minds."

"I didn't mention that if she showed up at the Olympics, I'd trip her back!"

"Christy!" her parents said together.

"She's only joking," I said. "Actually, what she would do is take Sonia out for a malted milk and then poison her."

She survived the trip to Chicago well enough. Dr. Hightower confirmed Dr. O'Halloran's diagnosis. I drove down to Notre Dame a couple of weekends to see her. She had recovered her high spirits and was obeying all the rules. I was a little too elderly for the campus life; however, there were a couple of good concerts and one good lecture, for which only a handful of the Domers showed up.

Geeks!

I told myself as I drove back late Sunday night—the rules I made for Christy didn't apply to me—that our relationship was unchanged. We were still good friends and still nothing more than that. It was harder each weekend to persuade myself that this was anything more than fantasy.

BLACKIE

25

We are very honored that you deign to visit us, Your Excellency, however informally."

"You will, of course, have an aperitif. Some sherry, perhaps?"

One of them was Father Luis, the other was Father Ramon, trim men of medium height, sallow skin, and dark brown hair. Not twins exactly, but so similar in posture, accent, and voice that I could not tell them apart. That was, perhaps, part of their game. Their residence was an elaborate mansion two blocks down the street from Forty Holy Martyrs. They had greeted me in a drawing room that would have been worthy of Philip II.

A couple of centuries ago, they would have worked for the Inquisition. Now they were trying to subvert the whole Church so they could run it. They had lots of clout in Rome, but were not smart enough to know how to use it. Besides, the Church was now too confused to be open to subversion.

I accepted a very small glass of sherry, a beverage from which my attendant leprechaun did not deign to steal.

"We very much regret the difficulties with Bishop Quill."

"It is perhaps necessary to assert that our people had nothing to do with his appointment."

"In fact, we have learned from the highest authority that our people in Rome opposed the appointment."

"They foresaw the troubles which would occur."

"And warned others what would happen."

"Indeed."

This was nonsense. They were merely covering their tracks, as they always did.

"It is true that he came to us about a television station, which he proposed to build here in the parish to combat the godlessness in the secular capitalist media."

"It is also true that we ourselves have given some thought to such a project."

"We had not gone beyond remote planning. Naturally, we would have consulted with the Cardinal."

"Naturally," I agreed.

"Bishop Quill had certain peculiar mannerisms."

"He seemed to assume that because he had presented his plans to us, we accepted them."

"Ah?"

"We had in fact agreed to nothing."

"Nor would we ever have agreed to cooperate with him."

"He was, how should I say it, too, ah, unstable."

"We would have to raise large sums of money for such a project."

"A building, electronic equipment, staff."

"Television is very expensive, as I'm sure you know, Bishop Ryan."

"We would owe it to our supporters to retain control of the station."

"That would have been most difficult if Bishop Quill was, uh, involved."

"I take your meaning. . . . Therefore, you were not displeased to learn of the Bishop's unfortunate, ah, experience?"

I might just as well have suggested that the Pope was not Catholic.

"Quite the contrary, we deplore it."

"It is most unfortunate."

"Very bad for the Church."

"He was such a very peculiar man, was he not?"

"Yes, very peculiar."

"We trust he is recovering well?"

Why was everyone so eager to be reassured that poor Gus would not recover?

"As well as can be expected. The doctors are cautiously

optimistic."

"Thanks be to God!"

"He will be able to return to the parish?"

"Perhaps, though at the present time that does not seem likely."

Their relief at such good news was all too obvious.

"Such a tragic story."

"Yes, it is."

"I am told that there is some suspicion that your friends could have been involved in his kidnapping."

Shock, dismay, outrage. Always polite, however.

"Surely not!"

"A man of your sophistication knows how many false things are said about us."

"We would never be a party to such evil."

"We know of no one who could carry out such a convoluted crime."

"Why would anyone spread such rumors about us?"

"It is defamation."

They did protest too much. On the basis of the past history of their group, they would do almost anything to further its goals. However, they would stop short of murder. But this wasn't murder, was it?

"I quite agree," I said soothingly. "I merely felt that, in conscience, I had to warn you about the rumor."

"We are most grateful for the warning."

"We will take action to counteract it."

"We will delay the television station indefinitely."

"Please assure His Eminence of our continued respect and esteem."

I promised them that I would.

I left them, quite certain that they would be buzzing as soon as I was out the door. They would be on the phone to Rome immediately. Even if most Romans had closed their offices, the office of the Legion was always open for emergency phone calls from its worldwide troops.

On the way over to Peter Quill's house, I called Mike the Cop and told him to add the Legion of Corpus Christi to his list of suspects. To save another phone call, I also instructed him to look into Peter and Grace Quill.

The Quills, well-preserved, elegant folk, both with dyed hair and various kinds of cosmetic surgeries, were not especially pleased to see me. They were polite, but distant. They offered me a preprandial drink which, in view of the drive back to the city in rush hour, I declined. They seemed relieved that no pretense of hospitality was necessary.

"We understand your interest, Bishop," Peter Quill began heavily, "and we'd like to help. You must understand that we were never very close to Augustus."

"His mother practically excluded Peter from her life when Augustus was born," Grace continued impatiently. "Some sort of Catholic fortune-teller or mystic, or something like that, promised her before Augustus was born that he would be a priest and a bishop. All the family attention and concern and money went to him."

"He did not call us when he was appointed bishop," Peter said. "We learned that from television."

"Nor did he inform us that he had been appointed pastor up here," Grace continued. "We were not, need I say, delighted."

"You were not happy to have your brother in the parish?" I said with mock surprise to Peter.

"Hardly," he replied. "There has always been something a little strange about Augustus. I don't know how to describe it. . . ."

"Creepy," Grace snapped. "He always made me feel uncomfortable."

"I don't know that I would use that word, Grace. Perhaps unusual. It's not merely that he lacked most of the human graces. Many priests are that way. Rather, he really didn't seem to care much about people."

"Except the Pope."

"When our kids were younger," Peter went on, "and he used to come around to visit, he lectured them about the Pope until they were sick of hearing about him."

"So he was an embarrassment to you?"

"Definitely!" Grace exploded. "People blamed us for whatever he did. Guilt by association. It wasn't fair."

"Whoever said the world was fair?" Her husband shook his head sadly. "Women stopped coming to Grace's dress shop, though it is the most fashionable one on Green Bay Road. My brokerage business suffered too. We weren't in terrible trouble. Still, it wasn't easy."

"So unfair!"

"How's he doing, by the way?"

Finally, an inquiry about his brother's health. Not much love lost in that relationship.

"He's suffering from a serious psychotic episode. The doctors think he will recover eventually, though they are cautious."

Peter Quill nodded. "Poor Augustus . . . I suppose his career is finished?"

"Arguably."

"That was all that ever really mattered to him, wasn't it, Peter?"

"What surprises me is that he got as far as he did. Don't they recognize psychopaths in Rome?"

"Usually too late. It is not easy to diagnose a borderline personality, much less to understand one. . . . I assume that since the return of Father Dribben, your fellow parishioners are more sympathetic to you."

"Women are returning to my shop, Bishop. However, it's slow, very slow."

"My business is coming along too," Peter Quill added. "Not as quickly as I would like. Eventually, I am confident the nightmare will be over."

"That's what it has been, a nightmare!" Grace agreed.

"It's very awkward, Bishop Ryan," her husband went on. "He's my brother. I don't want to be disloyal to him. We never say in public what we're saying to you. Yet I was not sorry to learn what happened to him. If he had remained here much longer, he would have completely destroyed what we both had worked so long to build up."

"We even spoke of ways to get rid of him," Grace admitted. "Send him away somewhere for a long vacation, or catch him molesting little boys. We couldn't come up with anything. We were delighted that someone else got him."

"I don't ever want to see him again," her husband said. "The very thought of him brings the nightmare back."

"Do you know who did it, Bishop?" Grace asked. "I'd like to shake his hand."

The conversation might have been an act. However, there was so much explicit hatred in it, I questioned whether it could have been faked.

As I struggled with the rush hour, I pondered in dismay how much anger and hatred there was for Augustus O'Sullivan Quill in Forest Hills. Only the good Crystal seemed immune.

I informed Megan Kim, who was the officer of the day, that a young woman named Crystal Lane might show up at the rectory. She wanted to be a youth minister, but I had my doubts. Megan nodded solemnly.

I had no doubts at all. However, I wanted to put the Megan in a situation where they would feel constrained to defend her against my doubts.

Thereupon I reported to the Cardinal, who had just returned from the Chancery office in a not untypical state of gloom.

"Let's have the bad news, Blackwood. There's no reason why you should be the only one with good news."

I therefore reported the bad news.

"I never should have sent him up there," he admitted. "He was a lot crazier than I thought he was."

"Could not the same remark be made of many of your colleagues in the hierarchy?"

"Our colleagues, Blackwood. How many times do I have to remind you that you're a bishop too?"

"I must try to repress it."

"Today, I think that is an excellent idea. If you pretend not to be a bishop, maybe everyone will forget it and you won't have to put up with the shit."

"Arguably."

"It sounds to me like the case is insolvable. Maybe that's just as well."

"No mystery is insolvable," I said firmly.

"Well, then solve it, Blackwood. See to it."

"One other thing . . . I hired away Matt's youth minister today at his recommendation because she will be studying at Loyola. Her name is Crystal."

"So? You're responsible for the parish. Just so long as I don't have to be youth minister."

"She's patently a saint."

"How do you know that?"

"She's the only one I've talked to who feels sympathy for Gus Quill."

"All right, she is a saint. That's all we need around here—a saint! Sign her up! Meanwhile, solve this mystery. . . . See to it, Blackwood!"

"You've already said that."

JENNY

26

There is a terrible noise at the door. Someone shouting "Police!" I put on a robe and slippers and, still mostly asleep, go to the door. The police are there. They shout at me. I can't understand what they're saying. Something about kidnapping Bishop Quill. Do I deny that I threatened his life? I'm too sleepy to answer. A woman cop handcuffs me, hands behind my back. She gives the cuffs a cruel twist that hurts. A lot more terrible things are going to happen to you, sister, unless you tell the truth. They drag me downstairs. There's a TV camera taking pictures as I am thrown into a patrol wagon. Don't try anything, sister, says the woman cop, shoving me, or you'll really get hurt. I tell myself it's a dream, a terrible nightmare. Somehow I know it isn't. Where are you taking me? None of your fucking business, she says. Eleventh and State, says a male cop. We're going to put you in with all the other whores.

Where's Ned when I need him? Why isn't he here to protect me from these monsters? I am very angry at him. After what seems a long ride, we pull up to a building with blue lights on it. The TV cameras are there too. Someone shouts, Jenny, why did you kidnap Bishop Quill. They shove me into the building brutally and then into an elevator. I don't know what I've done wrong. However, already I feel guilty. I'm dragged into a room with no windows. Two men and a woman, all looking smart and tough, shove me into a chair. The woman sits across from me. Another man, much younger and not so tough-looking, comes in. They tell me their names. Two captains and a lieutenant. The young man is an assistant state's attorney. They warn me that I am already liable to charges of perjury for denying to the arresting officers that I had threatened to kill Bishop Quill. Would you please take off the handcuffs, I ask. The state's attorney says he thinks the restraints are unwarranted. The woman across the table tells him to mind his own fucking business.

I want a lawyer, I say, a memory from a movie or a TV program popping into my head. Why do you want a lawyer, the woman captain snarls, if you're innocent? Come on, the state's attorney says. You haven't read her the Miranda rights. You haven't told her she can make a phone call. You keep her in restraints that are not appropriate. You expect me to go to a grand jury with this stuff? You've already lost the trial. Whose side are you on? snaps the woman. The side of the law, he says. If she confesses, the woman replies, you don't have to worry about Miranda rights. The hell I don't. The media will convict her, the woman argues. Look, says the young man, either she gets her phone call or I get out of here. All right, let her make her fucking phone call. Privately and with the cuffs off. They call the cop who had handcuffed me. She removes them with another vicious twist. What the hell are you doing, says the young man. I'm an officer of the court. I have to note these things. Shut up motherfucker.

I do get in a phone booth. The young man gives me a quarter to make the call. I call Ned. The phone rings and rings. Isn't he home? I hang up and try again. This time he answers, his voice groggy. Has he been sleeping with someone else? Yes? he says. Jenny. The police have arrested me. I'm at Eleventh and State in handcuffs and my nightclothes. They've been brutal. Come help me, please. I'm not having a nightmare, am I? No, I say impatiently, it's my nightmare. All right, he says. I'll be right down. I'll bring Manny Horowitz, our litigator. Not a word till we get there. Incidentally, what is the charge against you? I don't know. Something about kidnapping Bishop Quill. Assholes, he says. I love you.

It is nice to hear that, but why isn't he here to protect me? I will not say a word to you assholes, I tell the cops, until my lawyer is here. They throw me into what they call a holding pen. It is filled with prostitutes who make fun of my nightclothes.

TOMMY

27

The first thing I heard was someone shouting that if I didn't open the door they'd break it down. I assumed it was a nightmare. Just in case it wasn't, I grabbed for a robe and stumbled to the door. I opened it. There were four cops and two Hancock Center security guards.

"Why did you threaten to kill Bishop Quill?" one of the cops shouted at me.

Then I knew it wasn't a nightmare.

"I didn't threaten to kill anyone."

"OK, motherfucker, you just committed perjury. We're taking you down to Eleventh and State and we'll beat the truth out of you, got it, asshole? Cuff him!"

The cuffs felt real enough. O.K., I tell myself, this is not a nightmare. They didn't read me my Miranda rights. Rogue cops.

"I want to make a phone call," I shouted at them as they wrestled me towards an elevator.

"Shut your motherfucking face." One of the cops nudged me in the back with his club. "You get to make a phone call when we want you to."

At that point I remembered that my father had made tons of money on suits against cops who had done only what these guys had already done. O.K., Dad, some more business for you.

There are TV cameras in the lobby. The whole business.

Convict a guy at the door of his house as you drag him out in his nightclothes, which in my case were shorts and a robe.

"Tommy, why did you try to kill Bishop Quill?" one of the dumb women journalists shouts at me.

"Get all of this down," I screamed at her. "It'll be great evidence for a suit against the Chicago Police Department. They haven't read me my Miranda rights or let me make a phone call, either."

"I'll Miranda you," said the cop with the billy club as he pushed me into the wagon.

"He hit me with that upstairs," I yelled at the reporter. "Ask the Hancock guards!"

Inside the wagon, he raised his club to hit me in the head. "Go ahead, asshole," I sneered. "You'll do time if you hit me."

I would later realize that was an absolutely stupid thing to say. I was angry, however, and testosterone had flooded my bloodstream.

Another cop grabbed his hand. "The motherfucker is right. We could be in deep shit."

"The Deputy Super said to play it tough."

"Yeah, who do you think gets fucked, us or the Deputy Super?"

Deputy Super, huh. That was interesting information.

At Eleventh and State, I beat the dumb woman reporter to the punch.

"They haven't read me my Miranda rights," I shouted. "They won't let me make a phone call, and they have beaten me with a billy club."

They pushed me into the building in a hurry, so I didn'

get a chance to score any more points.

Later, Mom would say to me, "Tommy, weren't you taking a lot of risks? Suppose he had hit you over the head?"

"Big judgment," I said.

"Scrambled brains," she said.

"Yeah," I said, realizing that I was an asshole too. However, I was not completely ashamed of myself.

"I want my lawyer," I bellowed when they got me off the elevator and dragged me down the hall.

I continued to shout and they continued to ignore me and shove me around. Finally, they pushed me into an interrogation room. Two very tough-looking cops and a young blonde were waiting for me.

"Shut up, asshole," said the cop who was apparently in charge. "WE do the talking in here."

"You haven't read me my Miranda rights, you haven't let me make a phone call, you're trying to interrogate me without my lawyer present, and one of your arresting officers attacked me with a billy club. I'm not saying a thing till my lawyer is present."

"Is that true, Captain?" the blonde asked.

"He's full of shit. And you stay out of this, understand?"

The young woman looked scared stiff, but she stuck to her guns. "I will not stay out of it. If you did not read him his rights, you have already lost the case."

"Fuck the case. The media have the story."

"Oh? You let him make his phone call or I will go out and tell the media that the State's Attorney is washing his hands of the case."

"Whose side are you on?"

"The side of the law, Captain."

The young woman lent me a quarter.

"Are you Tom Flynn's son?"

"Yeah. Do I look like him?"

"A little bit." She laughed to herself. "You certainly act like him."

Beth answered the phone.

"Flynn residence."

"Mom, it's Tommy. I'm at Eleventh and State, charged apparently with attempted murder and perjury. They haven't read me my rights yet, they wouldn't let me make a phone call, and a cop hit me with a club. I'm still in cuffs! We got a great case!"

"Tommy! Are you all right?"

"Having the time of my life! Let me talk to Dad."

I told Dad the same story.

"Why, Tommy? Why would they do such stupid things?"

"The Deputy Superintendent is apparently behind it. I think they want some kind of conviction in the media."

"The Superintendent is away. . . . All right, Tommy, I'm coming down there. I'll bring Cindy Hurley along to be your lawyer. Not a word to anyone till she arrives."

"Got it!"

"Tommy . . ."

"Yes, Dad."

"Don't do anything foolish. Rogue cops are dangerous cops."

That sobered me a bit.

"Not me, Dad."

Later, when my bloodstream had cleansed away the adrenaline and the testosterone, I realized how foolish I had been. Then revulsion, humiliation, and guilt overwhelmed me. I understood how the innocent people who had been convicted in the Communist show trials had come to feel guilty.

"Not a word before my lawyer arrives," I informed the assembled group in the interrogation room.

"And when will that be?" the captain sneered.

"When she comes," I replied.

"OK, smartass, we'll throw you in the holding pen with the bums and the drunks and the perverts."

"You heard that, Ms. State's Attorney?"

"I did. Captain, you shouldn't say things like that. Moreover, you shouldn't do them."

"What we do is our business."

"All right, you've been warned." She turned to me. "Who will represent you, Mr. Flynn?"

"Cindy Hurley."

She winced.

The holding pen wasn't so bad, except the men in there were so pathetic. There but for the grace of God goes Tommy Flynn. Then I thought for the first time of my young lioness. What would she think when she woke up in the morning and discovered I was in jail on a murder charge?

For the first time I felt the guilt and humiliation that would devastate me in days to come.

Hours later, still cuffed, I was dragged back to the interrogation room. Cindy Hurley swept in like the Golden Horde.

"All right, assholes," she shouted, "what the hell is going on here? Are you the state's attorney?"

"Yes, ma'am," the cute blonde replied in a trembling voice.

"I note that my client is in restraints. I note that you have observed this. I hold you responsible."

"Yes, ma'am."

"Actually, Ms. Hurley—"

"You're Tommy Flynn?"

"Yes, ma'am."

"I'm Cindy Hurley, your attorney. You won't speak till I tell you to speak. Got it?"

"Yes, ma'am."

In fact, Ms. Hurley was an attractive woman, also blonde, about Mom's age.

"Now, assholes, explain to me why my client is under restraints. He is a law-abiding young man with no criminal record. There is no reason to think he is dangerous. . . . You haven't a criminal record, do you, Tommy Flynn?"

"Some parking tickets."

She bit her lip to repress a grin, something that she would do often as the interrogation went on.

"Therefore I direct and insist that my client be released from restraints. We won't even begin the discussion until that occurs. You understand, Ms. State's Attorney?"

"Yes, ma'am. I agree."

The captain looked like he would willingly kill the two women who were ruining his game.

"You're going pretty far, counselor."

"You don't know any law, Captain. Neither did the asshole that assigned you to this interrogation. You've already gone too far."

The cop who had cuffed me was summoned to uncuff me

"Ms. Hurley—"

"Yes," she snapped.

"May I say something?"

Again she repressed the grin. "What?"

"This officer is the one who hit me in the back with his club and threatened to hit me over the head."

"Is he now? Officer, you seem to be missing your name card. I have your badge number already. Do you want to tell me your name?"

"Mason," he said with a ferocious scowl.

"Thank you, officer."

We arranged ourselves around the table, the captain across from me, the lieutenant next to him, Ms. Hurley next to me. The captain turned on the tape recorder and muttered the day and time and the names of those present.

"I want to add some things for the record," my lawyer said immediately. "My client has been dragged out of his bed in the middle of the night, put under restraints, beaten by a police officer named Mason, and brought here to the interrogation room without being read his Miranda decision rights. To my knowledge they have yet to be read. He was at first refused permission to make a phone call. I have reason to believe that all of this has been done at the connivance of the Deputy Superintendent, who at this moment is doubtless watching through the screen on the wall. All right, Captain, ask your first question. . . . Tommy, don't answer it till I tell you that you should."

"Finally," the cop growled. "Your name, sir?"

I remained silent.

"You can answer that, Tommy."

"Thomas Patrick Flynn."

"Your occupation?"

"Commodity trader."

"Is it not true, Mr. Flynn, that in front of Holy Name Cathedral on Sunday, September nineteenth, in the presence of several witnesses, you made a threat on the life of Bishop Augustus O'Sullivan Quill?"

So that's what it was about. I looked at my lawyer.

"Answer it, Tommy."

"No, sir, it is not true."

"We have witnesses—"

"My client denies having said it, Captain. Save your witnesses for the courtroom."

"Did you say anything about Bishop Quill?"

Ms. Hurley nodded.

"I believe I did."

"So you don't deny you threatened his life?"

"Captain, you need a course in logic. My client did not admit a threat. All he has admitted so far is that he said something about the Bishop. Wouldn't it be intelligent to ask him what he said?"

"All right, Mr. Flynn, what did you say?"

Cindy nodded again.

"To the best of my recollection what I said was that someone ought to kill him."

"You don't consider that a threat on his life?"

"Drop it, Captain. It won't fly. My client admits an angry comment about Bishop Quill, perhaps an imprudent comment. You can never twist that into a threat no matter how hard you try. You'd better have a lot more evidence to justify tonight's events."

Somewhere, deep down, the part of me that was worried

heaved a sigh of relief.

"Is it not true," the captain plunged ahead, "that you use scheduled drugs?"

Before I could deny it, Cindy Hurley exploded.

"You'd better have strong evidence to back up that question, Captain. Do you? Moreover, you better be prepared to explain to me how that's relevant to the present charge."

The captain fumbled the ball. Ms. Hurley was right. He was an inexperienced interrogator. She caught my eye and I shook my head.

"Everyone knows that those traders are all on drugs. It's pertinent because Bishop Quill was poisoned with an injection of heroin."

"Let me get this straight. Because my client is a trader, and because you have proof that all traders use drugs, you have reason to believe that he injected the heroin into the Bishop's veins?"

"I want to establish that your client had access to the scheduled drug that was used in the kidnapping."

Ms. Hurley laughed contemptuously. "He and maybe a half million other people in Chicago . . . You gotta be kidding. Tommy, you may answer the man's question about the use of drugs."

"I'm not sure what a scheduled drug is, Captain. I have, however, never used illegal drugs."

"Next question," Ms. Hurley snapped.

"Where were you on the night of October second?"

She nodded.

"I don't remember where I was. Probably in my apartment reading. That's what I usually do at night."

"So you have no alibi?"

BLACKIE

28

S omewhere, light years away, a telephone rang. Another hospital call. I was not on duty tonight, was I?

"Father Ryan," I said automatically.

"Blackie? Mike. We have a situation developing."

"Ah?"

"Eleventh and State has interjected itself into the Quill case. They've dragged two people out of bed, cuffed them in their nightclothes, alerted the media, and accused them of being involved in the kidnapping. They have no evidence except for hostile comments about the Bishop. John Culhane has already investigated them quietly and tentatively cleared them. It's a play to take credit for breaking the case without ever going to the grand jury."

"Despicable."

"Worse than that. To cover their asses, they've told the media that they have moved quickly in response to a demand for closure from the Catholic Church! It's been on TV all night."

I glanced at the clock next to my bed: 5:00 A.M.

"Which Catholic Church?"

"The Roman Catholic Church!"

"Ah, that one!"

"Has the Archdiocese put any pressure on anyone?"

"The Roman Catholic Archdiocese of Chicago?"

"Not the Greek Orthodox!"

"Certainly not! . . . Who did they arrest?"

"Thomas Flynn Jr. and Jennifer Carlson. They have implied a conspiracy between them."

Two of my parishioners! A great rage surged within me. This atrocity would not continue!

"John says they have nothing?"

"Nothing but a deputy superintendent who wants to make a name for himself while his boss is out of town."

"I see. . . . You may tell John that we will have a statement to make before the sun rises."

I thereupon ascended to the Cardinal's suite of rooms. Asleep, Sean Cronin looked remarkably peaceful. I shook him. He was reluctant to leave the peace behind. Finally he opened his eyes.

"It can't be the last judgment," he said, "because you don't look like the angel Gabriel."

Under the circumstances, that was not a bad line.

"We have a situation," I informed him.

"I assumed as much."

I told him what had happened.

"Bastards—push people around to get publicity and then blame us!"

"Indeed."

"We'll need a statement."

I recited what I had formulated on the way up the stairs.

"Yeah, that's good. Who should give it?"

"You would be overkill. I would be underkill."

"Jaime?"

"My very thought."

"See to it, Blackwood. I have an hour's sleep still coming."

Thereupon I descended to Father Keenan's quarters. He would think that a sunrise statement in front of the Cathedral would be fun.

JENNY

29

They take me back to the room without the windows. My hands are still bound behind my back. I need to go to the bathroom, but they won't let me. A little bald man with elfin eyes says, I am Emanuel Horowitz, your attorney. They won't let me go to the bathroom. He looks around at the cops. Officers, he says, we must straighten a few things out before our little conversation begins. You will release my client and permit her to go to the women's washroom, where she may wash her hands and comb her hair. Otherwise, there will be no conversation. Do I make myself clear? His voice is so calm and soft they do not seem to hear him. The fuck we will, says the woman captain. Madam, my attorney replies, I must ask you not to use such language. I am an Orthodox Jew and I find such language personally offensive. My client is clearly a lady and I'm sure she finds it offensive. Please refrain from using it. I'm a lady too, the captain says. Madam, the lawyer replies, I assure you that you are not.

Somehow, he gets his way. When I return from the washroom, my hair combed and the belt on my robe tied properly, I feel a little better—brutalized, humiliated, violated, but awake and alive. The boy who is the state's attorney even smiles at me. Now we may begin our conversation, the lawyer says.

JAIME

30

(Television scene in front of Holy Name Cathedral just before sunrise. Father Keenan is a tall, handsome, self-assured young man with blond hair and natural presence.)

J.K.: I'm Father James Keenan of the Cathedral staff. I have a statement from the Archdiocese of Chicago. *(He pauses to let the solemnity of this fact sink in and then begins to read.)*

We have learned that the Archdiocese is being blamed for the arrest of two Cathedral parishioners during the night in connection with the Bishop Quill case. It has been said that the police had to pull them out of their beds and handcuff them in the middle of the night because of pressure from the Archdiocese. We categorically reject that allegation. It is a lie. We have no complaints against the careful detective work of Area Six. We agree with Area Six that there is no substantial evidence against these two people. We are unable to understand the reasons for this carefully staged attack on their rights and on the rights of the Archdiocese. We demand that whoever is responsible for the allegation of pressure from the Archdiocese retract that allegation. *(Another pause)*

This is the end of our statement.

(The sun peeks up to survey the situation. Apparently she is pleased because she continues to rise.)

(Questions surge from the media vultures, irritable now

235

after a long night of running around. Father Keenan smiles charmingly but shakes his head.)

QUESTION: Has Cardinal Cronin seen this statement, Jaime? *(It's the question he has been waiting for.)*

J.K.: He has approved every word.

QUESTION: Has Bishop Ryan seen it?

QUESTION: Did Bishop Ryan write it?

J.K.: Who?

QUESTION: Bishop Ryan?

J.K.: *(Wicked grin)* Who's he?

(He turns and walks back into the Cathedral. Madam Sun, now patently pleased, sheds her nightdress of clouds and rises higher in the sky.)

The Cardinal helped himself to another cup of tea.

"The young man is good, Blackwood. You've done a fine job of training him."

"He needed no training," I said, stating only the obvious. "I think we have won this one."

"Arguably."

This stealing my line was becoming a bad habit. We watched the scene at Eleventh and State as the valiant Cindy Hurley attacked the police department.

"Now we must see to the healing of those who have been savaged. It will require discretion," I remarked to the Cardinal.

"Why would the cops try such a stupid trick?"

"Mostly for the media. Do not think that they have lost. Even if they had no evidence against their two victims, even if they are forced to release them, even if they never bring them before a grand jury, the element in the police department who sponsored this caper will still look to the public like they have acted vigorously. They have created the impression that these two innocents may well have conspired to poison Gus Quill."

"Won't they sue?"

"By the time the case is settled out of court, the public will have forgotten what it is about. The Deputy Superintendent has carried the day, though he may well have overextended himself this time. I suspect that he is not very bright. We will have to await the return to the city of the real Superintendent and the comments of the Mayor."

"That Carlson woman is gorgeous, isn't she?"

"I did notice that."

"How old is she?"

"Timeless."

TOMMY

31

Captain, this is an outrage. All you have is one quote from my client that only proves he was very angry at Bishop Quill. It was not a threat. You have no other evidence. This was not a fishing expedition. It was a deliberate attempt to intimidate my client. It failed. Now either charge him formally or release him."

Ms. Hurley's anger was not feigned. She was genuinely furious. I was exhausted and now feeling violated. These bastards, we'd get the whole lot of them.

"We have other evidence, counselor."

"The hell you have. I am willing to wager that Area Six

found nothing against my client."

"We have other evidence."

"Suit yourself, charge him if you dare. . . . Ms. State's Attorney?"

The cute blonde had been mesmerized by my attorney.

"Yes, ma'am?"

"I'm sorry to disturb your reflections. Have you heard anything you might want to bring before a grand jury?"

"Against your client?"

Ms. Hurley drew her breath impatiently. "Yes, of course, against my client!"

"No, ma'am. Nothing."

"All right. Captain, I am declaring this interrogation concluded. I am advising my client to walk out of this police station unless you and the idiots who dreamed up this fraud are crazy enough to charge him."

She stood up. I stood up. The cop looked confused. My knees were shaking.

JENNY

32

My wonderful Jewish lawyer has tied the police up in knots. The only evidence they have is the stupid comment I made at that party. I'm innocent. Why do I feel so guilty? Someone brings a note in to the captain. He glances at it and tells us that we may leave. We're not finished with you yet, he warns. Nor are we finished with you, officer, my lawyer says ominously. Outside, Ned is waiting for me. He puts his arm around me. I don't want anyone's arm around me. I feel soiled. I need a long, hot bath. Alone. He doesn't get it.

A boy joins us, wearing a robe and slippers. I'm Tommy Flynn, Ms. Carlson, he says. I'm from the Cathedral parish. They arrested me too. He is a cute little boy. I think I remember him. I just want to say, Ms. Carlson, that at this hour of the night or day, or whatever it is, and after all you've been through, you're the most beautiful woman in the world. I hug him and begin to weep.

I weep all the way back to my apartment. May I come in? Ned asks me. No, I want to be alone. All right. He just doesn't get it. I don't want a man slobbering over me. I want to be alone with my pain and my guilt and my humiliation. Forever. I don't want to see you anymore, I tell him. I am quitting my job. Go away. Don't come back. I take off his ring and try to give it back to him. He won't take it. I throw it on the sidewalk and run up the stairs, sobbing. As I close the door, I see him bending over to pick up the ring. He still doesn't get it.

The next morning Dr. Murphy says to me that I was cruel. You took out your trauma on him. You don't get it either, I yell. I'm through with him. Is that fair? I don't care whether it is fair or not. You're not really angry at him. You're angry at yourself. I am NOT! I leave her office and promise myself that I will never return.

TOMMY

33

Ms. Hurley gave them hell on television. "Rudy Giuliani is not mayor of Chicago, Rich Daley is. Ken Starr is not state's attorney, Dick Divine is. These things do not happen in the city of Chicago or the county of Cook. Mr. Horowitz and I are prepared to go into court to demand relief for our clients so that this will never happen again to anyone."

If we've won, I wondered, why do I feel like such a rotten jerk? I was dumb to say that about the Bishop, a real asshole. I made a fool out of myself with the cops. I just wanted to go home and hide for a couple of weeks. What an idiot I was.

My lawyer hugged me and told my father that it was a damn good thing for him that I had decided not to be a lawyer, because I was so much better at the game. Dad was pleased as punch. So was Mom, who also hugged me.

"Poor Tommy," she whispered.

Lawyer or not, she understood how I felt.

Like a total jerk.

I would certainly not be going down to the Exchange today. Or anytime soon. People would look at me like I was some kind of monster.

Christy? My young lioness?

I winced.

I was in no mood for her exuberance. I had barely thought of her during the night's ordeal. She was not important to me. She was still a kid. I did not want her slobbering over me. I could take care of myself. She had been a big mistake. I would have to get rid of her.

Dear Christy,
    As you've probably read in the papers or heard, I've been through a hell of a night. I have to put myself back together again. It will take time. I think we'd better break up. I'm sorry.
    Tommy

She didn't reply. Either because she was very angry at me or because she understood. I didn't care. It was all over with her. It should never have started. I was free again. Thank God.

BLACKIE

34

"T he poor guy has always been a locomotive out of control, Blackie," Ted Coffey observed. "He's run over a lot of people without noticing them. Small wonder someone wanted to destroy him."
    I was sitting in the parlor of St. Regis rectory, just south of Chicago Avenue and just east of Harlem Avenue in Oak Park. The homes around this, the mother church of Oak Park, were stately old Victorian mansions, just like the rectory. North of Chicago Avenue was the Frank Lloyd Wright historic district of Prairie School homes, none of which had ever attracted me as a place to live in. Across

Harlem was River Forest, once, long ago, the most presti
gious of the western suburbs and even now an elegan
place to live. St. Regis had spawned the other parishes ir
Oak Park and the newer ones in River Forest. It proudly
called itself the mother church of the western suburbs
Now, in a more yuppie and racially integrated neighbor
hood, it boasted modernity as well as history. I had decided
to pay a visit to Monsignor Theodore Coffey, J.U.D., the
acknowledged leader of all Catholic and ecumenical activ
ities in the two suburbs. Perhaps he could give me some
clues that would excite the image that lay latent, deep
down in the sub-basements of my brain.

"Was he morally responsible for what he did? How can
answer that question, Blackie? Is a diesel locomotive
without a motorman at the controls morally responsible?"

Ted, wearing gray slacks and a maroon-and-white St
Regis sweatshirt, was lolling in his recliner, the confiden
and able pastor of a hectic modern parish—and one much
less precious than Forty Holy Martyrs.

"Take the case of Tom Flynn and his family. Tom is a
great lawyer, a descendent of a powerful Oak Park family
a solid Catholic, with perhaps slightly old-fashioned ideas
about family life. He marries a pretty and lively wife—a
least they say she was pretty. I wasn't here in those days
Four kids are too much for her. I don't know. Maybe she
should have had no more than two. I guess Tom wanted
four. She flakes out. I mean, *really* flakes out. By the time
I get here, she's around the bend and over the top. Tom
stubbornly, too stubbornly, tries to hold the family together
Finally she leaves them more or less permanently in her
lesbian phase.

"I tell Tom he should get an annulment. He's sufficiently old-fashioned to hesitate. I really have to push him into it. He's been dating Beth for a year or two. He's enough of a hardhead that he doesn't think they'll fall in love. Naturally, they do. So we get him the annulment. No sweat. Whatever she may have seemed when they married, the poor woman has deep problems. You can imagine what all this is doing to the kids. Young Tommy, who has problems of his own, holds the family together. God knows what this does to *him*.

"Anyway, they have the marriage already scheduled and they learn that Mrs. Flynn, the first one, egged on by Father Innocent, the Franciscan out in Oak Brook who does these things, has appealed to the Rota and the annulment is annulled. The Chicago tribunal sends out the decision. It's horseshit, Blackie. Of the three judges who hear the case, two are senile and the other is Gus Quill. I'm sure we can win an appeal—which we eventually do. I tell Beth and Tom we'll go ahead with the marriage. I'll take the heat from downtown. Tom gets scruples. Beth insists. So does young Tommy. They get married and live happily ever after, until young Tommy gets arrested the other night."

"So I understand."

"Is Gus to blame? He's written an idiot decision because he doesn't give a damn about the people. Or is Tom, because he waited so long and exposed his kids to so much insanity? Or Beth, because she seduced Tom? Or Tommy, because he's worried about his kid sisters? How do I know!"

He walked over to the teapot and poured the two of us fresh cups of tea.

"The trouble with evil, even if it isn't evil for which the person is morally responsible, is that it generates more evil. Whoever put out the contract on Gus seems to be doing everyone a favor. Then they drag poor Tommy out of bed and make him the fall guy. You and Sean get him out with that statement, but the shadow still hangs over him, and he's all fouled up again. . . . His sister Amy tells me in tears that he has broken up with his girlfriend. How much can a nice young guy take? Whose fault? I don't know."

"Did downtown ever give you any trouble about Tom Flynn's remarriage?"

"Not a word. I bet they never noticed. . . . Now this woman they picked up—what a knockout she is—her husband was a preening little jerk who couldn't keep up with her in any way, especially sexually. So he beats up on her and blames her for his failure to get a Nobel Prize, which he would never get anyway. Then he runs off with a graduate student. Matt Dribben sends her downtown for an annulment. Again, no problem. Enter Father Innocent and this little academic prick and we get another appeal and another reversal, which Gus writes. Poor Jenny goes into a tailspin, a serious one. So Matt asks me to work on a reversal. We finally get that through and she pulls out of the tailspin. She's a classy lady. So they drag her out of her apartment in her nightgown with the TV cameras rolling and she goes back into the spin. Whose fault? Gus's? Her husband's? Father Innocent's? The whole Church's? Jenny's, for not being tougher? You tell me, I don't know."

"God does, fortunately."

Even in the seminary, Ted's laugh had been infectious. It had improved with years of hard and successful priestly ministry.

"Yeah, and He's on our side. She, as you would say. I don't know why I worry about these things. I do my best out here and hope it works out. Beth and Tom were one of my success stories. Her stepdaughters really love her. They pray she gets pregnant, like she wants, so they'll have a little sister. You don't get that usually from stepdaughters."

"Might either Tommy or Ms. Carlson have participated in this conspiracy against Gus?"

"Might they have?" He frowned and twisted in his chair. "Sure, they might have. They were both angry enough, and they both are clever enough. They'd have to put out a contract or get someone to put it out. Did they? I doubt it, but you never can tell about people. If they did, I don't blame them. I don't think anyone else would either."

"I think we have a mastermind behind this," I sighed. "I know Tommy well enough to know that he's not a mastermind. Ms. Carlson?"

"She might be. Always struck me as a deep one, but I still doubt it."

I sighed again. "So, it's almost anyone?"

"I wish I could help, Blackie." He squirmed in his chair, frustrated by his own powerlessness. "I really do."

"Tell me more about Gus. I didn't know him well in the seminary. I thought he was a creep who they shouldn't have ordained."

"Between you and me, I learned later that most of the faculty thought so too. However, he manipulated the rector like he has manipulated a lot of other people ever since. Somehow, he created the assumption that he would be ordained and the rector didn't try to fight it. That was the technique right up to being made bishop here. Thank God he'll never succeed Sean."

I grunted my assent.

"In his first assignment, a black parish—as we called it in those days—on the South Side, he persuaded the pastor, a nice old guy, without too much smarts, that the Cardinal, the old Cardinal, wanted him to work at the Chancery. He edged his way into the matrimonial court, where they say he was an absolute disaster. They made him a clerk to keep him out of trouble. . . . Is it true he tried to take the Cathedral away from you?"

"He apparently believed that he had been given the job."

"That's the technique. You're the first person I know who stood up to him."

"In fact, the Cardinal did."

"He should have stood up to the Vatican and refused to accept him. He should never have sent him to Forty Holy Martyrs."

"It did give the Cardinal a chance to reappoint Matthew."

"Come to think of it, you're right. Does Cronin really think that way?"

"Without my help, sometimes."

That took Theodore back a moment. And contributed nicely to my image of gray eminence, which was not without its uses.

"Well, you beat him anyway."

"Go on with the story."

"This next time around I'm involved and I'm ambivalent about it even today. The Chancellor called me and told me that the Cardinal wanted to send me to Rome to study canon law. I liked my work in the barrio, loved it, as you know, and didn't want to go. I argued for three days. Finally, the Chancellor said, 'You're going,' and that's that. Just before Sean came here. He would have let me out in a minute. So, anyway, lo and behold, Gus has been telling everyone that the Cardinal wants to send him to Rome to study canon law. He says it so often and with such conviction that everyone believes him. They figure he'll goof up during the first semester over there. Then the appointments come out, and lo and behold, he goes to Rome and I'm left in the barrio. Great, I won my argument. Then the Chancellor calls and says the Cardinal doesn't want to be unfair to me. 'We're sending two to Rome this year,' and that's that."

"Amazing."

"He plays the same game in Rome, but this turns out to be a plus for me. I'm scheduled to go to the College of Noble Ecclesiastics to study for the diplomatic service. Can you imagine me spending my life with those creeps?"

"In truth, I cannot, Theodore. You would drive them crazy with your energy and disregard for rules."

"You got it, Blackie," he says with his contagious laugh. "I tell Sean Cronin that I'll leave the priesthood. He's new in the job and he doesn't know what to say. Fortunately, Gus has been scheming to get himself appointed to the Rota. He pulls it off again. Sean says he can't afford to give up two priests, so I come home to work in the matrimonial court for a while. Then I get back in the barrio part-time. Then they send me out here. An exciting life. Poor Gus sits around Rome and does nothing but write incoherent opinions, almost always minority opinions. So, I owe him."

"And the Cardinal."

"Indeed, yes. And the Cardinal."

"Indeed" was my line, but I have no patent on it as I do on "arguably."

He refilled my teacup and brought out a few shortbread cookies. In a package. One makes do with whatever one can.

"Not to put too fine an edge on things, Theodore, but we have no idea how many people he might have screwed during his life as, to change the metaphor, he roared down the railroad tracks."

"Most likely someone in Chicago, don't you think? Someone who couldn't stand to have him around as a bishop."

"Arguably."

"It strikes me as the kind of thing your friends the Legion of Corpus Christi up there in Forest Hills might try. They could see Gus manipulating their bosses in Rome to give him the TV station they want to build."

"A point I had not considered."

"Stay for lunch? We've got chocolate ice cream."

"My weaknesses are known all too well, Theodore. I must, however, return to do my hospital visits."

"Stay in touch. If I get any bright ideas, I'll call you."

I drove up to Chicago Avenue to turn on Harlem. Then I remembered the existence of Peterson's Ice Cream on Chicago, just east of Harlem on the Oak Park side of the line. My late father had often argued that it was the best ice cream emporium in the metropolitan area. He was, in this matter, as in so many others, quite correct, even taking into account his native West Side bias.

So, in honor of the old fella, I consumed a large malted

milk as an early lunch. Then I drove down Harlem, under the L tracks near where the missing L train had been found, and to the Congress Expressway (as we Democrats call the Eisenhower Expressway) and returned to the Cathedral.

I reflected that I still knew nothing about the assault on Augustus O'Sullivan Quill.

35

"Ms. Carlson to see you, Bishop," Megan O'Connor informed me crisply.

"Very well."

"Bishop Blackie," the proto-Megan whispered into the phone, "she's like totally ravishing."

"If you say so, Megan."

Nevertheless, I did put on my Roman collar.

"She's in your parlor," Megan said with a significant roll of her eyes.

"Don't worry, Megan, I'll leave the door open."

"You always do that when there's a woman in there."

That was true.

"I'm sorry to disturb you, Bishop," Jenny Carlson said to me meekly. "I thought you might want to talk to me."

"I always want to talk to a parishioner," I said.

She was, through no fault of her own or conscious effort, a deeply disturbing woman. In a gray business suit with a long skirt, she seemed rather prim. However, she quietly radiated an intense sexual appeal that filled the whole office. Men would go crazy for a touch of her hand. How old was she? Somewhere between thirty-five and fifty, with no clear hints in her smooth complexion and finely carved figure as to which number would be closer to the truth. After a moment, one did not care.

"Not much of a parishioner, I'm afraid. I didn't attend Mass for a long time. I came here a few Sundays with Ned. Now that we have broken up, I've stopped attending."

"You will, however, begin again next Sunday."

"Yes, Bishop, I will."

"Ravishing" was too mild a word. How could her first husband have left her?

"Thank you for the help when I was at Eleventh and State. Mr. Horowitz, my attorney, said that it was the statement from the Church that forced the police to release us."

"We were later supported by the Mayor and the real Superintendent."

And by the subsequent quiet transfer of the Deputy to a harmless desk job.

"I want to apologize for all the trouble I've caused by my stupid comment at the party in Forest Hills. I'm afraid I lost my temper."

"Ah."

"I'm not angry at him anymore. I was then. And again when the police released us. However, now I merely feel sorry for him."

"And forgive him?"

She paused, thought for a moment, and then said firmly, "Yes, I forgive him. Why not? I did it to myself, the way I reacted to the reversal of my annulment. That should not have mattered as much as it did to me. Anyway, it was reversed. Father Dribben and Monsignor Coffey got it reversed."

"So I am told."

The virtuous Mary Kathleen, whom I presumed Jenny had been seeing, had done her work well with this woman.

"My anger was really at my husband. He appealed the annulment, though he had already remarried, out of pure spite."

"Ah."

"Anyway, I know you're still investigating the case. I hope you find out who kidnapped Bishop Quill. It will remove suspicion from me and from poor little Tommy Flynn."

I did not think of the legendary Tommy Flynn as either poor or little, but what did I know?

"You have very good reason for suspecting me, Bishop."

"Why would that be so?"

"You know I hated Bishop Quill. If you've seen my work at the Reilly Gallery—"

"Very interesting work," I said quickly.

It surely was. It did not fit with the demeanor of this pious matron, but it did fit all too well with the erotic aura that surrounded her. Which was she, fire or ice, or arguably both?

"You know what a twisted imagination I have. I could have cooked up that scheme or a dozen others like it."

There was no question about that.

"Perhaps," I answered, "I would prefer the word 'fantastical' to 'twisted.' However, there is some reason to doubt that you would have the ruthlessness to carry them out."

She smiled wryly. "Probably not, Bishop Ryan. However, you can't assume that, can you? . . . If you have any questions you want to ask . . ."

If this woman had told me that she had just flown across

the Atlantic Ocean without the benefit of an airplane, I would not have doubted it.

"Do you speak Spanish?"

"Only a few words."

"Do you use drugs?"

"No, I don't even drink much. I'd be afraid of drugs."

What else? Quick, Blackwood, start thinking!

"When was the last time you were on an L train?"

She smiled.

"I don't think I've ever been on one."

There was a hint there, perhaps not pertaining to her. A picture of an L train in the back of my head.

So she could smile.

"We have nothing on you, Ms. Carlson—"

"Jenny, please, Bishop—"

"We have nothing on you, Jenny. No one does. Area Six, once again in firm control of the investigation, has nothing on you, though for reasons of discretion and prudence, they're not about to say that."

"And are still watching me—"

"Not systematically."

"I hope they find out who really did it. I'd like my name cleared, though somehow that doesn't seem as important as it used to be."

She stood up, ready to leave.

"You have indeed broken up with Ned?"

She shrugged listlessly. "I just don't need a man in my life now."

"That can hardly be a permanent orientation?"

"My shrink doesn't think so. I stopped seeing her after . . . after I was arrested. I had to go back to her like I had to go back to Ned's firm. I don't know what will happen."

"We will leave it, for the moment, in the hands of God, who doubtless has Her own plans for you."

God is notoriously empirical and pragmatic, as I argued in my little book about William James, in his style of telling the stories of our lives. He would not like an ending to this story that excluded Ned.

"You will be at the Eucharist next Sunday and thereafter?"

"I promise, Bishop Blackie."

I escorted her down to the Megan's lair.

"Megan, would you give Ms. Carlson a box of our collection envelopes? She has undertaken to attend the Eucharist every Sunday."

Jenny Carlson laughed happily. So she could laugh too.

"She's already in the parish," Megan insisted, "I've seen her in church."

Typical of women of her gender and ethnic group, Megan always had to argue.

"Now she is formally a member of the parish. So we make it official."

"Course, I saw her in church." Megan had pulled a registration card, but still had to have the last word. "She's the best dressed woman at Mass."

Jenny laughed again. "You're a sweetheart, darling."

"Well, the Bishop says we have to be friendly to new parishioners. You know what bishops are like."

"Oh, yes," Jenny said. "I know what bishops are like."

After Megan had registered her and given her the collection envelopes, I escorted Jenny Carlson to the door.

"I'll be looking forward to seeing you at the Eucharist,

hopefully along with Ned."

Her face turned pink. "Maybe, Bishop Blackie, maybe."

"She is," I remarked to Megan, "merely a prim and proper middle-aged woman."

"So's Annette Bening."

My generation would have said Sophia Loren, not that it mattered.

Back in my room, as I flipped on my computer, I pondered the interview. If she had been involved in the assault on Gus Quill, it would have been a very clever ploy to confront me in my fortress and admit she might have been, and also to proclaim, with apparent spontaneity, her forgiveness of Gus.

And to sign up for the parish and jest with irrepressible Megan.

Or she might have been exactly what she purported to be, a lovely and lonely matron pining for lost love—lost but not irrevocably lost. I hoped that was all she was and I hoped that she would recover Ned. Yet I could not be sure. I would have to leave her to Area Six and John Culhane.

A few minutes later Milord Cronin, freshly returned from a confirmation, ambled into my room.

"Was that Jenny Carlson leaving the rectory?"

"It was. She formally joined the parish. So we registered her and gave her collection envelopes."

"Yeah? . . . You know she looks like an attractive but very prim and proper middle-aged matron."

"So," I said with a loud sigh, "does Annette Bening."

B ishop Blackie," Megan Flores, a.k.a. Megan Flower, said, "that terrible Tommy Flynn boy is down here flirting with me and disrupting my work."

"Are you bragging or complaining, Megan?"

She giggled. "He says he wants to see you."

"Then I had better come down, had I not?"

"O.K."

"Like Megan O'Connor goes," Megan Flores warned Tommy as I drifted into the office area, "you're much too young for me."

"Either too young or too old, Bishop Blackie," he said to me. "That's the story of my life."

"Arguably," I said with considerable skepticism in my voice.

In the security of my office, he collapsed.

"I'm a wreck, Bishop," he confessed. "A shambles. I know that I ought to shake off that stuff, but every night I dream someone is knocking at the door. How come people don't tell us how awful it is to be dragged away by the cops, with the TV cameras catching every move, every word, every expression?"

"It's a horror they want to forget, Tommy Flynn."

"I want to forget it too. I feel shattered. Everyone is nice—Mom and Dad, my fellow traders—they all hate the cops too. I take positions now more than I trade. My nerves are shot. I don't trust my instincts."

"You're losing money?"

"No, not really. I'm still doing all right. The fun has gone out of it."

"Perhaps it will come back."

"I suppose so. . . . When I try to read at night, my imagination replays everything that happened, all the mistakes I made, what an idiot I was."

"The conventional wisdom is that you were brilliant."

"They got it wrong. . . . I stopped going to my shrink—did I tell you I finally got one? She's very good. I made an appointment with her for the day after tomorrow. She'll say the same thing."

"Your lioness?"

"It's all over, Bishop. We broke up after the . . . incident. I have too much to straighten out. I don't need her daffiness. She's just a kid."

"Yet older than the worthy Megan who unanimously agree that you are too young for them."

"They're only kidding. . . . I sent Christy an e-mail the morning after and told her that we were breaking up. She didn't reply, which proves that she's very angry at me. That's good. I don't want to hurt her any more than I already have."

Noble words, huh?

"Or perhaps, like the skilled hunter she is, she is merely biding her time."

That stopped him. He pondered the possibility, not without some pleasure, I observed.

"No way," he finally decided, "she's not that clever."

"I have always judged her to be extremely shrewd under that, ah, daffy enthusiasm. Lionesses tend to be very shrewd."

"I don't think the metaphor goes that far."

"Well, it's your metaphor."

"I'm not here to talk about metaphors, Bishop Blackie. . . . First thing, how is poor Bishop Quill doing?"

"Right now the doctors say that he is a little better than might be expected, sometimes even quite rational."

"Yeah, I'm glad to hear that. I felt kind of sorry for the poor guy. He's an idiot, and maybe a dangerous idiot, but no one deserves to have their personality blown away."

"Tommy Flynn, you are growing up!"

"Maybe . . . I apologize for my stupid remark about him that Sunday. I didn't mean it even then. Temporary temper."

"So you've forgiven him?"

"Why the hell not?" he said with a deep frown. "Why the hell not? I maybe had reason to be angry at Dad and at my mother—I don't mean Beth—but the Bishop was only a cog in the annulment machine. As it turned out, we didn't need him anyway. The family is happy now. My real mother is even talking about marrying the guy she's with now. Maybe she's grown up too."

Tommy Flynn's trauma had improved his human sensitivities. Or maybe only permitted them to come out into the open. Nonetheless, I suspected that, in fact, he was experiencing the delayed effects of his first love. I had little doubt that the Fighting Irish would return to fight another day.

"A happy ending."

"A human ending, like in a really good novel. Nothing's perfect, but things get a little better, like later Stephen King."

"Arguably."

"Look, I know you'll eventually solve this mystery."

At that point, he knew a lot more than I did.

"I have a reputation to uphold."

"So you have to suspect me, don't you?"

"We are assured by Area Six that there is nothing to link you to the assault on Bishop Quill other than your unwise remark on these very premises."

"Yeah, but you're smart enough to know that I might have faked that so I could throw people off the track."

I was not, in fact, that smart.

"You're capable of it, I agree."

"I'm a pretty clever guy, when you stop to think about it, Bishop Blackie. I'm not bragging. A guy has to be clever to succeed in my business. I know how to take smart risks and win. Well, I used to. I could have cooked this whole caper up, know what I mean?"

"And so you did?"

"Hell, no! I'm just saying I might have, and you should keep your eye on me if you're professional about solving this thing."

"I'm not a professional, Tommy Flynn. I see things. Try as I might, I can't see this one yet. I will, however. I doubt very much you'll be in the picture, however."

"I sure hope I won't. . . . Are there any questions you want to ask me?"

Could he and the startling Jenny have contrived this common approach? Hardly. Were they both trying to discharge residual guilt from their arrest trauma? Was I a shrink? What did I know?

This time I would not try to fake questions.

"None at all at the moment. Should there be any, I'll feel

free to call you."

"Yeah, thanks . . . I'm not sure why I'm even bothering you. Like I said, I'm a mess, a total geek."

Ah, the Fighting Irish word. You came, Tommy Flynn, because you wanted to be reassured that you had not heard the last of that young woman. No way.

"Time and counseling will help, Tommy."

"I guess so. It's not like I was a prisoner of war or anything."

"A trauma in the middle of the night is a trauma in the middle of the night."

Especially if your earlier family experiences inclined you to expect the worst.

"Yeah," he said as he stood up to leave.

At the door of the porter person's room, he added, "See you around, Megan."

"Not if I see you first, señor."

At the door, I offered him the consolation he needed. "I am prepared to take a position with you, Tommy Flynn."

"Yeah?" His eyes lit up at the prospect of a contract offer.

"I want to go long on Christina Anne Logan."

He thought about it.

"I don't gamble with princes of the Church."

37

I stared out the window on Wabash Avenue, neither the Magnificent Mile nor State Street, that great street, but a workaday Chicago street, stretching for its final leap to glamour. It never looked like much out of the window of my study, and probably never would. On a late November day when there was what the Irish would call a fine, soft rain in the air (meaning a torrential downpour), it looked like a bland wall to Dante's Purgatorio—though not D. M. Thomas's—dull, dreary, and depressing. I sighed loudly though presumably only God could hear me, and I doubted She paid much attention to my sighs.

The problem with the strange case, as Dr. Watson would have put it, of the bishop and the L Train, was not that there were no motives or an absence of people who rejoiced in the decline and fall of the Most Reverend Augustus O'Sullivan Quill, J.C.D., D.D. Quite the contrary, there were tons of people, as the Megan would have said, who rejoiced in his decline and who declared that they would cheerfully take credit for that decline. They felt that whoever had cooked up the scheme was a genius and should be richly rewarded, instead of being turned over to the Chicago Police Department and the State's Attorney for the county of Cook. All available suspects, with only two exceptions, would have cooked up the plot if they had had the opportunity. In the words of Ted Coffey, "Blackie, the guy was a frigging genius. You and Cronin owe him a debt of gratitude."

Such a marvelously forgiving folk, these Chicago Catholics. Milord Cronin and I dissented from this conventional wisdom. However much an idiot Idiot was, he had, as a creature of God, certain basic human rights. Those rights had been violated—cruelly and shamelessly. We could not accept this, no matter how many times he had violated the rights of others. Moreover, he was a priest of the Archdiocese. Milord Cronin had a duty to protect and care for his priests. As his gray eminence, I shared in some way in that responsibility.

Besides, I did not like unsolved mysteries.

Earlier in the day, after my visits to the local hospitals, I had paid court to the Reilly Gallery, to collect my dues of apple-cinnamon tea and oatmeal-raisin cookies. I had discussed the mystery with Mike the Cop and his beauteous childhood sweetheart and present wife, Annie Reilly. With the Irishwoman's determination to stand by her own kind and to repeat that loyalty as though it were the only observation on the case that really mattered, she had insisted that "Jenny Carlson wouldn't hurt a fly."

"Ah," I said, for the sake of the argument, if for no other reason, "the valiant Jennifer is a woman of considerable depth, imagination, and passion, all of which our mastermind certainly has. Mike, you have seen some of her computer graphic art—do you consider her capable of twisted fantasies?"

"She's a wonderful woman," the good Annie interrupted as she replaced the oatmeal-raisin cookies that the leprechaun who haunts me had deftly stolen. "If she was going to kill anyone, it would have been her worthless husband!"

"I like her and I like her work." Mike did not dispute his wife, wisdom in any man, especially if he's Irish. "We will sell a lot of it here. There's mystery in her, Blackie. She has the kind of fantasy life that could come up with anything. And the kind of passion."

"She has a good man who loves her," Annie protested. "Why should she put that in jeopardy?"

"I understand," I noted, "that they have broken up."

"She's seeing your sister. No way will Mary Kate tolerate that."

It was true that my sister could be very directive when the mood and the situation suited direction—in my case all the time.

"My people could find no trace of an anti-Quill conspiracy up there," Mike reported. "A lot of hatred, a lot of complaints, and a lot of satisfaction that he's gone and Father Dribben's back. No conspiracy. That doesn't mean there wasn't one. If there was, we'll only find out by accident when someone breaks down and talks about it."

"I feared as much. . . . On the other hand, to return to those who were arrested," I continued as Annie refilled my cup with apple-cinnamon tea, "the young Tommy Flynn seems utterly transparent."

Ms. Reilly firmly believed that caffeine was not good for one, even though I argued that the medical research had shown that *real* tea was an effective preventive for heart disease and cancer. I could no more persuade her to accept that finding than I could persuade any woman that one did not catch colds from going outside without a hat.

"Tommy," Mike pointed out, "comes from a long line of Irish political fixers. His father is, among other things, your classical Irish political lawyer, as was his grandfather and his great-grandfather before him. While the present generation is honest, sternly so, the same could not be said of its predecessors."

"Ah . . . I assume Tommy became a trader to break the family tradition."

"There is not that much difference between an Irish political lawyer and an Irish commodity trader," Mike continued. "Their strength is their ability to push the envelope farther than anyone else, and cover it with charm."

"Tommy is a sweet boy," Annie turned her defense now to a male of the species. "He always is so polite and friendly when he rides down on the elevator with us."

The Reillys, like Tommy Flynn, lived in the John Hancock Center, our city's proto-skyscraper.

"That's what I mean." Mike nodded his head as if his wife had made his case for him. "He's a charmer and a fixer and an operator. Nothing wrong with that, God knows. He is not, however, as sweet as he might appear."

This was characteristic dialogue between Sean Cronin's gray eminence and the head of both the North Wabash Avenue Irregulars and Reliable Security. Mike never cleared anyone. There were those who said that he was Watson to my Holmes, or Flambeau to Father Brown. Annie, however, had often suggested that I was his Captain Hastings.

"I think that young woman he's dating is just wonderful," Annie continued. "I'm sure they'll get back together again too."

"The girl next door—"

"She defines the term 'Fighting Irish,'" Mike agreed. "The winning goal on a broken leg . . . If I had to hunt for suspects, I'd take a close look at those Corpus Christi priests up in the North Shore. They have a lot of money. He was after it for his TV station, which they thought would embarrass them. You'd never get anything on them, Blackie."

"Arguably not . . . When it is a question of their protecting their work, they are notoriously flexible in their ethics. They certainly weren't unhappy that Gus Quill is, so to speak, no longer in play. They are quite devious, but perhaps not all that smart. However, they are smart enough to know that if they should fund a TV station to compete with the good Mother Angelica, it must be theirs, not anyone else's."

"I think Cardinal Cronin would be great on TV. He should have his own program. And, Blackie, this is absolutely the last of the cookies—don't give me that leprechaun stuff either."

"There are, of course, Gus's worthy brother and sister-in-law, the pious Peter and Grace Quill, though like Fathers Ramon and Luis, as they call themselves, their ability to devise a grand plan is questionable."

"I have something on them for you, Blackie." Mike reached for a stack of papers. "They are under considerable financial pressure. Peter went bearish in the market because that was what all the clever talking heads said a wise person would do. He lost a lot of money, both his own and his clients'. Her dress store up there on Green Bay Road has been quite successful. But it hardly covers for Peter's mistakes. They would have bounced back if the Bishop hadn't alienated just about everyone up in Forest Hills."

"And now that he is incarcerated in St. Joseph's Hospital?"

"Out of sight, out of mind. Peter and Grace have benefited greatly from his kidnapping. A murder would have done them more harm, but a disappearance seems to have suited them just fine."

"All too many folks," I agreed, "seem to think that the destruction of a mind is not as serious as the destruction of a body."

"It's a crazy case, Blackie," Mike said. "I don't think I've ever run into anything quite like it."

"There are numerous folk up in Forty Holy Martyrs who do not regret the sad fate of their sometime pastor."

"Why would they connive to kidnap him? Hadn't the Cardinal ordered him to restore all the people he had fired?"

"Perhaps they didn't think the order would have any effect. Certainly Gus had not obeyed it at the time of his disappearance. I have the impression that they wanted him out of there, regardless. Whether they would have and could have organized so quickly such an elaborate scheme seems problematic."

"Then who would have?" Annie demanded as she discovered some cookies of whose existence she had perhaps hitherto been unaware.

"That is the problem," I agreed as I bit into one of the treasures. "There are lots of people who would like to have disposed of Gus Quill, but no one who clearly had the ingenuity and the resources to do so. We are back to our anonymous mastermind."

"And that could be almost anyone who had found good reason to seek revenge against Bishop Quill," Mike concluded. "Blackie, I think it might be insolvable."

"There is no such thing as an insolvable mystery," I said firmly.

"You were never a cop," Mike said with a laugh.

"It is curious, is it not," I went on with more determination than I felt, "that the only folks with whom I have spoken who are no longer angry at Gus, and who feel sorry for him, are the two that your sometime colleagues down on South State Street arrested?"

"Tommy Flynn is probably too besotted with the tigress next door to think of anything else," he admitted. "Jenny Carlson is another matter altogether."

"She's a good woman!" Annie insisted.

"Doubtless she is a disturbing and admirable woman," I said. "Yet is so profoundly mysterious—"

"That man of hers will have his hands full," Mike agreed. "If he gets her back."

"You two are terrible! Just because a woman of her age is naturally erotic, you think she is a femme fatale!"

"I wouldn't dare suggest that!" Mike grinned.

"And the question is whether she wants him back!"

"Erotic appeal," I said, falling into my Solomon mode, "is a blessing limited neither by age nor by gender. . . . Yet there is something about the fair Jenny that suggests a link between passion and anger—"

"With a husband like hers, she should be angry!"

I did not say that the anger could easily be transferred to a more vulnerable target.

"I have some more information about the parish staff for you, Blackie. How did Father Dribben put up with those people!"

"Good staff are hard to come by in the contemporary Catholic parish. Good staff and emotionally balanced staff even harder to come by."

"There's nothing wrong with the Megan," Annie interjected, still defending womankind of whatever phase in the life cycle.

"Inarguably . . . the Good Matthew managed to keep his unruly team in line by a blend of patience and wit, both nearly inexhaustible."

"That nun . . . Joe Anne Reed?"

"Former nun."

"Whatever. She participated in some demonstrations in which church property was defaced. Her husband, the former priest—"

"Orlando Carlin, the director of adult education."

"He has a bit of a wandering eye."

"That does not surprise me."

"Herman Crawford, the organist—"

"Is gay. That, too, does not surprise me."

"He is currently unattached. The chairman of the finance committee is a high-powered corporate officer. Nothing on him. He doesn't need the job. On the other hand, Larry Henning, the chairman of the parish council, is from the west side of the parish. . . ."

"Which means?"

"That he is a relatively small-time staff number cruncher in a big firm. A lot of his personal status is tied up with that parish council."

"Indeed!"

"Your bishop friend was a threat to all of them. Some of the more conservative parishioners might have tattled to him. Even the threat to tattle would have been enough to put them in jeopardy."

"Which of them might have come up with such an elaborate plan?"

"Only the finance committee chair could have carried it off, but why should he bother?"

I sighed.

"My conclusions exactly."

I wandered back to the Cathedral rectory, turned on my computer, listed the suspects, and then turned off the computer without bothering to save the file. The quick image of a solution, which had often teased me in other similar matters, had turned itself off. All I knew was what I knew the day I had found Gus Quill in the alley behind North Central Park Avenue—that an ingenious but vain mastermind was behind it.

So I sat there and watched the rain fall on Wabash Avenue and the living and the dead.

With no warning, the image machine turned on again and remained on. An L train.

The picture was quite impossible. No way it could be true. How could we ever prove it, even if it were true? Vanity! Oh, yes. There was a marvelous way the mastermind could exercise vanity, a way to leave a hint that he could point to eventually, when it was safe to do so. And then laugh at all of us.

I pondered the solution. It fit all the known facts. I hesitated to move out of my comfortable easy chair. A brief period of resting my eyes was certainly in order, was it not?

Reluctantly, I forced myself to rise. Leaving Jaime Keenan and the Megan in charge, I walked to a certain store. After considerable searching of its wares, I found the area of my interest. Within that, I at first found nothing. Then, after a more detailed search, I found exactly what I knew should be there. I purchased the item and I slowly walked back to the Cathedral. The Megan were all present in their little hutch, babbling away. The presence of only one was required. The rectory had become the functional equivalent of a mall.

"Tell Father Keenan I'm back, and I'll be with the Cardinal."

"Yes," they said hardly affording me any notice.

I rode up in the elevator and interrupted Nora and the Cardinal in their afternoon tea, real tea. I accepted the offer of some. No cookies were in sight. I gave Sean Cronin my purchase. He and Nora inspected it. Both turned pale.

JENNY

38

Buy you lunch? I say as I lean against the door jamb of his office. Everyone is watching us, hoping . . . I do not know what they are hoping. I swore to myself I would never do this. Raw need is too much for me. I must have him again. It is Dr. Murphy's fault for forcing me to face my own passion. Tied up, he says. Supper, maybe. Fine, I reply. Where? he asks. Savarin? He smiles, as if he knows the implications. He ought not to take me back. I am emotionally unstable. He knows that. I am turning out wild and attractive designs now that everyone, even Donnie, likes. Annie Reilly is preparing an exhibition of my computer art, which reveals just how crazy I am and, even worse, how much I am preoccupied with sex. Everyone knows I'm unstable and will always be unstable. I no longer care what they think.

He is waiting for me at the restaurant, smiling faintly as I walk in right on time, trying to give the impression that I am a sophisticated woman of the world, though my legs are trembling. This is what being in love with a man is like,

I realize. It means your body cries out for him the instant you see him, that you want him inside you even as you sit down next to him, casually aloof while he orders drinks. The usual? he asks. I nod. However, it is my treat. He orders a bottle of expensive red wine. I do not argue about it. He says something nice about my latest design effort. Crazy woman, I reply. Gifted woman, he responds. Gifted and crazy. He shrugs.

I forget all the possible apologies I had rehearsed. Do you have the ring with you? Yes. I hold out my left hand. May I have it back? He removes the ring from its box and slips it on to my ring finger. I dissolve into warm surrender. We should marry, Jenny. Oh, yes, I say as I weep. Soon. Then I won't be able to act like an idiot again . . . and I'll be in your bed every night. He nods solemnly. I'll like that very much. When? I take a deep breath. Before I came over here I called Bishop Blackie and asked him to pencil in a date the week before Christmas. He laughs happily.

That was audacious, Dr. Murphy says the next morning. His love wasn't in doubt, I reply. Mine was. I knew he'd take me back. You had a fine domestic evening? Wonderful.

TOMMY

39

I knew I was in truly serious trouble. My rejected lioness had phoned me the night before.

"We just totally have to have lunch tomorrow," she instructed me.

"After work? One-thirty at Trader's Inn?"

"Yucky!"

"How about the Italian Village on Monroe, across from the bank?"

"I know where the Italian Village is," she said firmly.

My throat was tight and my hands were wet when I hung up. I knew that the call would come. You don't get rid of a young lioness like Christy Anne Logan without a struggle. She would want to talk it over, find out why I had broken up with her, and offer me a chance to change my mind. I dreaded such conversations. They never worked out. How could I dig in my heels and tell her stubbornly that it would never work out between us? A woman always designed such tête-à-têtes so that the man would look bad to himself and to her friends. Then she could return to her coven and tell them how awful he was.

Well, in Christy Anne's case to her pride of lionesses, all of whom would say that they knew I was no good the first time they met me.

The first time they thought I was adorable. But what did it matter?

Someone in the back of my head whispered to me that I was full of shit. The humiliation of my arrest and the continued suspicion of the police, some of whom trailed me most of the time, perhaps waiting for my first purchase of a scheduled drug so they could arrest me, had shaken the foundations of my personality, down there in all the sub-basements where the rats ran around amid the sewer water.

I was making no progress with my shrink, who now seemed to have abandoned objectivity and to be on Christy's side, along with Mom and my sisters.

"Ja," said the shrink, "once more you are not a man, once more you are afraid of the Woman. You fear that you cannot cope with her."

"Precisely," I would agree fervently.

Christy Anne strolled into the third floor of the Italian Village ten minutes late, a deliberate ploy so she could make a dramatic entrance.

Dramatic it was. She was wearing a shiny, metallic black pantsuit with a crimson sweater, thick crimson belt, crimson earrings (perhaps rubies), and crimson lipstick. She was a sophisticated woman of the world, almost thirty perhaps, with thorn-stick cane. No, she was a late adolescent, giving such an excellent imitation of a woman of the world that you had to look very closely to notice how problematic this role was for her.

"You're gawking, Tommy Flynn," she instructed me as I helped her into her chair.

"So is everyone in the room."

She snorted derisively. "You're the only one with your mouth hanging open."

These young lionesses can be tough. I was in for a long lunch.

"How's your leg doing?"

"It's healing nicely," she said with an impatient frown. "That's what Dr. Hightower says anyway. He's letting me swim at last. I totally have to exercise. Would you believe it, Tommy Flynn? I've put on four pounds!"

"It doesn't show," I said gallantly. In fact, it didn't show.

"I feel totally gross, fat, pudgy, ugly. I have to order a salad today."

"You're wearing a girdle?"

"Certainly NOT!"

"Well, then you don't look fat, pudgy, and ugly."

She snorted again, as if to say, a lot you know, Tommy Flynn.

"What's happening on the Olympic front?"

"Oh, *that!*"

I ordered a bottle of red wine, which, strictly speaking, she could not drink because she was not quite twenty-one. Despite her good intentions, she ordered ravioli with meat sauce.

"You're not driving?" I asked as the bottle arrived.

"I took a cab down from my parents' house." She waved away my concern. "I'm not crazy, Tommy Flynn."

"I never thought you were. . . . Now, about the Olympic tryouts."

"You keep saying 'tryouts,' Tommy Flynn. I'm like, totally, going to make the team! That's a given!"

No false humility for this child.

"O.K."

"I can start training for them again in February, so I'll lose the weight and be fine. No problem! Doc Hightower says that occasionally on a cold, damp day, I may feel a little twinge. I tell him that it will remind me of winning the national championship."

What else would she say?

"And the Stanford girl, er, woman?"

"Sonia . . ." she sipped the wine. "Well, you do have good taste in wine anyway, Tommy Flynn. . . . Oh, Sonia's no problem. Our team wrote letters to the Soccer Federation asking them to give her another chance. So they postponed her suspension till after the Olympic tryouts. She's like on the phone to me in tears. . . ."

"She's taking Irish-Catholic charity now, is she? Will she make the team?"

Christy shrugged. "Maybe, but I don't think so."

As we talked, I realized how captivating this young woman was, even in ordinary, small-talk conversation. I was sinking deeper into trouble.

"She goes, like, can we be friends? I'm fersure. She's, like, you can trip me or something if you want to. I go, that's not the way we Irish-Catholic women do it. I'll take you out for, you know, a malt some night and poison it. It took her a moment to realize I'm joking."

"Italian women, actually."

She waved her hand, "Regardless. Anyway Jesus said we're supposed to forgive, so I'm counting on some extra favors from Him."

She accepted the offer of Parmesan cheese.

"How could He refuse?"

How could anyone refuse?

She dug into the pasta like it was going out of fashion.

"I'm starved," she said. "Two o'clock is kind of a late lunch for me."

"I'm sorry."

"No problem." She waved a fork laden with pasta.

"Now, Tommy Flynn," she said after a gulp of wine, "there's absolutely no way we're breaking up."

"Oh?"

"I'm, like, how can we break up when we're going to be married at the end of May right after I graduate?"

"What!"

"That's all settled, Tommy Flynn, so don't even argue

about it."

"But—"

"My mom is, like, the woman always has to bring closure to a romance. So, I'm bringing closure. It's simple. Besides, this virginity stuff can't go on forever—I want a man in my bed with me!"

"Men," I stammered, "are crude, smelly, and don't clean up."

"Amy says you're fastidious."

"She doesn't know the meaning of the word."

"Well, actually, she goes, my brother is obsessive."

"We're too young," I said.

"*You* may be too young." She paused before bringing a forkful of pasta to her mouth. "I'm not too young at all. I'll be three weeks younger than Mom when she married Dad."

"Megan at the Cathedral says I'm too young for her and she's only sixteen."

"Well, maybe you are too young for her, but not for me."

This was outrageous. I had been backed into a corner. She couldn't do this to me.

"We hardly know one another."

She waved away that suggestion with a shrug of her strong and shapely shoulders.

"Maybe you don't know me, but that's all right, you can find out about me. I know you, however, and that's that. Besides, Mom and Dad know you too, and they, like, totally love you. My dad goes, Christina, you'll never find another young man so perfectly suited for you. And I'm, like, tell me about it, Daddy."

"Oh."

"And your family thinks it's wonderful. Your dad goes, it's time Tommy settles down."

"Settles down!"

"Well, you know what he means. . . . This stuff is really good."

She continued to destroy the ravioli.

"Besides," she went on in serene confidence, "we have to start dating again. I'll totally need some foreplay to prepare for marriage. You can't expect me to do it all on our wedding night."

I gulped and choked on my wine. The best thing I could do now was to run.

"Foreplay?" I sputtered.

"You know, mess around with my boobs and stuff."

The image of engaging in such amusements affected me like a blow to my head. I was reeling. I felt my fists clench.

"Are you all right, Tommy Flynn? I don't want you choking to death on me!"

"I'm fine!" I gasped.

When I had recovered, I fell back on my last line of defense.

"Christy, I can't even think of anything that serious with these police charges hanging over me."

"Foreplay isn't serious," she said, her eyes averted and a tint of red in her face, "it's just playing around a little."

"I mean marriage!"

"Oh, *that!* Don't be silly. Bishop Blackie will solve that. He always solves mysteries."

That her presumed intended was being shadowed by the police was a matter of no concern to her at all. Like my shrink had said.

"I don't know, Christy—"

"Besides," she said jabbing her wine glass at me, "you, like, totally know that if you marry me, you'll never regret it a single day for the rest of your life."

There could be no question about that.

However, I weakened not because she spoke the truth, but because young lionesses have such sad eyes when their hearts are about to break.

"I don't know, Christy," I said again. "I could probably make some time this afternoon."

Defeat and pain in her wondrous blue eyes, she put down the wine glass.

"For what?"

"To go shopping for a ring. Do you want to come with me so I don't make any mistakes?"

"No way!" she said with a triumphant grin. "Surprise me. I'll like whatever you like! It doesn't have to be too big!"

No way it didn't have to be big. I'd call Mom and ask her if she could spare me an hour from the law to validate my choice.

"You can, like, give it to me this evening before we have supper at Mom and Dad's."

"I can indeed."

We were both flooded with tears.

"I suppose you can give it to me at Ghirardelli's."

"Funny thing, I thought you would suggest that."

So you see how tricky God is.

BLACKIE

40

Your problem, Ted," I said to Ted Coffey, "is not so much your vanity, though that's what did you in. Your problem is your illusions. You thought that if it hadn't been for Gus Quill, you would be in his place, the new auxiliary bishop and the putative heir to Cardinal Cronin."

"I don't know what you're talking about," he frowned at me. "You always were a little weird, Blackie."

We were sitting around the conference table in the Cardinal's office. Milord Cronin was wearing his ring and his pectoral cross, as he always did in such circumstances. Through the efforts of the worthy Jaime Keenan, I was wearing mine too.

"Arguably," I replied. "Nonetheless, as you yourself said to me, he almost blocked your study in Rome. He did interfere at the last minute with your appointment to the College of Noble Ecclesiastics. Instead of an exciting career representing the Pope around the world and dodging the daggers of your colleagues, you came back here to the matrimonial court, which, by your own admission, was unbearably dull. You were, however, a great success in working with Hispanic Catholics and became one of the most respected priests in the Archdiocese. You are a perennial member of the Council of Priests and have been its chairman twice. You have worked wonders in your parish in Oak Park, which was moribund when you arrived. You have helped countless people who have had troubles with the Church, of whom the Flynn family were but one example. That wasn't enough. You covered up your disappointment well. However, your frustrated ambitions, driven by your illusions, poisoned all of that."

"Sean, this guy is crazy!"

"My guess is that you had too much integrity to succeed in papal diplomacy and that you may have come to realize it. You were happy in your work and satisfied with the respect of your fellow priests. Yet your resentment of Gus Quill continued to fester in your soul. When he appeared in Chicago with his foolish assumption that he would be the next cardinal, you determined to finally undo him. In which determination you were quite successful. Presumably you had access to a drug gang from your service in the barrio. They may well have done the job at a clerical discount, or even free. Your plan was only marginally risky, and your young friends executed it brilliantly. Exit Gus Quill as a practicing bishop, much to the joy of all too many people."

"I'm getting out of here, Sean," he rose from his chair. "This is intolerable nonsense! I don't have to put up with it!"

"Sit down, Ted," Cardinal Cronin said firmly.

Ted Coffey sat down. Wondering, perhaps, if I knew the whole truth, he had become anxious and uncertain, his eyes flicking back and forth rapidly.

"Your weakness," I went on implacably, "is your vanity. It was a nice touch, a signature of a sort, to tell your associates to dump the Ravenswood Line train in the yards at Desplaines Avenue, on the fringes of your parish. No one would pick up on the clue, you assumed. Nonetheless, you put it there. So you could laugh at the stupidity of the police. And at my stupidity too. If you could not be a bishop in Chicago, despite your brilliance, you would show, to your own satisfaction, that my much vaunted mystery-solving skill was, if you will excuse the expression, fictional. It took me a long, long time to see your signature on the L train, a train you could easily drive by and gloat over long before the cops or the CTA would find it."

"This guy is as crazy as Idiot is," Ted snarled at the Cardinal.

"Arguably," the Cardinal seemed to agree—and stole my line without my permission.

"Once I realized how vain you were, I wondered if you might have left us another clue. I recalled that you had once written fantasy stories under the name of a certain Burke T. Burke. I wondered if you had tried to turn one of those admittedly ingenious fantasies into reality. I visited a science fiction bookstore specializing in old magazines, over on LaSalle Street. After considerable searching, I found an issue of a magazine called *Fantasy Mystery* in which there was a story by Burke T. Burke called "Getting Rid of Gus." You even called the doctor that your protagonist wanted to eliminate Gus Quill. You described Gus with both accuracy and venom. The disappearing L train was added to the story. Perhaps there is a story somewhere else from which you lifted that component. We are searching for it."

Sean Cronin opened the crimson leather cover of his notebook and edged a photocopy of "Getting Rid of Gus" towards Ted.

There was a long silence in the office, the silence of a graveyard.

"I would have made a better bishop than him. Better than you too."

"Arguably," I said, beating the Cardinal to the line.

I felt no particular happiness in the solution of the mystery.

"You caused great worry to the driver's wife and indirectly to your sometime parishioner, Thomas Flynn Jr., whose fragile sense of self was devastated by his arrest."

"He'll be all right." Monsignor Coffey shrugged that off. "I did you guys a favor by getting rid of Idiot. He's out of your hair permanently now. You should be grateful to me."

"Perhaps," I agreed. "Yet Gus Quill had the right to the integrity of his soul, such as it was, every bit as much as you and I do. You destroyed him or tried to because of envy and vanity and illusion. Added to the malice of that act, you did it to a man who, however flawed and inadequate, was a fellow priest."

"So what! You'll never be able to prove anything. Neither will the police! You wouldn't dare turn me over to them."

Finally, the Cardinal spoke in a calm, controlled voice.

"Ted, this story of yours would enable them to make a powerful case and to certainly solve the crime."

"You'd never turn a priest over on the basis of a bit of fiction he wrote ten years ago!"

"You're saying that I should become an accessory after the fact to your crime? If I learned one thing during the years of the pedophile mess, it is that a cover-up never works. As you yourself said many times at the meetings of the Council of Priests, we must always tell the truth."

"They'd never indict me!"

"Don't be so certain," the Cardinal said grimly. "They might not get a conviction, but then again, they might. My advice is that you get a good lawyer and plea-bargain with them."

"No!" He stood up, ready now to storm out of the office. "Why did you have to bother? Why didn't you leave me alone! Is Gus that important to you!"

I leaned forward and pointed my finger at him. "Like every human being, he is important! So are the two parishioners you have exposed to public suspicion and humiliation."

"I didn't intend that to happen!"

"It happened just the same," the Cardinal said coldly as Ted prepared to leave in righteous fury. "Just a minute, Monsignor, before you leave. I'm asking you to resign as pastor of St. Regis, effective at once."

Ted whirled on us.

"I'll fight you. I'll demand a trial."

"I hardly think so. If you do not resign, I will suspend you and appoint an administrator."

"Fuck you!" Ted Coffey exited in righteous rage.

I picked up the phone and called the Reliable Security number.

"Casey."

"Blackie."

"We found the L train story. It was written six years ago, after he became pastor of the parish in Oak Park. Sure enough, they parked the train in the Desplaines Avenue Yards. Why would anyone take such a chance?"

"Driven to it by his vanity." I put my hand over the phone to speak with the Cardinal. "Mike the Cop found Ted's L train story."

The Cardinal nodded.

"I assume he awaits your instructions."

"He does."

"Tell him to turn both of the stories over to John Culhane."

"Follow plan A," I said to Mike on the phone before hanging up.

"The arrogant bastard," Milord Cronin said through tight lips. "The arrogant, obnoxious bastard."

"In his own way," I agreed, "as self-deceived by his illusions as Gus Quill."

The Cardinal inclined his head in agreement.

"I presume the story will be leaked, Blackwood?"

"Too good not to be."

"I suppose so. Prepare some kind of statement. Innocent till proven guilty. Deplore the whole matter. Suspended until the civil authority makes further decisions. Will they indict him?"

"Oh, yes. He'll doubtless plea-bargain."

"I'll send Jaime out to Oak Park as administrator. He's from that part of the world. Do you mind?"

"It is time." I sighed heavily at my loss. Just to put it on the record.

"No one will know that you solved the mystery?"

"They will not learn it from me."

He laughed ironically and the hoods flashed back from his blazing blue eyes. "A lot of people will guess. As I have said on some previous occasions, I'm glad you're on my side."

"Arguably."

41

Some Sundays You permit matters to arrange themselves better than on other days. Thus this morning two couples, both very much in love, appeared at the rectory to make proper arrangements—and to be congratulated by the Megan—before they were ushered into the pastor's office, which had been redone to look like an aging parlor in an old-fashioned Irish house. The first couple were Jenny Carlson and her lover, who wanted to be married the week before Christmas, on the day Jenny had providently requested. The second couple were both parishioners, the boy and girl next door, even if next door was the John Hancock Center and the Water Tower apartments. I was exhorted to bless the engagement ring ("Isn't it totally excessive, Bishop Blackie!") and enter a date in late May for a wedding.

You have permitted these two matters to arrange themselves very neatly. The couples are quite different. The older couple are quiet, intense, and deeply passionate. The younger couple are exuberant, zany, and unpredictable. Yet in the most crucial matter they are both alike. Usually, when two people wander into a rectory in a romantic daze, both are focused on themselves and on the forthcoming event. With Your Grace they grow out of this. However, both couples this morning were focused on care and concern for the other. Their love models Your love for us and the way we should try to love You.

All very clever on Your part, if I may say so.

Then I took a taxi, driven by the ever faithful Mr. Woods, up to St. Joseph's Hospital, not trusting myself to drive in the falling snow. (Only, however, because my sibling had called and warned me "not even to think about it!")

Dressed in black trousers and white shirt, Gus Quill was sitting in a chair next to his bed, reading Graham Greene's *The Power and the Glory*. Next to him was a stack of so-called Catholic classics.

"Blackie! Good to see you again! Very generous of you to come up here in the snow and on a busy Sunday before Christmas. . . . Do you know this book? Fascinating! I had no idea it existed!"

I admitted that I did and sat down on the other chair in the room.

We discussed Greene and J. F. Powers and Edwin O'Connor and the other authors Gus was systematically working his way through.

He had not put himself completely back together again. However, he was making progress. The various shrinks who presided over him went so far as to say "remarkable progress." Oddly enough, there were few traces of the old Gus. He was putting together a new persona. Or, perhaps, discovering an old one.

Remarkable.

"So it was Ted Coffey?" he said finally.

"It would appear so, if one is to believe the papers."

"What will they do to him?"

"They are negotiating a plea bargain. The state's attorney does not want to bring a priest to trial. He'll plead guilty and be sentenced to probation. The hang-up now is whether he will name his accomplices. In fact, he dare not do so, or they will doubtless kill him. The state's attorney knows that and will back off from such a demand."

"And the Church?"

"Retire him with a full pension and ask that he leave town."

"Poor guy. I really feel sorry for him. I wasn't worth all that trouble."

"He was caught up in his illusions."

"Like I was, only mine were different. . . . Well, I think I'm getting rid of them, at least I hope so."

Mary Kathleen had predicted such a realignment might happen. She had also warned that it might be fragile.

"I suppose you solved the mystery?" he went on.

"My answer to that when asked is, What do I know about solving mysteries?"

He slapped his leg and laughed. "That's really funny, Blackwood, really funny. . . . Did you see the posters your porter persons sent up to me?"

The Megan, dubious despite my suggestions, had prepared posters for Gus's room: NUCLEAR-FREE ROOM, SMOKE-FREE ROOM, NOISE-FREE ROOM—THIS MEANS YOU, DOCTOR! and ANNOYANCE-FREE ROOM—THIS MEANS YOU, NURSE!

"They're very clever."

"Thank them for me. I'll thank them myself if I ever get out of here."

"I'm sure you will, Gus."

"One thing I want to ask you about. The desire I've always had to work with the poor—I don't think there was anything wrong with that, do you?"

"Certainly not."

"Would you think the Cardinal could find a way for me to do that when I'm feeling better?"

"I'm sure he would be delighted."

"Would you mention it to him?"

"Absolutely."

It is up to You, as all manner of things are. It is not, however, a totally improbable idea.

As I left his room, Gus Quill was fingering his rosary beads.

So what do I know?

The snow was falling heavily, but Mr. Woods was waiting for me. He drove carefully through the slush on Lake Park, picked his way along Fullerton, and then at last escaped to the relative freedom of Lake Shore Drive. The snow was falling so thickly now that one could barely make out the skyline and the green and red lights that festooned it for the season.

I asked to be let out at Chicago and Michigan.

I walked a couple of blocks down the Magnificent Mile, bright with the white lights the Mayor likes to put everywhere to celebrate the birth of Your son. I imagined hosts of angels at work above me, busy protecting cars and drivers and trying to make us human creatures realize once again that this is the time of the year when we should smile.

Then I walked back to the Cathedral to admire the Christmas decorations the Megan had created for the offices—exuberant and in good taste.

I want to pray for Gus Quill and Ted Coffey, for Jenny and her Ned, for Tommy Flynn and his lioness, for Sean and

Nora Cronin, for Mike and Annie, for all my family, for peace everywhere in the world where there is trouble . . . and for anyone else I ought to be praying for. And, oh yes, for Crystal Lane too.

It is late at night now. I can neither pray nor think any longer.

Good night.

Chicago, April 18, 1999
Third Sunday after the Feast of Our Lord's Resurrection.

Center Point Publishing
600 Brooks Road • PO Box 1
Thorndike ME 04986-0001 USA

(207) 568-3717

US & Canada:
1 800 929-9108

3721D